TALES OF SUSPENSE FOR BOYS

On the Run: Chasing the Falconers
by Gordon Korman

Goosebumps: Welcome to Dead House
by R. L. Stine

Animorphs: The Encounter
by K. A. Applegate

SCHOLASTIC INC.

New York Toronto London Auckland Sydney
Mexico City New Delhi Hong Kong Buenos Aires

ISBN 0-439-85860-7

On the Run: *Chasing the Falconers*, ISBN 0-439-65136-0,
copyright © 2005 by Gordon Korman.

Goosebumps: *Welcome to Dead House*, ISBN 0-439-56847-1,
copyright © 1992 by Scholastic Inc.

Animorphs: *The Encounter*, ISBN 0-590-62979-4,
copyright © 1996 by Katherine Applegate.

12 11 10 9 8 7 6 5 4 3 2 1   6 7 8 9 10 11/0

Printed in the U.S.A.   40

First printing, April 2006

CONTENTS

GORDON KORMAN

ON THE RUN

CHASE #1

CHASING
THE
FALCONERS

In memory of the irreplaceable Paula Danziger

ISBN 0-439-65136-0

12 11 10 9 8 7 6 5 4 3 2 1   6 7 8 9 10/0

Printed in the U.S.A.   40

First printing, April 2005

It wasn't a prison.

Not technically, anyway.

No bars, cells, electrified fencing, guard towers, or razor wire.

People who drove by probably never noticed the logo of the Department of Juvenile Corrections on the mailbox that stood at the end of the long lane leading to County Road 413. To them, this sprawling property was just another farm — one of thousands of dusty puzzle pieces that covered this part of Nebraska.

Farm. Aiden Falconer winced. He hated that word. Sunnydale Farm, they called it — a name so deliberately cheerful it turned his stomach.

His eyes took in the empty, far-flung acreage. This broad, flat land wasn't meant for crops. It was a barrier. Anybody trying to escape would have to cross that pool-table-flat boundary in full view of the supervisors, for too many miles and too many minutes. It was as effective as a moat full of alligators.

Welcome to Alcatraz Junior.

True, there were a few farmy things. A modest cornfield and a few acres of soybeans. Busy work for the "residents."

Inmates, Aiden thought bitterly.

Life at Sunnydale Farm was based on one simple principle: that the residents could not be allowed so much as a second of free time. For these juvenile offenders, time meant trouble.

So there was school. Seven hours, broken only by a twenty-minute Gulp 'n' Gag lunch. The rest of each day, from five A.M. wakeup until lights-out at nine, the eighteen boys and twelve girls worked the "farm" — tilling, planting, fertilizing, pruning, and picking. They tended the chickens and fought with the geese.

And they milked the cows.

Aiden hated milking duty almost as much as he hated Sunnydale itself, and his reason for being there. Okay, animals weren't clean freaks, but that barn stank to high heaven and was hot as a sauna. To enter it was to stop breathing until the chore was done and you could stagger out, blue in the face and gasping for air.

Milking was an art that he seemed incapable of mastering. Some of the residents could plunk themselves down on the stool, reach under the cow, and you'd hear *squirt, squirt, squirt*. Aiden would plaster his face against the flank of the beast, his hands working like pistons. The *squirt, squirt, squirt* never came.

The frustration was maddening. He was a Falconer, from a family known for its brains. His parents were both PhD's. Respected scientists.

Or at least they used to be. . . .

No. Don't go there.

The cow was losing patience with Aidan's incompetence. It happened just the way it always did. First the twitching. In a few seconds, it would turn its massive head and moo at him. Next, the shuffling and stamping. And then the kick. He would go one way, the stool would go the other, and the pail would be upended, spilling into the straw of the stall the few drops he had managed to squeeze out.

His escape came a split second before the cow went into total revolt. Aiden jumped up and fled the barn, feeling sick and breathless, his tan jumpsuit drenched with sweat.

"What a wuss." Miguel Reyes walked toward the

henhouse, carrying a sack of chicken feed. "No-body's scared of cows. Dumbest animals on the planet — next to *you*."

As he passed by, he made sure to whack Aiden on the side of the head with the heavy bag.

"Ow!"

"Are you okay?" Meg Falconer peered anxiously around the corner of the barn.

Aiden could never quite get used to the sight of his eleven-year-old sister in this terrible place. At fifteen, he was as old as most of the juvenile offenders banished to this prison camp. But Meg was just a kid, ripped out of sixth grade.

"Beat it!" he hissed at her. Boys and girls were supposed to stay separated except during classes and Gulp 'n' Gag.

Meg had never been big on following rules. She usually got by on a sweet smile and wide-eyed innocence — all fake.

"Are you going to let him get away with that?" she demanded.

Aiden stared at her. "This isn't some self-esteem game about standing up to bullies. That guy was in Juvie before this. For *manslaughter*!"

"But where does it stop?" she demanded. "Mom and Dad — framed! The two of us, stuck away in the back of beyond! We don't even know who we *are* anymore."

"If I pick a fight with Miguel," Aiden warned, "I'll know *exactly* who I am. I'll be the dead guy in the morgue!"

"Hey!" came an angry shout.

The supervisor who stormed over was named Ray. The residents called him Rage because he was always in one. In Aiden's opinion, that nickname could have gone to any of the other jailers at Sunnydale. There was a kind of permanent anger in the people who worked there — probably from dealing with delinquents like Miguel day in and day out. The "supes" got sassed so often that they lived in a constant state of being bent out of shape.

Ray was scowling as usual. "Well, what do you know — Eagleson and Eagleson. A regular family reunion."

Eagleson — that was their identity at Sunnydale. Falcon, eagle — like this was some kind of April Fools' prank. The court had ordered the change. After the media circus of their parents' trial, *Falconer* might as well have been *Dracula* as a last name. The judge said he didn't want the children suffering for their parents' crimes.

If this isn't suffering, then what is? Aiden wondered

angrily. *We're banished to this Old-McDonald-Had-a-Jail, mingling with dangerous offenders. While Mom and Dad rot in prison for something they didn't even do —*

He took a breath. The Falconer kids were at Sunnydale because none of their relatives would take them in. Who could blame the distant cousins for wanting to shield their own families from the scandal? A day didn't go by without Mom and Dad decried as traitors in every newspaper in the country.

Aiden and Meg had committed no crime. They were here because there was no other place for them.

"Sorry, Ray. It won't happen again — "

His sister cut him off. "That's funny, Ray. You're quick enough to catch us talking. But someone using a sack of feed as a deadly weapon — you missed that, didn't you?"

The supervisor's scowl deepened. "You little snot, how'd you like to lose your telephone privileges for a month?"

That shut Meg up. Those weekly phone calls were the only contact the Falconer kids had with their parents in prison in Florida.

All the contact we'll ever have . . .

Luckily, Meg had the brains not to fight with a

supe. She retreated to her work in the soybean fields, and Aiden steeled himself for round two with the cows.

But later, as he was busing his tray after Gulp 'n' Gag, Meg stepped out in front of him, her eyes like lasers. She grabbed both his wrists with such intensity that it took all his strength to keep the dishes and cutlery from sliding to the floor.

"We have to get out of here," she murmured urgently.

"Get a grip," he whispered back. "There's no way out of this place."

"We *have* to!" she insisted. "We're Mom and Dad's only chance."

For a second, he thought he might start losing it right there in the mess. Wouldn't *that* show Miguel and the others how tough he was. "The appeal — "

She shook her head fervently. "The government will never let them go. The case is closed. We're the only ones who can prove our parents are innocent, and you know it!"

Classic Meg. She didn't live in the real world. Escape was impossible. But even if they could get away, then what? How would two kids come up with evidence that would clear the Falconers after so many top lawyers had failed?

And then there was the question he dreaded most of all. The unthinkable thought, the one he dared not ever speak aloud, even to his own sister.

What if he and Meg set out to exonerate their parents, only to discover that they had been guilty all along?

"**D**ude, your house is on TV!"

With those six words in the school hall, the nightmare had begun.

A group of students had gathered around the wall-mounted screen in the media center. The sound was muted, but Aiden could see it — his own front door.

His first thought was idiotic: *New paint job still looking good* . . .

Not *What's going on?* or *Why is my house on CNN?* The paint job.

The camera pulled back, and he saw the police. More like an *army*. Scores of commandos in body armor surrounded the Falconer home, shields deployed, weapons pointed. A roadblock cut off their quiet street. Choppers circled overhead.

What the — ?

The rest was a blur. Exploding tear gas canisters. The battering ram reducing the door to toothpicks.

His parents hustled out in handcuffs by an FBI agent the size of Shaquille O'Neal.

And then the call over the P.A.: "Would Aiden Falconer please come to the main office? Aiden Falconer . . . "

Like things were totally normal. Like they were going to tell him that Mom had forgotten to sign his field-trip form.

That was March 7. The day the world ended. The day life changed forever for Aiden and Meg.

The details came twenty-one hours later. At long last, they were allowed to see their parents in a windowless maximum-security cell guarded by two soldiers armed with automatic rifles.

The charge: passing classified information to enemies of the state.

"Classified information?" Aiden stared at his father. "What would you be doing with classified information? You're a teacher at a college nobody's ever heard of! And you write detective novels!"

"*Bad* detective novels," Meg added breathlessly.

The Falconers told their story. Husband and wife professors — both respected criminologists. Three years before, they had been approached by an old family friend who turned out to be an undercover CIA recruiter. Their country needed their expertise,

Agent Frank Lindenauer told them, in the global war on terror.

For the next eighteen months, the two professors worked for the government. They developed profiles for United States operatives to identify terrorist sleeper cells throughout the world. It was going beautifully, Lindenauer assured them. Thanks to the Falconers' work, the CIA had the foreign extremists on the run.

And then everything fell apart.

Somehow, the Falconer profiles had fallen into the hands of the terrorists themselves. Knowing what the Americans were looking for had surely helped them avoid capture.

Now the Department of Homeland Security accused the two criminologists of aiding the enemies of their country. The crime was treason.

"So?" wailed Meg. "Just get Frank Whatsisface to explain that you're the good guys!"

That was the problem: Agent Frank Lindenauer had disappeared off the face of the earth.

For months, the Falconers and their lawyers tried to reach him, with no success. Worse, the CIA claimed it employed no such operative. He was the professors' only contact — the one person who could back up their story.

During the trial, witness after witness detailed how the Falconers' work had become a training manual for sleeper agents. Captured extremists testified that the profiles were widely used in the terrorist world.

Without their CIA handler, the Falconers had no way to defend themselves. It was over before it started. But the sentence was beyond their wildest nightmares:

"You are remanded to the custody of the Department of Corrections for a term of not less than the length of your natural lives."

The gavel came down like a pistol shot. It was a moment that happened on television a dozen times a day. But TV never showed the real story — the shattered lives, the ruined families.

What happens to a son and daughter when two loving parents are suddenly shut away for good?

At least the juvenile authorities got one thing right: They kept Aiden and Meg together. Mom and Dad weren't so lucky.

The foster homes were a disaster — accusations and fighting on the inside and encampments of reporters on the lawn. Falconer wasn't a name anymore; it was a glowing neon sign. After a few false starts, the judge decided that the only option was to get these kids out of the spotlight. They had to disappear, taking their notorious pedigree with them.

That's Sunnydale, Aiden thought bitterly. *The place you go when you want to be nowhere.*

Gang members, purse snatchers, and car thieves made great camouflage.

The TV was barely watchable, with faded color and a jumping picture. Yet to the boys of Sunnydale, it was Disney World — their only entertainment besides bragging, threatening, and fighting. The two fuzzy channels were their sole connection to the world that lay beyond the endless fields.

Nowhere was the pecking order more obvious than around the TV. At six foot four, Latrell Chambers was able to claim for himself the only halfway comfortable chair. It didn't hurt his reputation as a tough guy that he used to belong to an infamous Seattle gang. Miguel was right up there, too, on a lumpy couch with a great viewing angle. Gary Donovan — armed robbery — had a beanbag chair that he defended with both fists. And so on down to Aiden, pretty close to rock bottom — obstructed view of a picture that was pretty obstructed to begin with. Only Seth Lowinger, computer hacker, had less status. He didn't watch TV at all.

Aiden wondered what the atmosphere was like in the girls' lounge. Was his eleven-year-old sister subjected to this kind of ugliness and intimidation? With Mom and Dad out of the game, Aiden had to stand up for Meg. But how could he do that when he could barely stand up for himself?

A half-eaten pear came sailing through the air and knocked the old-fashioned rabbit-ear antenna off the top of the set. Instantly, the picture dissolved into snow, and a howl went up from the spectators.

Gary Donovan smacked Miguel in the back of the head. "What's the matter with you, Reyes? It took us weeks to get that stupid thing exactly right!"

Miguel tossed his wadded-up napkin at the blank screen. "For what, yo? To watch reruns of *Touched by an Angel*? When I get out of here, I'm going to kick back with my brother in New Jersey. He's got, like, seven hundred channels, plasma screen, satellite dish, the works! That's for me."

"Dream on," sneered Latrell. "They're never going to let you out of here — not till you turn twenty-one, anyway."

Aiden waited for the explosion and fistfight, but Miguel just laughed.

"This cage can't hold me," he boasted. "I'm just chilling, that's all."

There was a lot of hooting and jeering, and Miguel was pelted with apple cores and candy wrappers.

Aiden spoke up. "You know a way out?"

Miguel snorted in his face. "Look at the big escape artist! You don't have the guts to milk a cow, Eagledink. You'd wet your pants before you hit the cornfield."

"Shut up, Reyes," snorted Gary. "There's no way out, and you know it. Not unless you can walk thirty miles in a Juvie jumpsuit without being seen."

"That's why you guys are a bunch of felons," said Miguel. "No creativity. Look around you. You see a cage. I see wood, and hay, and papers. One match, and this whole dump *burns*."

Gary opened his eyes wide. "You want to *torch* the place? And escape while the supes are manning the bucket brigade?"

Latrell gave a disinterested yawn. "You're talking nonsense, man. You've got a rap sheet like the *Encyclopaedia Britannica*. Slap an arson on there, and they'll put you in the adult system no matter how old you are."

Miguel shrugged. "Gotta catch me first." He waved at Aiden. "Hey, Eagledink, go fix the antenna. And get it right this time."

Aiden did as he was told, but he never took his eyes off Miguel. "You're kidding about that, right? The fire? That can't work, can it?"

Miguel chuckled his contempt. "What are you in for, Eagle? Spitting on the sidewalk? Jaywalking? I know everybody's sheet in this place except you and your little sis. What did you do — whack your parents or something?"

Suddenly, there was nothing more important to Aiden than taking the antenna and ramming it down Miguel's throat. He was on the boy like a flying squirrel, almost screaming with rage.

What happened next was shocking and lightning fast. Miguel shrugged him off as easily as he might have flicked away a crumb. The punches were airborne like missiles, compact, bony fists slamming into Aiden's cheek and chin.

Aiden tasted blood and prepared himself to shed more. *I don't belong with these criminals,* he thought with amazing detachment. *How can I ever hope to defend myself against them?*

Latrell grabbed Miguel by the back of his collar and hauled him off Aiden. "Cut it out, fool! You want the supes on our necks?"

Gary hauled Aiden to his feet, but his real concern was for the antenna, which was bent like a pret-zel. "Aw, man, you broke it!"

Somehow, the TV picture was now clearer than it had ever been. That, Aiden assumed, was the only reason why he was allowed to go on living.

The incident did nothing to improve relations with Miguel. "You'd better watch your back, Eagledink," he promised grimly. "When you least expect it, this is the face that's going to be coming up behind you."

3

If there was a force that could overpower Aiden's anger and resentment at the fate that had overtaken his family, it was sheer boredom. The routine at Sunnydale was so repetitive, so dull, that days slipped into weeks, and weeks slipped into months without anybody noticing how much of life was being wasted.

It had been over four months since the Falconers' arrival at the farm. The corn was getting higher and the days were getting shorter. Other than that, there was very little indication that time was passing at all.

Even the changes didn't seem like changes in the great numbness that was Sunnydale. Gary completed his term and was released. The very next day, his replacement showed up. Eugene from Boston, aggravated assault. He looked and acted exactly like Gary and even inherited Gary's spot in the pecking order and seat at the TV.

Last Wednesday, Aiden and Meg had spoken to

their father in prison in Florida. Dr. Falconer had tried to sound upbeat. "Hang in there, kids. You won't be in that place forever."

Meg had cried, and Aiden had come pretty close himself. The awful flip side of that statement was obvious: Dad would be in *his* jail forever, and Mom in hers. Life meant life.

Every night at Sunnydale, two residents were se-lected to see to the animals' food and water supplies overnight and into the morning. Turndown service, the supervisors called it.

Aiden found no humor in their gag. The duty was creepy in the extreme. There was no electricity in any of the outbuildings, so the barn and coops were pitch-black.

Aiden entered the gloom of the henhouse, hold-ing up the kerosene lantern, leading the way for Seth Lowinger, his partner tonight. The hens stirred as the intruders passed from roost to roost, filling water cups and feed trays.

Seth, whose crime was creating a high-tech com-puter virus that had shut down every ATM in eleven states, couldn't figure out how to open a sack of chicken feed.

"You just tear it, Seth," Aiden told him. "Where the stitching is."

"I don't see any stitching," Seth complained. "What — over here? It won't tear."

Aiden bit back a sarcastic remark. He would not become like Miguel and the others and make fun of someone who was even lower on the totem pole than he was.

He set the lantern down on the floor and ripped open the heavy paper. As he handed the feed back to Seth, the bottom of the bag knocked over the kerosene lamp. The little glass door fell open, and the flame licked out to the straw-strewn floor.

Aiden quickly dropped to his knees to beat out the small fire. All at once, Miguel's words echoed in his ears: *One match and this whole dump burns. . . .*

Suddenly, he was frozen, staring transfixed at the fingers of flame rising from the parched-dry hay.

"Hey!" cried Seth. "*Hey!*"

It jolted Aiden out of his reverie. But by the time he moved to put out the fire, there was no stopping it. Miguel had been right. The farm was a tinderbox.

Aiden pounded at the flames with the feed bag, but the blaze was spreading faster than he could stamp it out, accelerated by the spilled kerosene.

A tinderbox . . . a tinderbox . . .

There was nothing in here that would contain a

fire. In a matter of seconds, half the floor was burning.

Seth was in a full-blown panic. "It's going up the walls!"

The sensation that overtook Aiden was like walking from semiconsciousness into terrifying reality. This was nothing that he and Seth could handle on their own. It was no longer a mishap that could be covered up.

"The supes!" he choked in the thickening smoke. "Get the supes!"

Seth was uncertain. "What are you going to do?"

"I'll — I'll take care of things here." It was pure babble, but it was enough for Seth. He raced out into the night. The rush of air from the door fed the flames, which were reaching for the roosts. The hens scattered in agitation.

Aiden was sure there were a million things he should be doing. Yet in this frantic moment, only one thought possessed him. He had to save the chickens.

The chickens didn't agree. Or at least they were so worked up by the smoke and fire that they could not be herded toward the door.

The moment was as absurd as it was awful. His parents were locked up for life; he and Meg were exiled to a prison farm, a place he had just set on fire. And what was he doing? Rampaging around a smoke-filled henhouse, windmilling his arms and screaming in an attempt to scare the chickens outside.

He burst through the door, kicking the last bird ahead of him. A horrifying sight met his eyes. The coop was an inferno, the sheets of flame bent diagonal by a strong wind. As he watched, a gust jumped the blaze to the top of the log rail fence. The ancient wood was like kindling. The fire tightrope-walked across it, advancing quickly and steadily toward —

"The barn!"

It would be next, with the cows trapped in their stalls. Aiden loathed those animals, but they couldn't be left to die. Not that way.

He threw open the door and barreled into the manure smell. It was so dark that he moved by touch alone, pawing at stall barriers and big bodies.

"Everybody out!"

His cries had little effect on the sleeping cattle. He pounded on their sides and kicked at their legs with all his might — anything to start them ambling toward the door and safety.

Now he could see smoke curling in through the

gaps between the wallboards. The outside structure was on fire. There wasn't much time.

"Come on, you idiots! *Move!*"

There were nine cows at Sunnydale. He had to drag them out one at a time. One head-butted him into a post, one tried to bite him, and four kicked him after he had led them outside. Some gratitude.

By this time, the entire chicken coop was engulfed in a pillar of flame twenty feet high. Its collapse was spectacular, sending a fountain of sparks up into the night sky.

Aiden gawked, awestruck, as the wind scattered the thousands of airborne embers. They sailed high over the main house and then descended like a blanket to cover the wood-shingle roof. There was instant combustion.

His alarm soared to a new and more urgent level. This wasn't about chickens and cows anymore. That house was full of people!

And the next thought, far more terrifying:

Meg.

The girls' dormitory was smaller than the boys', but with identical rows of bunk beds on each side of the room.

Meg was the only girl in bed, staring at the blank piece of paper that was supposed to be a letter to her mother.

What's there to say? she thought morosely. *That I hate it here? It'll only make her feel worse.*

One thing was clear. No matter how terrible Sunnydale Farm may have been, a federal penitentiary had to be a thousand times worse.

She sniffed. Smoke. Leticia was probably lighting up again. The girl must have a ten-year supply of cigarettes hidden here somewhere. The supervisors searched the place twice a week and still couldn't find anything.

She peered through the door to the adjoining TV lounge where the rest of the girls were gathered. Odd — no one was smoking. A few of them were painting their toenails. That blew Meg's mind. Convicted of robbery, assault, drug dealing, and grand theft auto, they were acting like this was a gigglefest slumber party.

When she heard the yelling, she rushed to the window and threw up the blinds. Whatever was happening, it was on the other side of the building, where the animals were. But the yard looked somehow — wrong. There was an eerie reflective glow.

The northern lights? In Nebraska?

A groaning sound filled the room. The floor shuddered.

An earthquake?

And then the ceiling disintegrated, and it was raining fire.

A large chunk of burning roof tile hit the pillow inches from her head. With a cry of shock, Meg hurled herself to the floor and rolled for cover. But there was no cover. Hot sparks singed her face.

Out in the TV lounge, there were screams, followed by a mad scramble.

Breathing into her T-shirt, Meg took a quick inventory of herself. Nothing broken, nothing burning. A large chunk of roof barred the way to the lounge — the only exit. A wall of flame.

"Help me!" she screamed. "I can't get out!"

There was no response, no sound at all. They had abandoned her here.

She looked around wildly. There had to be a way out. "There's a solution for everything," Mom had always said, "if you're willing to take the time to think it through."

She yanked the top drawer out of the nightstand, dumped the contents, and raced over to the window. Swinging with all her strength, she began to hack at the glass. To her dismay, it broke but did not shatter.

It was security glass, she recalled in growing panic, with wire mesh embedded in each pane.

With reserve power she didn't know she had, she picked up the entire nightstand and flung it. It struck the window and bounced away.

She stepped back. *Can't get through the door; can't get through the window. No other exit.*

Unbelievable. She was going to die in this fire.

And all because I didn't want to paint my stupid toenails!

"Meg!"

Out of the fire itself appeared a steaming, smoldering shape, staggering directly through the burning roof tiles that blocked the door. Meg looked on in amazement as the flaming blanket was flung aside to reveal Aiden, wild-eyed and desperate.

"How did you do that?" she blurted. "Why aren't you dead?"

In answer, he ripped the blankets off two bunks and dragged her into the adjoining bathroom. He turned the shower on full blast and crammed both of them into the spray.

She stared at him. "This is safe?"

"In *The Case of the Pharaoh's Mask* — " he panted.

"Dad's *book*?" She began to beat at his chest and face with her open hands. "You got this from Dad's book? Are you crazy? The biggest fire he ever survived was a backyard barbecue!"

Aiden was too exhausted to answer, but his expression said it all. Maybe this wasn't safe, but it was infinitely safer than staying here to burn.

He draped one of the dripping blankets over her head and wrapped himself in the other one.

"Hold your breath!" he said harshly. "And whatever you do, don't stop!"

They ran, bursting through the flame-obscured doorway. Cowering under the wet wrapper, Meg couldn't see. But she knew when she was in the fire. There was extreme heat, and, most terrifying of all, a total absence of air — a baking vacuum.

And then it was over. Aiden ripped the blanket away, revealing the TV room, with the blaze miraculously behind them. "Roll!" he commanded.

She did. At that moment, she would have obeyed if he'd asked her to fly.

They pounded at each other's wet clothing, beating out any smoldering spots.

"Are you okay?" he rasped.

But Meg was listening to something else — an all-too-familiar creaking sound from above. The rest of the roof was about to cave in.

She grabbed her brother's hand. *"Run!!"* The two

of them blasted out of the building. The roar that came from behind told them the roof was collapsing in their wake. But they never looked back.

Outside was pure chaos, with the helpless supervisors squirting extinguisher foam on a fire that had already consumed everything in its path. The outbuildings were ashes. Cows, geese, chickens, and residents milled around in the confusion. Aiden got no more than fifty feet from the house before collapsing to the dirt, physically and emotionally drained.

"It's okay," Meg soothed. "We made it."

"How can it be okay? Look around you!"

Meg shrugged. "What do we care if their jail burns down?"

"But it's all my fault!"

Meg goggled. "You torched the farm?"

Aiden gasped out the story of the mishap with the kerosene lamp. "I could have put it out! I was *going* to — I just waited a few seconds! But by then it was too late. The supes are going to kill me!"

Meg drew him to his feet and led him farther away from the remains of the building. "The supes are never going to see you again," she said. "We can be a long way from here by sunup."

Aiden was horrified. "You mean take off? Don't you think we're in enough trouble already?"

"We're the only ones who *aren't* in trouble!" she argued. "They have no real right to keep us here. Besides, there is no 'here' anymore."

Aiden was racked with guilt. "Aren't you listening to me? I have to turn myself in. Somebody could be dead in that fire. It was almost *you*."

"The girls all got out," she reasoned, "and the boys had plenty of warning." She took hold of him by the shoulders. "Listen, bro. You just saved my life. Now I'm going to save yours. Let's blow this Popsicle stand."

His eyes were hopeless. "We'll never make it."

"The supes have their hands full," she insisted. "You think we'll be the only ones missing when the ashes cool? Besides, when they investigate, they'll hear that the roof fell on me, and you were in a barbecued chicken coop. Maybe they'll think we're dead."

"Even if we can get away," Aiden argued back, "we're in the middle of nowhere. We have no place to go, no money. You're in your pajamas. I'm in a jumpsuit that might as well have a sign that says JAILBIRD."

"This is what we've been praying for — a chance to get out of here, to help Mom and Dad! I don't know how we'll do it, but we definitely can't if we're locked away." She played her trump card. "This place is dust. God knows where they'll send us next. We might not even be together. This is a gift, Aiden. Say thank you and fly."

Over Meg's shoulder, Aiden saw the east wall of the main house collapse in a cascade of smoke and embers.

Whatever lay ahead, this chapter of their lives was over.

They sprinted for the cornfield.

We're fugitives.

The thought bounced off the walls of Aiden's brain as he and his sister tramped through fields that seemed to have no end. The harvest moon and a billion stars lit their way for a while. But when the clouds rolled in, the prairie night wrapped them in velvet black. Soon their faces were scratched from the tall cornstalks.

One advantage of the zero visibility was that Aiden had finally stopped glancing over his shoulder, expecting to find Ray and the other supervisors bearing down on them. He wasn't any less scared, but why look when there was no chance of seeing anything anyway?

"This can't still be our cornfield," Meg complained. "We've been walking for ages."

"This is Nebraska," Aiden reminded her. "You can cross the whole state without leaving cornfields."

In three hours they had not yet come to a single road. But they knew one was not far away. They could hear distant sirens as emergency vehicles converged on Sunnydale Farm. Aiden pictured a fire truck roaring up to the facility to find every man-made structure already gone.

"My feet are killing me," groaned Meg. "I think my slippers disintegrated an hour ago."

Aiden was shocked. Because he was wearing work boots, he'd assumed that Meg was, too. But no, she had on the thin slippers that were issued to the residents for use in the main house — flimsy, barely socks.

"We can't stop," he told her. "Want to wear my boots for a while?"

"Those clodhoppers? I'd be crippled in an hour."

And they pushed on.

They reached their first road after midnight and trudged along the soft shoulder. Where they were headed was anybody's guess. At this point, the only important direction was *away*.

It was easier going, but the appearance of every set of headlights had them diving into the corn. For all they knew, word of the fire had spread via the media, and the entire county was searching for escapees from Sunnydale.

Fugitives have no friends.

But they couldn't stay hidden forever. Especially not in the daylight. Come sunup, they had to find a way to blend in, to look normal.

"We need clothes," Aiden decided.

"No problem," Meg said sarcastically. "I'll weave a new wardrobe out of some of this corn silk."

"I'm serious. We need to be able to walk around without attracting attention. We can't look like we just broke out of jail."

"It's no big mystery, bro. There are no stores, and even if there were, we have no money. Whatever we get, we have to steal."

Aiden made a face in the darkness. She was right, of course. She usually was. But the idea of stealing made him feel unclean. At least before, he and Meg hadn't belonged in the juvenile corrections system.

If this is what it takes to survive as fugitives, pretty soon our rap sheets will be twice as long as anybody else's.

As the adrenalin of their escape wore off, weariness set in. There were times that Aiden was pretty sure he was asleep on his feet, awakened only by the fresh twist of a leg cramp or the mild sting of yet another mosquito bite. At one point, Meg almost wandered out into the middle of the road, and

Aiden had to grab her and steer her back on course.

Not that there were cars anymore. His watch told him it was after three. Even the distant sirens had stopped by this time. Either that or they were now out of range. Only the chirping of locusts and crickets proved to Aiden that a world existed out there in the darkness. It was a tiny comfort to know that he and Meg weren't completely alone in the universe. In this spot, at this moment, it sure felt that way.

Five A.M. — twenty-four hours since they'd last slept. God, Meg looked tired!

Then it hit him. *I can see her.* Sunrise wouldn't be for another hour or more, but after a night submerged in black ink, even the faintest predawn glow brought the world into sharp focus.

Her voice startled him. "A house." He would have bet all the money he didn't have that she'd been sleepwalking.

Then he spotted it, too — a small wood-frame farmhouse with attached shed and a large modern barn in the back. The windows were dark, and — this was the kind of coincidence that always happened in Dad's detective novels — there was a carousel hung with clothes just outside the shed.

"Jackpot!" breathed Meg.

They approached cautiously. It was still mostly

dark. But farmers were notoriously early risers. It would be a tragedy to get caught clothes-napping after making it so far.

Meg whispered a logical concern. "What if nothing fits?"

"It's still better than burned pajamas and a jailbird suit." Her brother pulled down a pair of khakis and a T-shirt.

Meg scowled at the label on her own selection. "Fatso! Hey, can you reach those shorts?"

The dog came out of nowhere, an oversize German shepherd in full flight. Against the backdrop of stillness, the barking was like the roar of carpet bombing exploding all around them.

The Falconers dropped the clothes and ran. The animal bounded after them, and Aiden realized with a sinking heart that there was no way they could escape. Two kids, exhausted and sleep deprived, didn't stand a chance against a full-speed attack dog.

As they scrambled around the laundry carousel, Meg reached up and yanked on a large white sheet. It billowed down, engulfing the leaping dog. The shepherd yelped and hit the ground, wrapping itself in linen.

It was all the time Aiden and Meg needed. They

raced into the barn and clambered up the ladder to the loft. Through a small window, they could see the white sheet jerking around like a spastic ghost as the dog struggled to free itself.

"It'll come after us," quavered Meg.

"Shhh. I don't think it can get up the ladder."

Crouched amid the bales of hay, Aiden was aware of an all-too-familiar smell. He looked down into the barn. Cows. Was there no escaping them?

"Someone's coming!" Meg hissed.

Sure enough, a light was shining in the house. Then the porch lamp came on.

The Falconers threw themselves flat to the floor of the loft and prayed.

A woman's angry voice called, "Fool dog! Are you into my laundry again?"

The animal did everything but talk. In the chorus of barking, Aiden could almost hear it: *Call the police! There are two escaped convicts hiding in our hayloft!*

But all the woman could see was her soiled sheet. "Bad dog! And stay away from that barn. You *don't* rile up the cows before milking. What's gotten into you?"

Aiden sneaked a look. The woman had gone back inside. A second later, the chastised shepherd slunk into the barn. Parking itself at the bottom rung of the ladder, it glared up at the loft, sniffing and growling.

"Now what?" whispered Meg.

Aiden wasn't sure. How long would the dog wait there for them? Hours? Days? Mom and Dad had traveled a lot on the lecture circuit, so the Falconers had never had a pet. How patient could man's best friend be? And how long before the people who lived here figured out that the shepherd was trying to tell them something?

Aiden would not have believed it was possible to sleep in this situation. But the next thing he knew, it was full daylight, and Meg was flaked out in the straw beside him, dead to the world.

He gave her shoulder a gentle shake. "Meg — "

She started. "I'm awake!"

"Shhh!"

There was a mechanical hum coming from the barn below, and the occasional clanking noise. Milking machines.

Aiden risked a look down the ladder. A chorus of angry barking rose to greet him.

"Get out of here, Sparky!" snapped a man's voice. "Every time you chase a rat up that ladder, we have to put up with your infernal racket!"

The two rats in the loft looked at each other hopelessly. How were they ever going to get out of there?

At last the milking was over, and the cows were taken out to pasture. Sparky never moved a muscle. He sat like a sentry, practically hugging the base of the ladder.

"We're going to have to run for it," whispered Meg.

"We wouldn't stand a chance."

It was high noon before the farmer, his wife, and three children piled into a huge SUV parked in the driveway.

"Sparky! Where is that dog?"

The eldest son ran to the barn, grabbed Sparky by the collar, and hauled him away to the car.

The Falconers did not allow themselves to breathe until the sound of the motor had faded into the distance.

They scampered down the ladder and out of the barn.

"It's a good omen," Meg decided. "It means we're lucky."

Of all the words that described their situation, "lucky" was the one Aiden would have picked last.

Back at the carousel, they selected clothes at their leisure. Aiden's khakis were loose, but a tackle harness made a suitable belt. The items Meg selected fit perfectly. There was even an old pair of sneakers that cradled her cut and bruised feet as if custom-made.

She looked hopefully at her brother. "I'm starving."

"No way," he said firmly. "For all we know, they've got a burglar alarm in that house. Or an old grandmother."

"Or another dog," she agreed, chastened. "But Aiden — look!"

Hanging on wall hooks were three well-used mountain bikes.

"We don't need them," Aiden said stubbornly. "Everybody's been treating us like criminals. Let's prove them wrong."

"They're speed. And the faster we get away from here, the safer we'll be." Meg could see she was getting through to him, and hurried on. "Besides, we're only *borrowing* them. We'll just ride to the nearest town, someplace where we can get on a train or bus."

"Yeah, but a train or a bus to *where*?" Aiden voiced the concern that had been eating him up inside since they'd first turned their backs on the burning wreckage of Sunnydale. "Where is this mystery destination of ours?"

"Florida," Meg replied readily. "That's where Mom and Dad are."

A wave of tenderness washed over him. His little sister had so much spirit. She was bent down by these past months but never broken.

"To do what?" he asked gently. "To bust them out of jail? You're talking about federal prisons, Meg. You can't knock them out with a kerosene lamp. Besides, that's the first place they'll look for us."

Her expression grew stormy. "Well, what's *your* plan, besides shooting holes in mine? Our parents are in jail because we can't get our act together to get them out!"

Aiden knew he had to reach her — really reach her — and right now. "There's nothing I wouldn't give for the four of us to be together as a family again. But to say that Mom and Dad are where they are because of us — you'll drive yourself crazy thinking that way. This is *not* within our power to change. Our parents are locked up because Frank Lindenauer wouldn't come forward to admit they worked for the CIA. That's it."

"Well, then, that's what we have to do," she said simply. "We'll find Frank Lindenauer."

Her brother stared at her. He did not have the heart to drag her back to cruel reality again. To explain that if teams of lawyers and private investigators couldn't find Lindenauer, what chance did two kids on the run have? She would have to face it sooner or later, but not today. Today the poor kid had to win at something.

"We'll take the bikes," he conceded.

After drinking deeply at the garden hose and inhaling a few not-quite-ripe peaches from the tree in the front yard, the Falconers returned to the road, this time on wheels.

Once he was riding down the two-lane highway, Aiden's spirits improved. Being on a bike again just seemed so — normal. It was something from his regular life, not this improbable nightmare that had replaced it. The wind in his hair felt great.

Meg had to feel it, too. *At eleven years old*, Aiden thought, *this is what she should be doing, not fleeing for her life*. Meg was too young to really remember the summer the Falconers had vacationed with "Uncle Frank" — the only time Aiden remembered meeting Frank Lindenauer.

It was amazing. After all the years the Falconers had known the man — even before they knew of his CIA connection — they didn't have a single photograph of him, or a single document with his name on it. Nothing that would prove his existence.

Yet Aiden recalled that vacation vividly. He'd been six, and Meg not quite two. The memories of the house were the clearest — a pretty white cottage with red shutters, on the Vermont side of Lake Champlain. The Falconers had gone back there for several summers after that. Enough years that Aiden had established his own secret hiding place behind a loose piece of paneling in his tiny bedroom. It made him blush to think of what passed for treasure in those days — bottle caps, rocks, Cracker Jack prizes, and a handful of pictures from his sixth birthday present, a little box camera. He could almost see the array of dumb family photos: Mom and Dad clowning around, Meg in her stroller, Uncle Frank and his girlfriend in lounge chairs —

Without warning, Aiden's bike veered off the shoulder and into the ditch, dumping him unceremoniously in the tall grass. He lay there, stunned, as Meg leaped off her own bicycle and rushed to his side.

"Aiden! What happened?"

He accepted her proffered hand and hauled himself to his feet. "I — " It hardly seemed possible after everything that had happened — the investigation, the defense, the trial. And yet it was staring him right in the face. "I think I've got a picture of Frank Lindenauer!"

Breathlessly, he explained to Meg about the summerhouse in Vermont.

She was furious. "Why didn't you remember that when it was important? When the trial was going on?"

"It wouldn't have made the difference between guilty and innocent," Aiden reasoned. "It's just a picture of a guy sitting by the pool."

"So what good is it to us now?" asked Meg, deflated.

"Maybe none. But it's someplace to start. It's our only clue." He looked hopeful. "A name can be faked, but you can't fake a face. If the picture's still there, we have someone to look for."

All at once, Meg was energized again. "Well, what are we waiting for?"

Aiden was actually laughing as he stood up and righted his bike on the pavement. There was something contagious about his sister's enthusiasm, but he had to bring her back to earth. "It's not as easy as you think, Meg. We haven't been there in years. I don't have an address."

She was unperturbed. "Vermont. East."

By the crazy logic of the fix they were in, it almost made sense. To stay here meant capture. They had to go somewhere.

Why not Vermont?

Agent Emmanuel Harris of the FBI took a sip of coffee and nearly sprayed it all over his desk. How was his lamebrain assistant ever going to make it as an investigator if she couldn't even remember that her boss took his coffee black? Black meant black — no milk, no powdered stuff, no sugar, no Nutra-Sweet. Harris was a tolerant man, but that didn't extend to coffee.

He was about to unleash his famous sarcasm, his fist hovering over the intercom button, when he spied the item on his computer screen. The Bureau provided its agents with real-time updates on all law-enforcement stories around the world. It was just a few lines — barely a paragraph. But the words jumped out at him — *Juvenile Corrections*.

GIBBON, NEBRASKA: A suspicious fire last night destroyed Sunnydale Farm, an alternative minimum-security detention facility run by the Department of Juvenile Corrections. No injuries have been reported, but seventeen of thirty inmates are still at large and possibly dangerous. . . .

"Not my problem," he said aloud, but made no move to scroll down from the report.

They were in the juvenile system somewhere. That was where they'd been bounced after the foster homes hadn't worked out.

Silly, he told himself. There were tens of thousands of teens in hundreds of facilities around the country. This was one little farm. The chance they were involved was less than slim. And yet . . .

He found himself dialing the number of the Department of Juvenile Corrections in Washington, DC. There was the usual runaround before Harris found himself on the phone with Deputy Director Adler.

"I heard you had a little trouble at Sunnydale Farm in Nebraska last night. Any idea if Aiden and Meg Falconer are among the missing?"

There was a long pause on the line. Then, "I can check the list. Give me the spelling of their last name."

With effort, Harris uncrossed his long legs and crossed them in the other direction. He was six foot seven, and the FBI didn't seem to have a desk large enough to accommodate him. "Falconer. As in the children of John and Louise Falconer."

"Oh!" The deputy director sounded ruffled. "*Those* Falconers. Well — uh — I'll have to look into . . . "

Harris wasn't listening any longer. The young Falconers' identity was probably under the highest level of secrecy. But he could hear it in Adler's voice. Something was up with those kids. And the department didn't want to admit it.

Adler was still hemming and hawing. ". . . so if you'll leave your number, I'll get back to you when I have more information." Then he added, "What's the big interest in these two, anyway?"

Harris let out his breath and realized he'd been holding it.

"I'm the one who put their parents away for life."

It wasn't a town exactly, or even a village. It was more a cluster of modest homes dotted around a gas station with a mini-mart.

Aiden and Meg left the road and struggled with their bikes over uneven ground and through dense underbrush. They were still too close to Sunnydale to risk being seen by the local population.

But as they circled around the back of the ramshackle garage, Aiden had a change of heart.

"I think we have to go in there," he murmured, gesturing to the mini-mart.

Meg was nervous. "Shouldn't we stay out of sight?"

"As much as we can," he agreed. "But look." He pointed to the flyspecked window at the rear of the store. Inside, tacked to the wall behind the cash register, was a large map. "It'll tell us where the towns are around here. We'll never get anywhere if we can't find a place with some transportation."

They stashed their bikes in an undergrowth of honeysuckle and crept toward the gas station, staying low in the tall grass. With Aiden in the lead, they came around the corner of the building and surveyed the terrain.

The mini-mart was empty. At the pumps stood a tall, gangly teenager in oil-spattered coveralls, filling up a Ford pickup and making small talk with the driver. His back was to them.

Aiden decided to chance it. Pulling Meg by the hand, he darted across the blacktop and eased open the door of the mini-mart. He was congratulating himself on their stealth when the bell sounded.

It was only a little ringer attached to the door. But to the two fugitives, it might as well have been a bomb blast. Aiden jumped, and Meg let out a yelp of shock.

The gas attendant looked over, and the Falconers rushed inside, faces averted.

From the grease pit adjoining the store, a voice called, "Be with you folks in a few minutes." Through the glass, they could see light coming from beneath an old Chevy.

"No hurry," said Aiden in a shaky voice. The two went straight to the map.

They were in a place called Buffalo County, Nebraska.

"No wonder they didn't need bars to keep us at Sunnydale," Meg whispered. "Where was there to go?"

"Shhh," Aiden cautioned. "Right there." His finger traced a single line marked with short crossbars. It traversed the county from east to west. "Railroad tracks," he told her. "And not too far from here. If we can find those tracks, all we have to do is follow them until we come to a station. Probably in" — he pointed — "Gibbon."

"Where's that from here?" asked Meg.

"South. We're headed east. That means we just

have to find somewhere to make a right turn and keep on going until we hit the tracks."

Meg nodded. "Let's get moving."

The country-western music coming from the radio in the grease pit was replaced by an announcer's voice. *"It's eighty degrees in Omaha, eighty-two in Lincoln, and seventy-six in Scott's Bluff. In news around the state, police and juvenile authorities continue to search south-central Nebraska, rounding up the runaways from the Sunnydale Juvenile Detention Center."*

Aiden froze with his hand on the doorknob.

"The facility burned to the ground under mysterious circumstances last night. No one was injured, but eleven of thirty young offenders are still unaccounted for.

"In national news . . ."

A sharp finger in the ribs brought Aiden back to life.

"Come *on!*" hissed Meg.

Aiden threw open the door. There, wiping his hands on a dirty rag, stood a burly middle-aged man with a smudged face under a three-day growth of beard.

His eyes narrowed at the sight of them. "Never seen you kids around here before."

Aiden was too devastated for speech. They had finally found a purpose — were heading toward something. They had a plan, no matter how flimsy. And it was all coming to an end because the local news in Nowheresville, Nebraska, came on at the wrong time.

Meg stepped around him and gave the man a dazzling smile with full teeth and dimples. "You can say that again, mister. We are *so* lost!"

He looked unconvinced. "Where are you heading?"

"We're staying at our uncle's place. He's got a pig farm outside Kearney. And — no offense, I'm sure it's a great place — but it stinks to high heaven. I mean, we were *choking*! So we got on our bikes and rode out. Aunt Cassie is going to kill us."

He studied her face. "That would be Cassie Whipple out at the old Ackerman property?"

Aiden held his breath and tried to communicate with his sister by telepathy: *It's a trap!*

He needn't have worried. Meg did not rise to the bait. "No. Cassie Ferguson. Aunt Cassie and Uncle Don. So anyway, we came in to check your map."

"So you know you kids are way off course. Kearney's twenty miles west of here."

"Yeah, thanks," said Meg. "Come on, bro, we'd better hit the road."

They breezed past him and walked quickly across

the blacktop, feeling the man's eyes — and the gas jockey's, too — burning into the backs of their heads. The instant they were around the side of the building, they broke into a full sprint to where they'd left the bikes.

A moment later they were speeding off down the road toward Kearney.

"Isn't this the wrong way?" called Meg.

"It's the right way to Aunt Cassie's house," Aiden shot back sarcastically. "We can't let that guy catch us riding east."

The last thing they saw before the gas station fell out of sight behind them was the big greasy mechanic dialing the mini-mart's phone.

"Aw, man, he's calling the cops!" Aiden groaned.

"Maybe he's calling his girlfriend," Meg suggested. "Or his mother."

"We've got to get off this road!" Even as he spoke the words, his heart was sinking. One thing they'd learned from the ride so far: Intersections were few and far between in this part of Nebraska.

They pedaled on west, unable to turn back. Aiden kept his eyes peeled for a way south — a dirt road, a cow path, anything that would get them away from here. The authorities were on the way. He had no doubt of that.

"Maybe we should ditch the bikes and cross these fields on foot," Meg suggested.

"We're too far out in the middle of nowhere. Gibbon is still miles away."

Going in the wrong direction, even when it was necessary, was driving Aiden crazy. *Pretty soon we'll pass the farm where we stole these bikes,* he thought miserably. *Then it's only a hop, skip, and jump back to Sunnydale.*

His ears strained to detect the faint whine of sirens. At any moment he expected a line of cop cars to explode from behind a stand of corn. The tension welled up inside him to the point where he almost wanted to get caught, just so the awful uncertainty would be over.

"Look!" cried Meg.

A road — a narrow, dusty two-lane thoroughfare, completely identical to the route they were on. But this one headed south.

They wheeled around the corner with new energy. Just the thought that every turn of the pedals was taking them closer to where they needed to be lent Aiden's feet wings. Meg must have felt it, too, because she was matching him rpm for rpm. In no time at all, they had covered so much ground that they could no longer see the turnoff behind them.

He caught a glimpse of his sister riding alongside him. Her face was glowing with effort and purpose. She flashed him a thumbs-up and called, "Vermont!"

He tried to look encouraging. Vermont, maybe. But Aiden would have settled for the heck away from here.

He pictured the mini-mart map in his mind, trying to estimate the distance to the train tracks. It was hard to translate inches on the poster into miles of lush farmland. But surely another hour or two would get them there.

When the horn sounded, it was a hammer blow to the heart. The pickup truck was practically beside them, its driver gesturing for them to stop.

Aiden pedaled harder, even as he knew that two kids on bikes couldn't outrun a motor vehicle. Stupid of them to get so wrapped up in the glory of their escape that they failed to notice a truck until it was upon them.

The driver rolled down his window. "I just want to talk!" he called.

"Keep going!" Meg screamed at her brother.

All at once, the pickup lurched ahead of them and screeched to a halt, blocking their way.

Both Falconers leaped off their bikes to avoid a painful collision.

Meg hit the ground running, but Aiden was pitched into the ditch.

The driver jumped out of his truck. "Hey!"

As Aiden struggled to climb the embankment, he suddenly recognized their pursuer. It was the teenage attendant from the gas station.

"What do you want from us?" Aiden demanded, steeling himself to fight for their freedom.

"You're from Sunnydale, right? The kids who ran away?"

"So what?" Aiden shot back.

"I was there. When I was fifteen. I did a year on that farm."

Meg turned around. "There's no such place anymore."

The teenager grinned. "No tears from this graduate."

"Is that what this is about?" asked Aiden. "An alumni meeting? We're in kind of a hurry."

The attendant turned serious. "You're in a *big* hurry. Jimmy — my boss — ratted you out. You've got to ditch those bikes. I'll drop them up north a ways — throw the cops off the scent."

The look that passed between Aiden and Meg spoke volumes. Ever since their parents' arrest, they had been mistreated, lied to, jerked around, ignored, and neglected. Worse, they had been treated as if they were guilty of some unspecified vile crime. It had never occurred to them that anyone might try to help them.

"Thanks for the heads-up," Aiden said finally. "Can you tell us how far the railroad tracks are?"

"Three, maybe four miles. But it's not safe on the road. Cut through the fields, keep low. And take these." He reached into the cab of the pickup and pulled out two shrink-wrapped submarine sandwiches from the mini-mart.

"We have no money," Aiden said stiffly.

The gas jockey smiled. "Jimmy's food tastes like wet newspaper. Trust me — you're paying exactly what it's worth." He loaded the first of the bikes into the truck's flatbed. "Now, take off."

Meg hated ham and cheese. But her mini-mart sandwich tasted like it had been prepared by a gourmet chef. She finished it down to the last crumb, then licked at bits of mustard on her fingers.

She turned a jaundiced eye on her brother, trudging beside her through the wheat field. Aiden still had three-quarters of his sandwich left. He was nibbling slowly, savoring every morsel, making it last.

"You're doing that on purpose," she said irritably.

"Doing what?"

"Waving that lousy sandwich in my face when you know I haven't got one."

"You had one. You ate it."

"Like a normal person," she insisted. "I didn't turn it into a three-day picnic."

"Do you want a piece?" he offered.

"No. It's yours."

"Well, then, let me eat it," he mumbled, mouth full. "My way."

But after a few more bites, he took the wad of clear plastic from his pocket, carefully unfolded it, and rewrapped the remaining half sandwich.

"Now what are you doing?" Meg demanded.

"Saving it for later. Who knows when our next meal will be."

She stormed ahead, putting her brother and his annoying habits out of her sight. Aiden always had to have a plan, even for something as stupid as a ham sandwich. What could you expect from a kid who used to sort his Halloween candy into alphabetical order and would still be eating the Zagnuts in April? It was almost as if his personality had been custom-crafted to get on Meg's nerves.

Hey, she reminded herself sharply, *he didn't get on your nerves when he busted through smoke and flames to rescue you.*

But even then Aiden had needed an instruction manual — the how-to he'd taken from one of Dad's cheese-ball detective novels. How was a guy like that going to get all the way from a wheat field in Nebraska to a place in Vermont he barely even remembered, with no money and no plan?

The challenge that lay ahead simply could not be met by a person like Aiden. This called for someone who could think on her feet and fly by the seat of her pants.

Someone like Meg.

It's my job to get us through this. I have to be sharp, on my toes. I can't let anything get past me —

"Meg!"

She looked back and realized instantly that between her and Aiden was a railroad track. She had actually walked right over it and missed it.

They made a left turn and walked along the line of the track. Somewhere on this shiny double rail to infinity lay the station at Gibbon, where two fugitive kids could hop a freight east.

Gibbon. It was still miles away. Ten? Twenty? Fifty?

Every time she pictured the mini-mart map, the dot that was Gibbon had somehow slithered farther away from them.

She swallowed her pride. "Hey, bro, how about we crack open that half sandwich?"

"We should probably wait," he warned, but finally gave in.

This time the food wasn't half as satisfying in her mouth, the ham too salty, the bread stale. Of course they should have held out longer. Why was Aiden always right?

She cast him a resentful look, and her eye was caught by a speck over his shoulder — a moving speck.

He was instantly alert to her distress. "What?"

She pointed. "I'm being paranoid, right? There are millions of reasons for a helicopter to be up there."

"Sure," Aiden said uncertainly, and couldn't name one. "But just in case — " He did a three-sixty. Nothing but acre after acre of golden wheat. Not a shrub, not a rock. Zero cover.

Eleven of us unaccounted for in a big open state . . . Meg felt the panic rising in her throat. Of course the juvenile authorities would search by air! At ground level, you could disappear into the Nebraska fields. But not when you were being hunted from above.

Aiden grabbed her arm and began running alongside the rails.

"Don't you think we have a better chance just lying in the wheat?" she cried. But then she saw it, too. About a quarter mile ahead, the tracks crossed a river via a narrow trestle bridge. If they could make it before the chopper got close enough to spot them —

They flew, with all the misery and horror of the past months acting as their booster rockets.

Meg risked a glance over her shoulder. The features of the helicopter were fully visible now. It was a bubble top, moving in a sweeping motion back and forth over the fields — a classic search pattern. She was sure she would have heard the clatter of the rotors except for the pounding of her own heart in her ears.

Their heavy footfalls made a gonging sound as the Falconers pounded onto the metal of the bridge.

Aiden swung a leg up to straddle the railing. "Get underneath!" he rasped. "Fast!"

Meg didn't have to be told twice.

They eased themselves over the side and climbed spiderlike along the support girders until they were well hidden by the top of the bridge. Gasping, they hung there, directly below the midpoint of the span.

"Do you think they saw us?" quavered Meg.

"We'll know soon enough."

They listened for several minutes. The sound of the chopper swelled and faded as it continued the track lines of its search. A good sign — it meant the crew hadn't noticed anything out of the ordinary.

Meg felt the muscles in her arms cramping up as she attempted to wiggle herself into a more comfortable position in the crook of two girders.

All at once, she detected a different sensation — a superfast vibration that seemed to permeate her entire body.

She looked over at her brother. "Do you feel like you're buzzing all over?"

The expression on his face was pure agony. "Hang on, Meg, and hang on tight! There's a train coming!"

Meg could hear it now, the great lumbering locomotive, the rumble of many hundreds of wheels, and the screech of brakes as the engineer slowed down to take the bridge. The roar drowned out the sound of the helicopter.

And it was growing louder. The vibration grew so intense that Meg was positive her teeth were jarring loose.

The train hurtled out onto the steel span above them. The noise was unimaginable — the squeal of metal on metal far louder than any jet engine. It was as if the bridge itself went into convulsions, shaking the Falconers like rag dolls in the mouth of an angry terrier.

Robbed of all but the barest consciousness, Meg shut her eyes and squeezed the girder. A single thought played like a tune through her agony: *Mom and Dad will never find out what happened to us. . . .*

The wild vibration acted like Novocain on her body. Numbness set in; she could not feel the girder. Her eyes blinked open, and she realized in horror that it was no longer there.

She was falling.

Then she was in the cool water, shocked to awareness and choking. The compulsion to swim for air was automatic. She broke the surface just in time to see a huge cannonball splash beside her. A second later, her brother bobbed up. The caboose cleared the bridge, and the noise began to fade as the train moved off.

"Are you okay?" Aiden spluttered.

She nodded. "The chopper?"

Treading water, they both peered up from their position in the shadow of the bridge. The helicopter was gone. The crisis was over as quickly as it had come upon them.

Typically, Aiden was agonizing over their close call, shivering and reliving every moment of the ordeal.

Leave it to him, Meg thought, *to obsess over something that didn't happen.*

"Aiden, we made it!" she interrupted. "What's the big deal?"

The big deal turned out to be this: They now had to finish their long walk to Gibbon in drenched discomfort.

The day was warm and sunny, but dusk was at hand, and clouds of mosquitoes rose from the fields, looking to light on any damp surface. The T-shirts dried after an hour or so, but the pants stayed soggy, clinging, chafing. The shoes didn't dry at all, squishing and oozing with every step.

The night was hideous. Aiden stumbled along the tracks, his arms windmilling as he slapped at the dozens of mosquitoes attacking his body.

"Do you have to do that?" Meg muttered into the deepening darkness. "They're mosquitoes, bro, not piranhas."

"That's easy for you to say. They're not eating you alive. I've got fair skin, and the water attracts them, you know."

She was unmoved. "If you didn't want to get wet, you shouldn't have fallen off that bridge."

"I didn't fall off," he retorted, killing three bugs with one slap. "I jumped off — to rescue you."

Meg bit her lip. Who was she crabbing at? The only person who cared what happened to her.

Soon it was every bit as dark as it had been the

night before — that suffocating unbroken blackness that made them feel they were the only two people left in the world. At least tonight they had the tracks to keep them on their course.

Just before midnight, another train came by, this one a westbound freight. Hiding amid the wheat, Aiden noticed in the passing glow of its single headlight that both his arms were covered in raised welts. The word "itch" didn't do justice to the feeling.

But the real enemy was not the mosquitoes, nor the chafed skin, nor aching feet. Lack of sleep was catching up with the Falconers. They had dozed only a couple of hours in the hayloft. The rest of the time, they had been not only awake but on the run, operating at top awareness and energy.

If we can't get a few hours' rest, something awful's going to happen, Aiden thought numbly. But how could they stop now? Miserable as it was, darkness was the best time for them to travel out in the open like this. *If we could only make it to Gibbon and stow away on a freight train. Then we could get some sleep.*

They saw their first electric light at about two A.M., a bare bulb outside a barn that housed a fertilizer wholesaler. Other signs of civilization flickered ahead.

"Is this the town?" Meg asked in dismay.

"Probably just the outskirts," he told her. "There's supposed to be a train station around here somewhere."

As they plodded on, the lights became more plentiful, and houses and low buildings appeared.

At last, there it was — a small, low, shedlike structure next to a level street crossing. On the side, a single lamp lit a one-word sign: GIBBON.

According to the schedule posted on the bulletin board, the first eastbound train of the day would stop here at 4:48 A.M.

"It's perfect," said Aiden. "It'll still be dark, with not too many people around. We can sneak into a boxcar without anybody seeing us."

"That's two hours from now," Meg calculated. "Let's find someplace to grab a nap in the meantime."

"No naps!" Aiden was adamant. "If we fall asleep now, a train wouldn't wake us unless it was running over our heads! We can't let the sun rise on us in this town. This is the first station east of Sunnydale."

"Well, can we at least see if we can get into the station? I'd give anything for a real bathroom."

The lock turned out to be broken, and they slipped inside with no trouble.

Just enough light was coming in through the high

windows for them to make out wooden benches and a small ticket and information kiosk.

By feeling her way along the wall, Meg located the ladies' room.

"No lights," Aiden reminded her. He sat down on a bench. No sooner was he settled onto the seat than his eyelids began to droop. He stood up quickly. *Great,* he thought. *Now I can't even trust myself to relax for a minute.*

There was a rustling sound behind him. He sat down sharply, no longer in danger of dozing. *Stay cool,* he told himself. *It's probably just a stray cat or a squirrel.*

Then it came again, and this time he was positive he heard a footstep. Somebody was in there! His imagination swelled with visions of muggers, murderers, and gangsters. But even if it was merely a homeless guy looking for a place to crash, that was almost as bad. He and Meg could not be seen by *anybody*

Avoiding sudden moves, Aiden shuffled over to the ladies' room and opened the door partway. "Hurry up," he whispered softly.

"Huh?" said Meg over the sound of running water in the sink.

"Let's go, Meg," he hissed. "Now!"

At the sound of her approach, he grabbed her wrist and began hauling her to the exit. There was the pounding of running feet, and the Falconers ran, too.

Aiden was reaching for the knob when the other figure slammed into him, driving him back into his sister. The three tumbled to the floor. A split second later, the intruder leaped on top of Aiden, pinning him. Aiden felt metal, cold and sharp, pressed against his throat. A weapon.

A rush of terror shot through him, and he found himself looking up through wide eyes at the face of —

"Miguel?"

"Eagledink?"

Meg's foot snapped out of the darkness and connected with the side of Miguel's head. The blow knocked him off Aiden and into the station door. In a lightning-fast move, he was on his feet again, brandishing a sharpened screwdriver at Meg.

Aiden jumped in between them. "It's only my sister! She didn't know it was you!"

The dark-haired boy lowered the weapon. "Little sis packs a wallop!" He squinted in the darkness from face to face. "I'm impressed, Eagledink. I thought a wimp like you would be back at Sunnydale, helping the supes clean up the mess."

"That shows what *you* know!" Meg said belligerently.

Miguel nodded. "I was worried. After what I said that time about the farm being a firetrap, I figured you'd be diming me as the pyro."

"I know you didn't do it," Aiden muttered, tight-lipped.

"Yeah? How?" Miguel's mouth dropped open. "Eagledink — *you*? I was just bluffing! You must be bugging to really try it!"

"It was an accident," Aiden insisted.

"However it happened," Meg put in, "we're not going back there."

"Amen to that," Miguel agreed fervently. "I hope this train's going to Jersey. The sooner I get to my brother's crib, the better. Where are you guys headed?"

"Delaware," said Aiden, at the same time as Meg said, "Virginia."

"Oooh, you don't trust me." Miguel grinned, taking mock offense. "Who can I tell without giving *myself* up? Like I care where you losers go. Hey, anybody hungry?"

"You've got food?" Meg asked anxiously.

Miguel pointed to a dark shape beside the information kiosk. "Candy machine."

"We don't have any money," said Aiden.

"My treat." Miguel jammed the screwdriver into the tool slot of the coin box and pried open the metal plate. Quarters cascaded onto the floor.

Aiden and Meg exchanged a look. They weren't thieves. Their honesty was what separated them from people like Miguel.

He read their minds. "You've got a lot of integrity for arsonists," he commented, investing some of his ill-gotten gains in a Snickers. "Remember, nobody's going to give you a reward for not robbing this machine."

Aiden hesitated. Was he crazy to think of himself and Meg as being better than Miguel? The three of them were fugitives, wanted by the law. And they were all guilty of stealing. The civilian clothes on their backs proved that. What was to be gained by denying themselves a couple of Mars bars? He and Meg were in a desperate situation. The odds against reaching Vermont had to be astronomical. It made no sense to tip them further. Why refuse nourishment just to preserve the fine line between themselves and Miguel? It probably didn't exist anyway.

"Why not?" he said with a twisted smile.

Meg had already scooped up a handful of coins and was stuffing them into the machine.

Miguel watched in amusement. *"That's* the spirit. It's a long way to Delaware. Or Virginia."

The four forty-eight pulled into Gibbon station a few minutes early. Truck farmers were spread along the road, their bushel baskets ready for loading onto the boxcars. The train crew was in position to open up cars five and six in the powerful spotlights of the work area. To anyone inside that brighter-than-day zone, this train had no engine, nor any caboose. The lights were blinding, the night around them inky-black.

Far behind the loading area, nearly a quarter mile to the rear, three shadowy figures slipped out of the underbrush and stole over to car forty-one, the third last on the long freight.

A hand reached up, released the latch, and slid the heavy metal door slightly open. An athletic silhouette hoisted itself up and inside, then bent down to assist two companions.

When the corrugated metal was pulled shut

again, it left no sign that anyone had ever been there.

The interior was pitch-black, darker even than the Nebraska night, and soundless, except for the ragged breathing of the three runaways.

Suddenly, a match blazed, illuminating all three of their faces. Miguel shone this temporary light into the four corners of the car. It was empty except for a few tattered sheets of newsprint and a single large crate pushed up against the front wall.

"Looks like we got the presidential suite," he said cheerfully.

"Let's just hope we don't get fleas," was Meg's comment.

"Let's just hope we don't get *caught*," Aiden amended. "What's in that big box?"

Miguel lit another match and went over to investigate. "Hey, Eagledink. What does T-N-T spell?"

"Put out that match!" rasped Aiden in a panic.

Miguel nearly choked on his laughter. "You are such a sucker! It's just some old tarps. Our beds, dummy."

Beside him, Aiden heard Meg snicker.

There was an abrupt lurch and a screech from the steel wheels. The train began to creep forward.

Miguel shared out the tarpaulins. They were

rough and stiff and smelled strongly of cabbages. To the fugitives, they were the softest of perfumed feather beds.

All three were asleep before the train had gathered full speed.

"Aiden — time to get your shoes on."

Six-year-old Aiden Falconer sat cross-legged on the shag carpeting of his small bedroom in the summerhouse. Spread out on the floor in front of him were a dozen color photographs, the boy's pride and joy. He had taken them himself, using his own camera, and his very first roll of film.

"Come on, Aiden. We have to be at the Colchester Grill at six."

"I'm busy," he called down the stairs. He hated restaurants where you had to sit in your chair the whole time, waiting forever for people to bring food you weren't going to like anyway. They never had hamburgers. And pretty soon Meg would be crying.

"Uncle Frank and Aunt Jane will wonder what happened to us."

"I'm not going." He selected a single picture out of his array — Uncle Frank and Aunt Jane. They were nice enough, he supposed, but so boring. Whenever they

were around, all Mom and Dad wanted to do was talk.
And eat dinner for three hours.

He prepared to rip the snapshot into a billion pieces.
But he could hear his mother's footsteps starting up the
stairs. Quickly, he collected his pictures, stuffed them
into the cigar box that held his summer treasures, and
stashed that in his secret hiding place. He got the loose
piece of panel back in its slot just as his mother burst
into the room.

"What is the matter with you, Aiden? We are going
out to dinner, and that's that."

She reached down and hoisted him high in the air. As
he swung around past the window, he saw the gleaming
waters of Lake Champlain on a summer afternoon. The
dock was festooned with hundreds of colored flags. At
the near end, the ferry was boarding for its trip to the
New York side of the lake.

"Come on, sweetie," his mother coaxed. "You'll have
fun."

As she held him, he had a strange feeling that he
should be hugging her harder, never letting go. . . .

Aiden awoke sucking air, because someone had
taken his mother away, and she was never coming
back.

"Hey — Eagledink!" Miguel was shaking him.

Aiden sat up in the darkness of the boxcar. The dream was still very real in his mind. *Colchester. The house was in Colchester, Vermont.*

Miguel brayed a derisive laugh. "You were crying for Mommy. You've got some serious hang-ups about your folks. What gives?"

Aiden looked around, orienting himself. A thin line of light showed at the edge of the sliding door. Daylight. He checked his watch: 4:05.

We've been asleep for eleven hours!

"Meg?"

"Still snoozing," said Miguel.

"No, I'm not," came her drowsy voice. "Where are we?"

"Stopped," Aiden said. It was only then that he realized it himself. The train was standing still. He turned to Miguel. "How long have we been stopped?"

"Don't know. I've been sleeping like you."

They could hear voices outside — Aiden listened — strident voices, barking orders. The rumble and slam of boxcar doors kept repeating itself, and — was that a siren?

"Something's up," Meg said nervously.

Miguel slid the door open a few inches and flattened himself so he could peer up the length of the train. "Cops," he said.

Aiden was horrified. "Searching the train?"

"No, dancing the hula. Get a grip!"

"*You* get a grip!" Aiden hissed angrily. "This is *your* fault! They probably saw the busted candy machine in Gibbon and knew we were on this freight!"

"Can we run for it?" Meg interrupted.

Miguel shook his head. "They're too close. We're trapped."

Trapped in a boxcar.

Something frantic rattled around in Aiden's head. He should know about this! This was familiar.

That's crazy! You've never been on a train that wasn't a commuter. What do you know about escaping from a freight car?

Then he remembered. Mac Mulvey, Dad's recurring detective hero, had once broken out of a locked freezer car via —

He looked up and there it was. The shaft of light from the open slider shone on an emergency hatch in the ceiling. He rushed over to the wooden crate and began positioning it in the center of the car.

"What are you going to do, Eagledink?" scoffed Miguel. "Mail yourself out of here?"

Aiden pointed straight up. Instantly, he had two helpers. When the crate was in place, he scrambled up the wooden side and balanced on the narrow rim. The trapdoor was held in place by a small latch. He popped the hatch, reached up, and took hold of the roof of the car.

Here goes, he thought. If the police were watching the top of the train, this would be his last act as a free person. *One . . . two . . .* — a silent prayer — *three!*

He heaved himself up through the opening and flopped flat onto the metal surface. He could see tall buildings in the distance — a skyline. They were outside a big city. But their immediate surroundings were lower and leafier. This was a suburban station. To his left, about a dozen cops patrolled the platform, searching the train. And they were only *two cars away!*

"Hurry!" he hissed, reaching down to help Meg and then Miguel to the roof of the boxcar.

He looked around desperately. To his right was an empty track. There weren't any officers on that side. But it was a twelve-foot drop to the ground.

A broken ankle — not a good idea for a fugitive.

"Follow me," he whispered.

Keeping low, he slithered forward on the metal roof, scrambling over the four-foot gap to the next car. Over his shoulder, he could see Miguel and Meg following him. The three snaked silently ahead, barely daring to breathe. Soon Aiden found himself on a different kind of surface — a thick lattice cage.

The powerful farm odor reached him almost immediately. A livestock carrier. Animals lowing wafted up from below.

He peered down through the bars. Didn't it figure?

Cows.

He slunk to the edge of the car and eased over the side. Using the steel struts as ladder rungs, he began to climb down. The cows mooed at him; one even pressed its snout right up to the opening and licked him. But he was able to clamber low enough to jump to the ground.

Miguel landed beside him a few seconds later. Meg came last. As her sneakers made contact with the gravel, she lost her footing and lurched toward the open track. Miguel grabbed her arm and propped her back into balance.

He gestured meaningfully at the spot where she had almost fallen. This was a commuter line. It had an electrified third rail. Had Meg touched it, she would have been seriously injured or even killed.

Her mouth formed the word "thanks," but she allowed no sound to come out.

Hidden behind the bulk of the train, they scampered the length of the station. A small metal ladder provided access to the outbound platform. They scrambled up, trying to look like local kids and not fleeing felons.

They were in luck. The vacant side was nearly deserted. At this time of day, people returning from a day's work in the city just wanted to get home. No one was hanging around.

They strode purposefully toward the stairway to the parking lot. It was a hundred yards away — a single football field. For the first time, Aiden allowed the notion to enter his mind that they might survive this latest close call.

They were halfway there — the fifty-yard line — when the bathroom door opened and out stepped a pudgy, middle-aged policeman. It was too late to turn, too late to hide. The only plan of action was to keep walking. As they drew close, Aiden noticed the fax in the officer's hand. The page was dotted with photographs — murky mugshots of the Sunnydale runaways.

Strangely — amazingly — the cop let them pass. They forged on, eyes fixed straight ahead. Was it possible that he simply hadn't noticed them?

Leather soles scraping against concrete — the

sound of someone turning around. Then: "Hey!
Hey!!"

They ran, flying across the platform and down
the stairs. The cop gave chase. "Police! Hey! Stop!"

In addition to being tougher than the Falconers,
Miguel turned out to be faster as well. He blasted
through the parking lot, opening a gap between
himself and Aiden and Meg.

He'll get away and we won't! The thought brought
Aiden hidden reserves of power, and he turned on
the jets and kept pace. Meg was hot on his heels.

Luckily, the policeman wasn't much of an athlete.
They could hear him puffing into his walkie-talkie:
"Lewin to Caldwell . . . Chris, I've got 'em . . . fast
little rats."

The parking lot was bordered by a small strip of
stores and restaurants. Beyond that, subdivisions began.

Miguel never hesitated. He barreled headlong
down tree-lined roads, wheeling left and right, nav-
igating as if he'd lived here all his life.

The Falconers followed like the tail of a comet.
They had no loyalty for Miguel Reyes; they didn't
like him, and trusted him zero. But he ran with the
kind of cool self-assurance that inspired confidence.
Besides, if anybody was an expert at fleeing the po-

lice, it had to be this juvenile delinquent. For good or ill, their fates had become intertwined.

Aiden looked over his shoulder. He could no longer see Officer Lewin. It brought some relief, but reinforcements couldn't be far behind.

Miguel sensed that, for the moment, the coast was clear. He selected one of the scores of identical homes and dashed for it, hopping the fence with an effortless vault.

Aiden was practically babbling as he scrambled over the obstacle. "What are you doing? There's nowhere to hide here!"

Miguel indicated the house, a well-tended brick colonial surrounded by sculpted bushes. "What do you call that?"

Meg jumped down beside them. "A houseful of people," she panted. "With a telephone for calling the police."

"For a couple of Eagles, you guys are blind as bats. There's a pile of newspapers on the front stoop. They're on *vacation*, brainiacs. Nobody home. No alarm, either."

"How do you know?" puffed Aiden.

"No stickers in the windows. Alarm people love stickers." He pulled a grapefruit-sized stone out of the garden and headed for the patio doors.

The Falconers exchanged uneasy glances. Taking clothes from a drying rack or bikes that you planned to return was one thing. *This* was breaking and entering.

But pretty soon the whole neighborhood will be crawling with cops!

Amazing, Aiden marveled. The only way to survive as a fugitive was by breaking even more laws.

If the police really want to reduce crime, they should leave us alone.

Miguel hefted the rock and deftly punched out a single pane of glass from the French doors. He reached inside and flipped the latch.

They were in.

They cleaned up the glass and took in the telltale newspapers. The next order of business, according to Miguel, was their appearance.

"What's wrong with how we look?" asked Aiden.

"Well, you're both pretty ugly," Miguel wise-cracked, "but that's not the problem. We match our mug shots, yo. Cops'll make us in a heartbeat."

He rustled through a few kitchen cabinets and drawers and came up with a pair of scissors. "Who's first?"

"No way," Meg said firmly. "I'm not letting this lunatic touch my hair."

Miguel shrugged. "No skin off my back, little sis. More time for me to split while the cops are cuffing you."

"There's too much at stake to risk getting caught," Aiden told her.

Meg hesitated. "You ever cut hair before?" she asked Miguel.

"I'm Vin Diesel's personal barber."

"Aiden — "

Aiden sighed. "Just do it."

Meg sat on a kitchen chair, biting back rage, as clumps of her long dark hair scattered on the floor. When she finally regarded herself in the mirror, she almost cried. She looked like a *geek*, with a Buster Brown cut that exposed her ears.

"You should stick to murder," she mumbled bitterly, "because as a stylist, you stink."

"Hey!" Miguel was upon her in an instant, grabbing a fistful of T-shirt and pushing her hard against the refrigerator. She felt the scissor blade pressing on the skin of her neck. "Don't you *ever* call me a murderer! You hear me?"

With cold steel against her throat, Meg was too petrified to reply.

"Let her go, man!" cried Aiden, struggling to remain calm. "She didn't mean it!"

Miguel's eyes burned feverishly. "It was *manslaughter*!"

"We know that," Aiden soothed. "We're all friends here. We've got to stick together if we're going to get out of this, right?"

"They don't send murderers to milk cows!"

Miguel made no move to release her. "You do hard time for that!"

"We *know*!"

The scissors hit the tile floor with a clatter. Meg fled to her brother's arms. The message flashed between them: *Who's the real enemy — the police or Miguel?*

"It was manslaughter," the olive-skinned boy repeated to no one in particular. Then, his voice barely audible, he added, "Jerk had it coming, anyway."

Soon Aiden's curly top had been reduced to a tight crew cut. Meg was amazed at how his entire appearance was transformed. Her brother had always had a serious yet somehow goofy look to him. Now his cheekbones seemed higher, his jaw stronger, his eyes more deep set. His appearance was older, more mature. Could one haircut have done all this, she wondered? Or had life on the run already aged her brother?

They found a box of color formula in the upstairs bathroom. While Aiden dyed his fair hair jet-black, Meg massaged hydrogen peroxide into the Buster Brown. Her scalp stung like crazy, but twenty painful minutes later she was a platinum blond.

Miguel gave himself a quick haircut using a portable sideburn trimmer. He loved the new him so much that he paid the trimmer the ultimate compliment — he pocketed it.

Meg started to protest . . . and then the doorbell rang.

A lightning strike could not have produced such electricity inside the house. Meg ran to the window, hoping against hope that she wouldn't see what she knew she would — a police cruiser, parked at the curb.

Miguel saw it, too. "Heat."

Aiden was well on his way to panic. "Why'd you have to take in those newspapers?" he confronted Miguel. "Now they know somebody's here!"

"They'd check an empty house twice as close, Eagledink," Miguel retorted. "Maybe notice that missing glass out back."

The doorbell rang twice more. Meg could hear urgency in its tone. Sucking in a breath, she headed downstairs.

Aiden realized his sister's intentions too late. "Don't do it!"

But Meg just knew, although she wasn't sure how: *Don't give the cops a chance to snoop around.*

And there was only one way to do that.

She threw open the door and peered up at a tall, thin officer. Her heart nearly stopped when she saw he was holding a faxed page with their mug shots.

Get out of here! Slam the door and run!

Yet there was no recognition in the young cop's eyes.

He smiled at her. "Pardon the intrusion, son. Is your mom home?"

Meg struggled to conceal her amazement. He thought she was a *boy*!

She conjured her best shy expression. "My parents are at work," she mumbled, peering alternately at the officer and the floor. *Don't let him get a good look at you. . . .*

"You're kind of young to be here all alone," the cop said kindly. "Who's watching you?"

"Carolyn. My sister. She's fourteen."

"Maybe I should talk with her."

"Sure," Meg agreed. "But you'll have to wait till she gets out of the shower. She takes, like, twenty showers a day." She wrinkled her nose. "Girls do that."

The cop grinned. "So I've heard. Have you seen anybody suspicious in the neighborhood the last couple of hours? Big kids, teenagers — two boys and a girl?"

She shook her head. "Burglars?"

"Nothing to get worked up over," he reassured her. "Just keep the house locked until your folks get home. And if you see anybody suspicious, you know the number to call, right?"

"Nine-one-one?" she ventured, almost too timidly.

"Good boy. Sorry to bother you." He started down the walk, tossing one last sentence over his shoulder. "Have your folks call the station if they have any questions."

When the door clicked shut, Meg nearly collapsed with relief.

Aiden and Miguel stepped out from behind the wall, regarding her in openmouthed wonder.

Aiden was white with fear. "Are you nuts? What if he wanted to chat with big sister Carolyn?"

Meg shrugged, not managing to look as cool as she'd hoped. "He didn't."

Miguel was staring at her with a new light in his eyes, something neither Falconer had seen before. Respect?

"Little sis," he said, "you've got it going on!"

Miguel couldn't find any money to steal, but he did unearth some travel confirmations. The MacKinnons of 144 Purple Sage Path, Hillside Park, Illinois, were at Disney World. They had flown United, rented from Hertz, and were staying at the Grand Floridian while the Sunnydale escapees "borrowed" their home.

"He's not just a thief and a killer," Meg whispered to Aiden. "He's also a pretty decent spy."

With the family on vacation, the house was empty of food except for three frozen pizzas — all gone by the time *Judge Judy* came on television.

"The legacy of Sunnydale," Aiden observed. "We can watch anything, no matter how boring."

"Bring on Dr. Phil," agreed Meg.

Miguel had a complaint. "Compared to my brother's setup, this dinky screen is a postage stamp."

The looting of the upstairs bedrooms was next. The MacKinnons had four children, and there were clothes for everyone. To Miguel's humiliation, he was a perfect fit for Mrs. MacKinnon's shoes.

He set to work in the garage blackening a pair of ladies' Reeboks with a tube of General Motors touch-up paint. Aiden and Meg channel surfed in the den, searching for details on the hunt for the Sunnydale escapees.

The Chicago news did a short account of the chase at the train station, but it was sandwiched between local crime pieces. CNN had nothing, although the scrolling updates at the bottom of the screen did mention that all but six of the missing juvenile offenders had been apprehended.

"I wonder who the other three are," mused Aiden.

"That's so like you, bro," Meg told him. "You worry about the wrong stuff. Who cares who else made it? *We* made it; that's all that matters. The big question is how do we get to Vermont from here? And" — she dropped her voice to a whisper — "how do we get away from that maniac? The sooner we kiss off Miguel, the sooner we can both breathe easier."

Aiden hesitated. He wasn't convinced that splitting from Miguel was the wisest course for them. As fugitives, the Falconers were completely clueless, flying by the seat of their pants. Miguel, on the other hand, had experience living outside the law. Yes, he was dangerous. But he might be a valuable guide.

For a while, anyway.

Miguel strolled into the room, modeling the painted Reeboks. "Check it out. I must be bad or something."

"Bad isn't the half of it," Meg muttered.

"Cheer up, little sis. You should be smiling. Why don't you ask me how we're going to get out of here?"

Aiden came alive. "You have a plan?"

In answer, Miguel jingled a set of car keys.

"But," — Meg was incredulous — "we don't know how to drive!"

"Speak for yourself. I was boosting rides when you were still playing with Barbies."

"Absolutely not," Aiden said firmly. "Come on, Miguel, these poor people! We break into their house, eat their food, steal their clothes. We're not going to rip off their car. No way!"

Dear Mr. and Mrs. MacKinnon,

There's probably not much we can say to make you forgive us for what we did to you. We're very sorry, but we had no choice. Someday, if things work out,

we hope we can pay you back. Trust me, no one
wants that more than we do. . . .

The car horn echoed through the house like an air
raid siren.

"Our chauffeur awaits," Meg commented dryly.

Aiden was still staring at the paper. *It's the only
way,* he thought, convincing himself for at least the
fifth time. *The cops will be expecting us to hop a train
or bus. This is our ticket out, our ticket east. . . .*

More honking. Hurriedly, he scribbled the rest of
the note:

Please believe me — this is not how we usually are.
We're not bad people but we're DESPERATE!!!

He put down the pen and said, "Let's go."

Miguel grinned down from the wheel of a black
Chevy Tahoe. "You navigate," he told Aiden, indi-
cating a tattered map spread across the passenger
seat. Meg climbed into the back.

They had delayed their departure until cover of
darkness. Opening the garage door flooded Purple
Sage Path with blazing light.

They can probably see us from the space shuttle!
Aiden thought nervously.

Now that the moment had arrived, abandoning their refuge seemed reckless and insane. Inside the MacKinnons' house, they were safe. Outside, anything could happen.

"Watch it," Meg exclaimed as the heavy SUV bounced over the curbstones. "You're on the lawn!"

Miguel snorted in glee. "This is grand theft auto! Gonna yell at me for tire marks on the grass?" He shifted out of reverse and roared off.

Navigation was bedlam, with Meg calling out street names and Aiden poring over the map, trying to place them in the spaghetti of roads and highways. The chaos just made Miguel laugh harder and drive faster. He was having the time of his life.

Nothing like an A-felony to bring out your inner child.

All at once, Meg cried, "Elmhurst Road — turn left!"

Miguel yanked on the wheel, and there it was — the entrance to the interstate, half a mile ahead. Flashing lights played off the tops of a parking lot of stopped cars clogging the roadway. There, before the ramp, were stationed four uniformed policemen, shining flashlights into windshields.

Aiden's formless fears suddenly crystallized with a crunch. "Roadblock!" he rasped.

Meg was incredulous "For *us*? But — " Her reasoning crumbled to dust. Of course the police would be expecting them to make a break for it. And where would the cops look? Freeway entrances near the spot where the fugitives were last seen.

Miguel threw the Tahoe into reverse, but it was too late. There were already several cars behind them.

Aiden looked around frantically. On their left, a two-foot-high concrete barrier separated them from oncoming traffic. On the right was a huge construction site — a deep ditch that took up an entire city block. "They've got us," he groaned.

"They've got squat," said Miguel, shutting off the headlights. With a grinding of gears, he shifted into four-wheel drive, swung out of the line of cars, and gunned the engine.

The Tahoe roared off the edge of the excavation. They were airborne, unconnected to anything on the ground. Through his horror and disbelief, Aiden felt gravity take over from the force of the car's forward momentum. They were falling.

The SUV lurched as its tires made contact with the dirt truck ramp. They rattled across the mud and rocks of the ditch, swerving at the last second to avoid cement mixers and portable generators.

Aiden peered out the back window. "I don't think anybody's following us. Hey, how'd you know that truck ramp was going to be there?"

Miguel's gaze never wavered from the obstacle course of construction equipment. "I didn't."

At the far side of the site, another ramp led back to street level. No sirens or flashing lights awaited them there.

They had dodged the bullet.

They crossed the city by dimly lit surface roads. They would have to get on the freeway eventually, but the metro area was an awfully large haystack, and three kids in a Tahoe represented a single needle. The Chicago grid hid them all the way to the Indiana border.

Later, as they stopped for a bathroom break, Meg whispered to her brother: "This guy was ready to drive off a twenty-foot cliff. We've got to ditch him before he gets us killed."

Aiden was toying with the idea that the opposite might be true. If they were to have a prayer of helping their parents, they would have to watch Miguel, to learn from him, almost *be* him in a sense.

To survive as a fugitive, you have to be a little bit crazy.

For the next two hundred miles, Aiden and Meg peered out the rear window of the Tahoe, expecting to see a line of police cruisers closing in on them, sirens wailing. But after a while, even fear becomes a routine emotion. Meg fell asleep just west of Toledo, Ohio. And somewhere along the south shore of Lake Erie, Aiden, too, surrendered to his overpowering fatigue.

Fevered dreams gave him little peace. Even as every broken line on the asphalt drew them closer to the east and their past with Frank Lindenauer, Aiden's time-faded memory tried and failed to paint a picture of the family friend who was the Falconers' CIA contact. The photograph — he could see the snapshot, but the face remained blank.

And the questions. Always the questions.

Why hadn't Lindenauer come forward during the trial? Was he sick? Dead? Suffering from amnesia? Or living in some isolated cabin where he simply hadn't heard about the Falconers' plight?

Oh, come on. He knew. Everybody knew. CNN called it the trial of the new millennium!

Why had he hung his friends out to dry that way? The one person who could have proved they were innocent . . .

If they were innocent —

How can you think that? Of course they're innocent! Does Meg ever have the slightest doubt about Mom and Dad? What kind of son are you?

"Eagledink." Miguel was shaking his shoulder.

"I'm awake." The digital readout said 3:34 A.M. Chicago time — 4:34 in the east. They were pulling into a highway service area. In the darkness, he could make out a few other cars and a lot of big rigs — truckers taking advantage of the empty roads. "Why are we stopping?"

"Gas," Miguel told him. "We should've boosted something with a little more fuel efficiency."

"We're broke," Aiden mused.

"We were stupid," Miguel commented. "We should've swiped some jewelry out of that house, pawned it in Chicago."

Aiden fought down his natural revulsion to crime. *This is your new reality. Get used to it.*

He said, "If we can steal earrings, we can steal gas. Just fill up and fly, right?"

Miguel shook his head. "Place like this, they've got cameras on the pumps. They'd radio our plate numbers to every cop between here and the George Washington Bridge. What we need is a credit card."

"Where do we get one of those?"

Miguel fluttered his fingers. "I have hidden talents."

Aiden was appalled. "Rip off somebody's wallet and buy gas while he's still looking for it?"

"You got a better idea, Eagledink?"

Aiden thought he had. Or at least his father had — in the continuing adventures of Mac Mulvey.

Meg jolted awake in the back of the Tahoe, groggy and disoriented. "Where are we?"

"Getting gas," Miguel replied.

She sat up. "I'm going to the bathroom."

"It's not that kind of pit stop."

"Huh?" They were nowhere near the gas pumps. The Tahoe was parked in the middle of a covey of transport trucks, hidden from the main station. She squinted out the window. Aiden was stringing a garden hose between the SUV and a large box van. "What's he doing?"

Miguel rolled his eyes. "He gave me some lecture about science. I told him to go jack the Magic School Bus — "

Now Aiden had one end of the hose in his mouth. Suddenly, he yanked it free. Pale liquid spewed from the nozzle. He jammed it in the Tahoe's fuel door.

"He's siphoning from the truck!" Meg exclaimed in amazement. "It's higher than us, so once he starts the gas moving, gravity will empty it into our tank!"

Miguel was impressed. "Maybe I should've paid attention in school."

Aiden appeared nervous but triumphant as fuel from the much larger box van drained into the SUV.

And then a fist the size of a small ham closed on his shoulder.

A force several times his own strength yanked him away from the Tahoe. The siphoning hose came loose, spewing a fountain of gas. Aiden wheeled to find himself grappling with the driver of the truck, a cement head and shovel jaw atop a broad ridge of plaid shoulders.

Aiden managed to spin himself free, only to be locked in the crushing bear hug of a second lumber-jack type.

"Aiden!" Meg sprang for the door handle. But

Miguel started the engine and stomped on the accel-
erator. The Tahoe squealed ahead, narrowly threading the needle between a tanker truck and a lumber
trailer.

The burst of speed plastered Meg against the
door. "What are you doing?" she shrieked. "Go
back!"

"He's done! Forget him!"

"*No!*"

Miguel aimed the Tahoe at the exit ramp that led
to the interstate. "What do you think those guys'll
do when they're through working him over?
They'll turn him in! You want to go back into the
system — a place with bars instead of chickens this
time?"

"I'm not leaving!"

"I'm not asking!"

They were on the ramp now. In another few seconds they would be hurtling east on the freeway,
abandoning Aiden to a beating and, worse, capture.
Unable to think of anything else to do, Meg reached
around the seat and clamped both hands over
Miguel's eyes.

There was a cry of outrage as he batted them
away. "You trying to get us killed?"

She lunged again, locking both arms around his

head. He struggled but could not budge her. "Are you *crazy*?"

She held on, wondering if she really *was* crazy. In another thirty feet they'd be on the interstate, surrounded by speeding cars. . . .

At the last moment, Miguel stomped on the brakes. The Tahoe spun out of control and lurched to a stop at the end of the ramp. Meg tumbled head over heels, landing on the floor mat in front of the passenger seat.

He glowered at her. "I've got no problem pitching you out that door *this minute*! You think I need some little girl slowing me down?"

Shaken and terrified, Meg glared right back into the teeth of his rage. "I'll crash the two of us, don't think I won't! *I'm not leaving my brother!*"

The punch in the gut knocked the wind out of Aiden, leaving him wheezing. The bigger of the two truckers held him in a full nelson, cursing and calling him every kind of punk in the book. The other man was more concerned with removing the siphoning hose from the box van's fuel tank.

Aiden knew he would never have a better chance. He brought his head forward and then snapped it back into his captor's shovel jaw. There were two grunts of pain — one of them from Aiden himself. The hold relaxed, and he exploded out of the tree-trunk arms.

The lumberjack brothers took off after him. But Aiden was flying, his high-stepping feet splashing in the puddled gas.

One thing I've gotten good at — running for my life.

Soon he was halfway across the parking lot. The question remained: Where was he running *to*? What could he do — hide in the woods outside some interstate truck stop? Miguel and Meg were gone, and he had no way to find them.

Then he saw it. Down the service area's exit ramp, the Tahoe was backing up at fifty miles an hour. He could see his sister's white face in the window and Miguel peering over his shoulder as he reversed at top speed.

Aiden waved his arms. "Over here!"

They came perilously close to flattening him. Meg threw open the rear door and he leaped inside.

Miguel put the SUV in drive and they squealed off toward the highway. "I thought *I* was bugging, but you Eagles are loony tunes."

Meg lashed out at Miguel, pummeling his arm and shoulder.

He deflected the blows into the dashboard. The windshield wipers jumped to life and the radio came on. "I went back, didn't I?"

Meg was out of control, spluttering tears of rage. "He was going to *leave* you!"

"I was caught — " Aiden reasoned.

"Traitor!" she roared at Miguel.

And then a newscaster's voice spoke a very familiar name, "Sunnydale."

"Quiet!" ordered Aiden.

Silence fell in the SUV.

"... *all but three of the missing residents are once again in custody*," the woman was saying. "*Still at large are fifteen-year-old Miguel Reyes, and a brother and sister registered under the name Eagleson. The Department of Juvenile Corrections has just confirmed that the Eaglesons are, in fact, Aiden and Margaret Falconer, ages fifteen and eleven, children of convicted traitors John and Louise Falconer.*"

Miguel pulled the Tahoe onto the shoulder in a screech of burning rubber. He turned on his passengers, eyes wide. "That's *you?*" he asked in horror. "Your parents are *terrorists?*"

"No — " Aiden began.

"But they helped terrorists. And you're calling *me* a traitor?"

"They're innocent!" Meg stormed.

"Innocent?" Miguel spat. "What does that mean? Remember Sunnydale? We were *all* innocent. Every place I've been — you can't find anybody guilty. If you go by the people doing time, crime is nothing but an ugly rumor started by a bunch of cops."

Meg was becoming belligerent. "Our parents were framed, and we're going to prove it!"

Understanding struck Miguel. "So *that's* the plan. You're going to ride in on white horses and rescue Mommy and Daddy."

"No," Aiden said patiently. "We're going to find evidence to clear their names."

"You're dreaming."

"Maybe," Aiden agreed. "But what else can we do? You know of another way to get justice?"

"Justice!" Miguel practically snarled the word. "You rich kids are all the same. Why are you entitled to justice? Where's my justice?"

"It's not the same thing," Aiden argued. "Maybe you had a good reason for what you did, but you still did it."

Miguel pulled out into traffic. When he spoke, his eyes were riveted to the horizon. He wouldn't so much as glance at Aiden or Meg.

"Yeah, I'm a real cold-blooded killer. Know what I'm guilty of? Shoving. Felony shoving. Aggravated shoving. First-degree shoving. If you lived with my stepfather, you'd be sick of being his punching bag, too. How was I supposed to know the jerk was going to fall down the stairs? Cops said he broke his neck — killed instantly."

"*That's* what happened?" Meg exclaimed in amazement. "You just defended yourself? You're innocent!"

"Don't you get it?" Miguel asked bitterly. "There's no innocent and guilty, just lucky and unlucky. Think my old lady's going to blow her savings on a lawyer for the kid who put her husband in the cemetery? Unlucky — same as your folks."

Aiden was thunderstruck. "Miguel — I don't know what to say. Being in jail for something you didn't even do — we both know what that's like."

Miguel twisted the radio dial, searching for music. "Listen, Eagle — Falcon — whoever you are. This car's rolling to my brother's place. Come, don't come — it makes no difference to me. But if New Jersey isn't in your travel plans, now's the time to do something about it."

Aiden and Meg said nothing. But as the Tahoe continued its long journey east, neither made any move to get out.

At the Department of Juvenile Corrections in Washington, DC, Agent Emmanuel Harris strode past the secretary without stopping.

"Sir!" she shrilled. "Deputy Director Adler can't be disturbed — "

Harris threw open the door, ducking so his head would clear the frame. "You *knew*," he accused, pointing a missile-like index finger at the thirty-something bureaucrat behind the desk. "You *knew* the Falconers were at Sunnydale. And you knew they were missing five minutes after that place went up in smoke."

"Sure, I did." In an attempt to look older, Adler sported a patchy mustache that almost — but not quite — filled in the space above his upper lip. "I also knew that information was classified for the kids' own good."

The famous sarcasm. "Yeah, we did them a real favor, throwing them in jail — "

"It's not a jail," the deputy director interrupted.

"No," Harris agreed. "From what I hear, it's a pile of charcoal."

"Aiden and Margaret Falconer were never in the system. They were at Sunnydale for their own protection."

"Surrounded by lowlifes," Harris added. "Like this Reyes kid with manslaughter on his rap sheet."

"They're not the little angels you think they are. They escaped from federal custody — "

"I thought they were never in the system."

"— and we're charging the boy with arson. We have an eyewitness who says he deliberately started the fire with a kerosene lamp."

"A kerosene lamp?" the agent exploded. "What is this, the dark ages?"

"Hard work and a simple life is a proven approach in dealing with young offenders," the deputy director said stoutly. "Don't tell me my job."

"You're not *doing* your job," Harris insisted. "You need to find these kids before they get hurt."

"We'll track them down," Adler said confidently. "We traced them from a couple of stolen bikes to the train station in Gibbon, Nebraska. The next day, they were spotted outside Chicago. The local cops set up roadblocks, but somehow the kids dropped off the radar. They had hooked up with Reyes by then."

Harris took a deep breath. "Suppose I can bring them in before they get into any more trouble. Could you look the other way on the fire? It was probably an accident anyway. What kid today knows how to use a kerosene lamp? You might as well hand him a flamethrower."

The deputy director regarded his lofty visitor with genuine interest. "You knocked off the biggest treason case in half a century. You're a hero in the FBI with a big future. Why can't you let go of these two kids?"

"Because I created them, that's why!" Harris snapped. "I made them what they are today — motherless, fatherless, homeless fugitives. Can't you get it through your head? Everything that happens to Aiden and Margaret Falconer — it's on me!"

Aiden had never been to New York City, but he recognized the skyline instantly from pictures and TV. As the tops of the gleaming towers sprouted from New Jersey's horizon, he allowed himself the tiniest breath of relief.

The East. We made it.

The nightmare of their near miss in Chicago was

over. From here, the country's busiest hub, trains and buses connected passengers to every conceivable destination. Including Vermont.

Miguel had become bubbly the minute they'd crossed over from Pennsylvania. "Wait till you see the sweet setup Freddy's got — flat-screen TV, surround sound, quicksand couch — you *sink* into those pillows!"

Now the Falconers were his best buddies. The bullying and intimidation evaporated the closer they got to his brother's house. For Aiden, the picture of Miguel holding a scissors to Meg's throat wasn't likely to fade anytime soon. But he had to admit that life in the Tahoe was certainly more pleasant when Miguel was in a good mood.

Union City, New Jersey, reminded Aiden of *The King of Queens* — endless tracts of long, narrow houses stacked close together like dominoes. Miguel pulled into the driveway of one of a row of identical cracker boxes.

"A millionth of a tank of gas to spare!" he declared triumphantly. He was positively beaming.

This was it — the end of the line for Miguel. Aiden was surprised at the lump in his throat. As nasty and unpredictable as Miguel was, it was comforting to have a partner who knew the ropes. Without him, the Falconers would be totally on their own.

So they allowed themselves to be coaxed up the front walk. "You guys kick back, maybe watch a movie, while I talk to Freddy. He's a smart guy. He can help you get where you're going."

A young dark woman who was very pregnant answered the door. "Angie!" cried Miguel, enfolding her in a big bear hug. "Look at you, girl! Why didn't Freddy tell me?"

Aiden couldn't help noticing that Angie did not seem happy at the sight of the newcomers. "Come in, come in," she said furtively, rushing to shut the door behind them. *"Freddy, we got company!"*

Miguel didn't pick up on her discomfort. "So, when's the baby due?"

"Uh — three weeks. *Freddy!*"

The house was small and shabby, with cracked plaster walls dividing the space into tiny rooms. At the end of the hall, Aiden could see an enormous TV screen — the subject of Miguel's endless bragging at Sunnydale.

"You *idiot*!"

Coming down the stairs was a man in his early

twenties — an older version of Miguel on a sturdier, more muscular frame. Despite the similarities in appearance, their expressions could not have been more different. Freddy Reyes was an unhealthy shade of purple.

"Are you crazy, coming here? Bringing *them*" — pointing at the Falconers. "Did anybody tell you who their parents are?"

"They're my friends," Miguel said defensively. "You know how it is when you're with people on the inside."

"Didn't you think the cops would come to me when you went on the lam?" Freddy demanded. "They've been here three times already, and that's just when they've knocked on the door! Angie and me — we see them cruising by, keeping an eye on the place."

Aiden felt his heart lurch. Any passing police officer would find a stolen SUV parked in plain sight on the driveway.

"I'll move the car," Miguel promised. "Park it on another street. I'll be careful."

"You'll be more than careful!" Freddy thundered. "You'll be *gone*!"

"What are you talking about, Fred?"

"You can't stay here, man! I'm still on parole. If they catch me with you, I'm back in the can. I can't risk that — not with a kid coming!"

The blow was so hard, so unexpected, that even Aiden felt the sting. For Miguel, coming to New Jersey to live with his brother had always been the pot of gold at the end of the rainbow. He had contemplated it, fantasized about it, obsessed over it — in custody, and on every mile of their long flight from Nebraska. And now the dream was in ashes, just like the juvenile detention facility that had once held him.

Miguel was shattered. "That's crazy, Freddy!" He searched his brother's face for some sign of softening. There was none. "Well, what about Ma? Could I stay with her?"

"Ma's on antidepressants — like she has been ever since you whacked her husband. I swear, Miguel — you go over there, and I'll beat your lousy head in. Leave us all alone — you're not part of this family anymore!"

"But — " It was barely a whisper. "What am I going to do? I've got nowhere to go. No money — "

Freddy pulled a wad of cash out of his pocket, peeled off a couple of bills for himself, and pressed the rest into his brother's palm. "I wish it could be different, kid, but you gotta get lost. If anybody asks, you never saw me."

Miguel stared blankly down at the bills in his hand. It would have been impossible to tell he was crying, if not for the trembling of his shoulders. One time at Sunnydale, Gary Donovan had smacked him with a planting spade hard enough to open a four-inch gash on his head — sixty stitches. Miguel never uttered a peep. Aiden remembered thinking that no amount of pain would ever get tears out of this guy.

I was wrong.

Miguel might have stood rooted to the spot forever if Meg hadn't taken his arm and led him out of the house. He followed meekly, without protest.

Aiden brought up the rear, but at the door, he turned angry eyes on the elder Reyes. It was stupid, he knew. He always criticized Meg for speaking up out of pure brash emotion, when no good could possibly come of it. But this had to be said.

"Ever heard of self-defense?" he challenged. "Big family man — why didn't you get a decent lawyer for your own brother? Better yet, why didn't you keep your stepfather off him before it came to that?"

Freddy's eyes bulged. "I should turn you in right now!"

But Aiden was already on the cement path back to the car.

Miguel slumped in the Tahoe's passenger seat, his head lolling against its rest. He reminded Aiden of an old *Far Side* cartoon of a boneless chicken ranch, with formless poultry flopping limply around a farmyard.

But there's nothing funny about Miguel's life right now.

Meg was trying to urge him behind the wheel. "We've got to get out of here. You heard Freddy. The cops could come around any minute."

"I got nowhere to go," mumbled Miguel. "Back into the system — that's as good a place as anywhere else."

Aiden would not have believed he'd ever be capable of such sympathy toward the bully who had once made a career of tormenting him. Yet he recognized Miguel's despair almost instantly. It was the combination of misery and hopelessness Aiden and Meg had felt during the trial, in the foster homes, and at Sunnydale. He knew from bitter experience that nothing he could do would cheer Miguel up. The best he could hope for was to show the boy he wasn't completely alone.

"There's a lake house in Colchester, Vermont," he said slowly. "Our old summer cottage. We think there might be a clue there — a picture of a guy who can prove our parents are innocent."

It felt good to say it out loud — almost as if discussing it made it real.

Not just the distant memory of a six-year-old.

"What's your point, Falcon?" Miguel groaned. "It's been a rough day."

Meg supplied the answer. "Are you up for a road trip?"

Aiden Falconer had never driven a car in his life. Now he had no choice. Miguel was utterly defeated and deflated. Once the terror of kids who were terrors themselves, he now couldn't muster the will to haul himself out of the Tahoe's passenger seat. So Aiden took over the wheel.

He had no license, of course — he was only fifteen. But that was minor compared with the stack of crimes he and Meg had committed so far. Even *that* seemed small in the face of their larger mission. Vermont was just a few hundred miles away. Vermont, Colchester, the house on the lake. And the secret hiding place.

He backed out of the driveway with agonizing slowness, still managing to knock over a garbage can. A half mile down the street, he pulled into an abandoned strip mall. There, he drove the huge SUV in circles, building his confidence and skill.

Before getting on the turnpike, they stopped for gas. Aiden couldn't believe how easy this was when you had actual money to pay for it. Miguel still hadn't moved from the seat, but he had no problem buying their fuel. "Take it all," he mumbled, tossing wadded up bills at Aiden. "I don't want *anything* from Freddy."

While Aiden watched the attendant fill the tank, Meg invested in a road map at the mini-mart. They found Colchester near the top of Vermont, about three hundred fifty miles away.

"Six hours' drive," Meg estimated. "If you don't wrap us around a telephone pole."

"Or get pulled over," Aiden added nervously.

It took them almost nine. Aiden missed a couple of exits, and his inexperience made it difficult to navigate back to the right road. A steady soaking rain began to fall, slowing them down further.

It was night by the time they reached the outskirts of Colchester. A 7-Eleven served as their pit stop for hot dogs and directions — a simple left toward the eastern shore of Lake Champlain. It was too dark to begin the search for the vacation house, so they pulled into a cheap motel for the night.

The desk clerk regarded Meg suspiciously. "I'll need your dad to come in and sign for the key."

"Oh, that's okay," she told him. "He gave me the money."

The old man shook his head. "State law. Got to be eighteen to check into a hotel, dear."

Meg thought fast. "Okay, but if the baby wakes up, Dad's going to be mad. She's been crying since Yonkers, and we finally got her to sleep."

The clerk peered out the window at the Tahoe, which was being buffeted by sheets of blowing rain. He took a key from the drawer and placed it on the counter in front of Meg. "Room twenty-two," he said kindly. "There's a canopy by the soda machine so the baby won't get wet."

"Thanks, mister." Meg's big mouth had never let her down.

She hoped Aiden's memory was just as reliable.

The rain continued all night, playing a soft but persistent drumroll on the roof of the Olympia Motel. It did nothing to disturb the exhausted fugitives. This was their first night in real beds since Sunnydale. They slept like the dead.

But in the morning, Miguel began to examine their surroundings with a more critical eye. "This place is a hole, yo. You took me out of Jersey to come to this dump?"

"We took you out of Jersey because you wouldn't leave your brother's driveway," Meg shot right back.

Miguel was offended. "I was just chilling. I don't need help from anybody, least of all some *girl*!"

He had been gradually coming alive in the course of yesterday's drive. Now he was back to his old self. Meg liked him better sullen and silent.

There was little chance of that now. "Vermont, huh? I'm not impressed. Let's see if there's any action around." He was about to throw open the tattered curtains when he jumped back, cursing.

"What's wrong?" asked Aiden.

"Cops! And they're — oh, man. Not good!"

Aiden and Meg peered out the streaming glass. Two cruisers, lights flashing, and two uniformed officers to match. There was no question about it — they were heading toward —

"The car!" groaned Meg. "Can they tell it's stolen?"

"They can if the MacKinnons came home from Disney World," Aiden reasoned.

Miguel paced the small room like a caged tiger. "We gotta get out of here!"

Meg felt the panic rising inside her. *No escape through the front door . . .*

Then she saw it. "The bathroom!"

A narrow window led to the alley behind the motel. Aiden got there first. He leaped onto the toilet seat, flipped the latch, and pushed. "Stuck!"

Over the years, dozens of sloppy paint jobs had sealed the frame shut. Aiden pulled out the keys to the Tahoe and began to chisel at the layers of enamel.

"Hurry!" Meg urged tensely. One of the cops was on his way to the office.

In a minute, he'll know exactly where we are!

Aiden and Miguel grabbed the handle and pulled with all their strength.

And then the first cop was jogging back toward them. Meg heard him call to his partner, "Twenty-two!"

"Guys — "

There was a crack as the window jerked open. Miguel climbed onto the toilet tank and wiggled through the opening.

"Meg!" Aiden cried.

She didn't wait for an engraved invitation. She bolted into the bathroom a split second before the cops entered with their passkey.

"Police! Freeze!"

But Meg wouldn't have stopped for a stampede of elephants. Aiden practically threw her out the window into the rain. She hit the ground, reached up, and pulled him through. He landed right on top of her. She felt her ankle twist, a stab of fire, as the two of them went down.

No time for pain. Not now . . .

And then the first officer was glaring at her through the glass.

"Run!" she yelled, hauling Aiden to his feet. They sprinted after Miguel, who was already halfway to the woods.

A quick glance over her shoulder. *Where are the cops?*

"Look!" Aiden pointed. The two officers were rounding the corner of the building in hot pursuit.

The Falconers blasted into the trees, pounding blindly through mud and wet underbrush. Bracken and low branches scratched at their faces and bodies, but they blundered on, not daring to slow down. A cry of shock rang out somewhere in front of them.

"Miguel?" Aiden panted.

Meg looked around desperately. There was nothing but trees and brush — and the rapid rustling of their own frenzied movements.

And then the forest floor disappeared beneath them.

She heard another scream — her own. The next

thing Meg knew, she was flat on her back, hurtling down a steep bluff toward the lakefront. Thirty-six hours of steady rain had converted the slope into a black diamond ski hill, coated with slick muck instead of snow.

She called to Aiden, just a few feet away, but no sound came out. Her words were sucked right back inside her, along with her breath, as she plunged ahead. She could see Miguel ahead of them, a slime-covered rocket sled, racing wildly out of control.

Frantically, she tried to dig her arms into the grade to slow her descent. Instead, she accelerated. The tickly sensation of free fall — that roller-coaster feeling — took hold in her stomach.

But a roller coaster is a controlled drop! Who knows what's at the bottom of this slide? Rocks? A barbed wire fence? A brick wall?

Determinedly, she kicked a sneaker deep into the mud. All at once, her momentum halted. The world twisted violently, and she bounced head over heels, her slide now a roll. Lake Champlain became a spinning blur, and she lost all sense of where she was.

She cried, "Help!" Or maybe it was just her mind screaming as she tumbled toward —

Toward what?

Suddenly, it was all over. She was sprawled across the broken line of a paved road —

With a big pickup truck coming right at me!

Two sets of hands grabbed her wrists and yanked her up and out of the way just before the pickup roared past.

"You okay?" Aiden gasped, his face white behind a layer of sludge.

She nodded, gasping for breath. "Where are the cops?"

"We gotta disappear!" Miguel scouted the area. They were right at the shore — a small neighborhood of docks and beach cottages. "This way!"

The Falconers had no choice but to follow. Surely the officers would be here soon. Or their colleagues would, answering a radio call to be on the lookout for three dazed and filthy kids.

Moving like a cat, Miguel led them to a small marina by the ferry pier. Without hesitation, he burrowed under the tarpaulin that covered the open stern of a sailboat. He lifted the sheeting, beckoning Aiden and Meg to join him. The hatch was unlocked, and the three fugitives scrambled into the cramped cabin.

They were quite a sight — wild-eyed from the chase and caked with mud.

But we're safe, thought Meg. *For now, anyway.*

Aiden looked haunted. "I — I think I saw it," he rasped, struggling to catch his breath. "No — I'm sure of it."

"Saw what?" asked Miguel.

"The house — just past the ferry terminal on the lake side." He clasped his sister's hands, dribbling wet muck on the deck. "We made it, Meg. We're here."

Agent Harris knew it was a long shot. Still, in law enforcement, sometimes it was better to be lucky than smart.

SEARCH PARAMETERS: _____

He typed "Chicago," and then "three juveniles." The computer searched the FBI's database of crime reports from coast to coast. More than six hundred hits registered. Another waste of time.

He frowned. How had the Falconers avoided capture for so long? The Chicago police had been right on their tail. There were officers watching the airports, train stations, and bus terminals. If the fugitives were still in that neighborhood, surely they would have been found by now.

Of course, Aiden and Margaret were with the Reyes boy. He was a hardened criminal, with a rap sheet and a half. He might know a few tricks that wouldn't occur to a couple of professors' kids.

Hmmm ...

Eyebrows raised, Harris added "stolen car" to the search keywords.

Suddenly, there it was — a 2003 Chevy Tahoe, taken from a suburban Chicago home and recovered at a motel in Colchester, Vermont. Officers there pursued three juveniles, who were still at large.

It was them. It had to be.

All the flights to Burlington, Vermont — near Colchester — were delayed because of high winds and heavy rain. Wherever the fugitives were hiding, they were probably soaked to the skin. The airline said it had been pouring up there for a day and a half. The National Weather Service was predicting no letup in the storm.

Finally, a break. A friend in the military offered Agent Harris a seat on a helicopter transport to Ethan Allen Air Base on the west coast of Lake Champlain in upstate New York. From there, a one-hour ferry ride would take him straight into Colchester.

The flight was a nightmare. Howling winds blew

the chopper around like a kite. The ride was so bumpy that his entire Starbucks Extra-Dark Roast emptied itself onto his pants, one slosh at a time. Agent Harris considered wasting good coffee a crime against humanity, but today he didn't mind. He was too airsick to drink it anyway.

He landed in Plattsburgh, New York, to find that all ferries to Vermont had been suspended due to the bad weather. Standing in the blowing rain in front of the locked ticket booth, he used language not at all becoming an agent of the United States government.

He was in luck, though. There was one rental car still available in the city of Plattsburgh — a Mini Cooper. He practically needed a shoehorn to cram his six-foot-seven frame into it.

The route around Lake Champlain would take him almost to the Canadian border, eighty miles out of his way.

Would the Falconer kids still be in Colchester by the time he got there?

The inside of the sailboat had become a sauna. The tarpaulin sealed the air inside, making the cabin as stuffy as a tomb.

Aiden was too anxious to notice that it was impossible to breathe.

They were being hunted — there was no question about that. Police sirens — distant, yet not distant enough — wailed all day long. Car doors slammed and voices spoke over walkie-talkies. As the storm pounded Lake Champlain, the boat bobbed in the waves, jerking its mooring lines and bumping up against the dock. To Aiden, every jolt, every sound was the SWAT team, preparing to swoop down and arrest them.

Seasickness amplified their discomfort. When they got used to the motion, hunger came.

Miguel gazed bleakly around the small refrigerator. "What kind of people own this crate? They got food to put on food, but no food to put it on."

It was true. The tiny galley had plenty of condiments — ketchup, mustard, and a hot sauce that claimed to be banned in thirteen states. Beyond that, there was nothing more than a half sleeve of moldy saltines.

"Just be grateful they're not the kind of people who enjoy boating in the rain," Meg replied grimly.

By late afternoon, the sirens had ceased. In fact, there were very few sounds at all from the world outside the sailboat. Whatever vacationers were still around had given up on the day. With the ferries canceled and the rain still going strong, the lakefront was deserted.

Even so, the fugitives waited until night had fallen before creeping out from under the tarpaulin.

Meg shuddered from the onslaught of blustery rain. "I was looking forward to getting out of that floating coffin. Now I'm ready to go back."

The summerhouse was smaller than Aiden remembered it, and the gleaming white paint had faded to a sort of air-pollution gray. But this was definitely the place. Same wooden shingles, same lamppost mailbox, same makeshift boat dock out back.

Getting in was Miguel's department. It took even less time than the MacKinnon home. He just pushed open a window, climbed inside, and helped Aiden and Meg in after him. "Hicks," he muttered. "They never lock anything."

Meg flicked the light switch. Nothing happened. She tried the one in the living room. Same result. "Power's off."

There was just enough glow from the street lamps to look around.

Aiden was mesmerized. *The outside may be differ-*

ent, but in here it's exactly like it was nine years ago.

Same shag carpeting. Same 1970s furniture. Even the muskie was there — a hideous two-foot-long openmouthed fish mounted on a wooden plaque. It still held the place of honor in the foyer. Mom used to be so grossed out by the thing that she claimed she could actually smell it decomposing.

Miguel squinted in the gloom. "Kind of a dump, yo."

"Nothing worth stealing?" Meg asked sarcastically.

Miguel shrugged. "I thought you Falcons were high society."

"Our parents are college professors," Aiden told him. "You know, before . . . " His voice trailed off. "I'm going to find my old room."

"I'll go with you," said Meg.

"I'll check out the TV," Miguel decided. "Maybe they've got some DVDs we can fence."

Upstairs, the outside lamplight shone a dull orange through the dormer windows. It was claustrophobic — the A-frame roof cut the bedrooms in half. Aiden remembered it being so *big*.

"Okay," Meg said. "Where's this famous hiding place?"

Aiden scanned the tiny room with anxious eyes.

Nine years was a long time. It was more than possible that someone had repaired the wall between then and now.

Funny — he had always known that. Yet right now the feeling that rose in him was close to panic.

If we can't find that picture, we're stuck. No leads, nowhere to go, no light at the end of the tunnel . . .

Being a fugitive wasn't fun, but at least they had some direction — the goal of saving their parents. If that turned out to be a dead end, they'd have nothing. They'd be wanderers. Worse, hunted animals.

Then he saw it. By the foot of the small desk, a square of paneling was attached at an odd angle. He dropped to his knees and began prying at it.

It didn't budge. Someone had nailed it into place. Had that person also removed his shoe box of treasures?

Can't think about that now. . . .

"Help me," he said, and Meg joined him on the floor.

There was a cracking sound, and the piece broke away from the wall. Aiden peered into the hole. This was it — the moment of truth.

"Yes!"

The cigar box was faded and dust-covered. But it was exactly where six-year-old Aiden had left it.

Reverently, as if handling an ancient artifact, he took it out and opened the lid.

There were a few rusted bottle caps, a penny minted in 1916, and a yellowed book of matches from the Colchester Grill. A couple of toy soldiers and a small cluster of amethyst crystals he had once discovered on the underside of a stone.

"Not exactly the crown jewels," Meg commented dryly.

Most of all, there were pictures. *Terrible* pictures, although back then Aiden had been so proud of them. They were blurry and clumsily framed, with subjects' heads cut off and large pink fingers in the way.

But as Aiden flipped through the stack, he realized these *were* the crown jewels. No, much more valuable than that —

The photographs showed the most notorious traitors in half a century, Doctors John and Louise Falconer, laughing, posing, and playing with baby Meg.

Oh, God, was there really a time like this? A time before trials, and prisons, and foster homes, and the Department of Juvenile Corrections? Were we ever really this happy?

Meg was choked up, too. "I forgot how they look when they smile."

And then the picture was right before their eyes in the dim light: a man and a woman, clad in bathing suits, relaxing on a hotel pool deck. The man was pale and lean, with long reddish-brown hair and a full beard.

Uncle Frank. The man who had started in motion the series of events that destroyed the Falconer family.

The only person who could save them.

Miguel pulled the carton from the back of the closet and dumped out its contents. *Junk*, he thought, riffling through the pile of expired coupon books, broken swim goggles, single gloves, and cheap toys.

He stood on tiptoe and felt around the shelf. Something heavy bounced off his forehead and hit the carpet. What the — ?

It was a thick hardback novel. He squinted at the cover in the dim light. *The Venus Flytrap Gambit — A Mac Mulvey Mystery*. At the bottom it said, *by John Falconer*.

Their father. He wasn't just a teacher; he was an author, too. Miguel remembered hearing something about that back when the Falconers first got busted. Not that Miguel was a news junkie, but you had to be deaf, dumb, and blind to miss *that* story.

Were Aiden and Meg lying about not being rich? You sure couldn't tell by this house. But this wasn't their real crib. It was just someplace they went for the summers.

"Rentals!" he spat in disgust. Little sis hit it right on the nose. There was nothing to rob in this dive. No cash, no jewelry — nothing worth the space it would take up in his pockets.

A noise startled him. He hadn't heard the others coming downstairs. "No offense," he added loudly. "I'm sure your family had some laughs in this — "

The face appeared out of the shadows. Chalky white skin on a completely shaved head.

A cop? Or some homeless guy who moved in when the summer people left?

"Yo, who are — ?"

A large hand with the power of a robotic claw grabbed Miguel by the throat. He tried to yell for help, but no sound came out.

Miguel Reyes had been in many fights in his fifteen years. He had been picked on by his stepfather, by gang kids, and by inmates at three juvenile prisons. But he knew instantly that something was different now.

This assailant was no bully. He was an assassin.

He's trying to strangle me!

Unable to breathe or struggle free, Miguel felt around for a weapon. There was nothing — just *The Venus Flytrap Gambit.* His hand closed around the thick novel. It would have to do. Lack of oxygen was sapping his strength. His vision was darkening around the edges. It was now or never.

With all the force he could muster, he swung the book at the bald head, aiming the corner of the hardbound cover at the man's eye. There was a cry of pain. Miguel sucked in a huge breath as the constricting grip released his throat.

He tried to kick at his attacker, but the powerful hands caught his leg in midair and hurled Miguel into a bookcase. Magazines and cheap knickknacks rained down on him.

"Help!" He realized right then how much he needed it. Whoever this bald guy was, he meant business.

Those two pampered kids upstairs were all that stood between Miguel and murder.

They heard the sounds of the struggle, followed by Miguel's muffled cry.

Aiden was instantly on his feet, stuffing the photograph into his pocket. "The cops!"

Meg looked around. The stairs were the only way out. Except — "The window!"

"What about Miguel?"

"We can't help him," Meg reasoned, remembering Miguel's own logic at the truck stop. "If the cops have him, he's already done."

With effort, Aiden and Meg managed to get the window open and scramble out into the rain. The A-frame roof was so steep that Meg had to slither snake-style as she led the way to the overhang of the front porch. She let herself slide until she was able to wrap her arms and legs around the wooden post and shinny to the ground. An anxious moment later, Aiden jumped down beside her.

"Let's get out of here," hissed Meg.

"Wait." Aiden looked around. The lakefront was still deserted. "Do you see any police cars?"

"If we can walk, so can the cops," Meg argued.

"Yeah, but why would they?" Staying flush against the front of the house, Aiden peered in the window. From the outside, the interior seemed pitch-dark, but he could hear the bump and crash of slamming doors and toppling furniture.

A fight?

No, more like a chase through rooms and hallways. Miguel wasn't going down easily.

But why would he resist arrest when there's no hope?

"Where's the girl?" roared a man's voice.

"What did I do?" Tough Miguel's reply was a plaintive whimper.

"Where's your sister?" the voice demanded.

He thinks Miguel is me!

Then it happened. A sudden flash of yellow. A short, sharp crack.

Gunshot.

With Meg hot on his heels, Aiden barreled in the front door just as the shooter moved to make his escape. There was an audible crunch as Aiden's forehead collided with the bald man's jaw. The pistol dropped to the floor of the foyer with a clatter. Aiden was jolted back into Meg, sending her sprawling onto the stoop.

The intruder recovered quickly and lashed out with a lightning fist. The hammer blow caught Aiden in the cheek, knocking him into the wall. His head struck something round and hard, and he saw stars. A rail?

No, it's the muskie! The preserved body was solid as granite.

"Get the gun!" cried Meg

But Aiden was too slow. By the time he spotted the pistol on the linoleum, the attacker's hand was already closing on the grip.

The blast of terror was as cold as liquid nitrogen. In less than a second, the muzzle would swing up at Aiden, and his life would be over.

With a desperation and purpose he would not have believed possible, Aiden wrenched the mounted muskie off its wall hooks. Before the man could point the weapon, Aiden raised the trophy high and slammed it down on the side of his opponent's head.

The frame snapped in two. The assassin went rigid and dropped like a stone, out cold. The wood *and* the muskie itself landed on his unmoving back.

Mom always said this eyesore served no earthly purpose, Aiden reflected. *She was wrong.*

But there was no time to think about that now. "Miguel!" He hauled Meg to her feet, and the two of them stepped over the unconscious intruder and ran into the house, calling for their companion.

"In here," came a weak voice from the kitchen.

In the laundry alcove, Miguel lay propped against the washing machine. Even in the gloom, they could see his face was pale, almost ashen. Blood oozed from a bullet wound in his shoulder. The entire front of his T-shirt was stained crimson.

Aiden got under one shoulder, Meg the other, and they were able to hoist him to his feet. Miguel howled in agony at the sudden movement.

"We'll get you to a hospital," promised Aiden.

"What about Hairless Joe?"

"Forget him," soothed Meg.

"He had a *gun*!"

"I had a fish," Aiden replied.

Miguel saw his attacker prostrate on the floor with the fossilized muskie on his back. "You know this guy?"

Meg shook her head. "Do you?"

"Figured him for a cop. But cops don't whack people." He regarded Aiden. "This guy thought I was you. Somebody wants you dead. Both of you."

Aiden and Meg exchanged an uneasy look. Tens of thousands of people wished harm on their parents. But on *them*? It was hard to fathom.

"Maybe we should tie him up with the curtain cords," Meg suggested. "Make him tell us what's going on."

"We've got to get Miguel to a doctor," Aiden argued. "That's the most important thing."

"Take his piece at least," Miguel rasped. "He could come to any minute."

Aiden had never touched a gun in his life. He picked up the weapon with two fingers, handling it like a sleeping tarantula. The metal felt cold, malevolent. This was an instrument of evil, a delivery system for harm and death.

Once outside, he hurled it into Lake Champlain. It was a relief to be rid of it.

The relentless rain cranked Miguel's suffering beyond the tolerance level. There was simply no way to keep his shoulder dry. Aiden couldn't help noticing how much red-tinged water was dripping down from the bloodstained T-shirt.

He needs medical attention. And fast!

Heart sinking, Aiden looked for a house with some lights on. Why wasn't anybody home? Just then, a car turned onto the shore road, heading away from them.

"Wait here!" Aiden shrugged out from under Miguel and took off after the white Mercedes. *"Stop! Come back! My friend's hurt!"*

With the windows shut and the wipers on maximum, there was little chance of the driver hearing his cries.

Aiden broke into a full sprint, splashing through puddles that were more like ponds.

Don't be stupid! You can't outrun a car. You'll have to find some other way.

He dashed to the side of the road, scooped up a fistful of rain-drenched turf, and flung it with all his might at the receding sedan. It hit with a splat, showering mud and grass over the rear windshield and trunk.

Aiden had just an instant to consider that the owner of a gleaming white Mercedes probably wouldn't think much of being muck-bombed by a total stranger.

And then the brake lights flashed on.

It was well after dark by the time Agent Harris made it to Colchester. Because of the storm, the bridges across the top of Lake Champlain were closed. He'd had no choice but to drive all the way north around the lake. This included a one-hour wait at the Canadian border and another delay crossing back into the United States.

The wind had subsided, but the rain was still pouring down when he finally turned onto the main shore road. Suddenly, his headlights illuminated a running figure, dead ahead.

With a cry of shock, Harris stomped on the brake

pedal. The wheels locked up, sending the Mini Cooper into a slide. At the last instant, the man vaulted up onto the front of the compact vehicle. He bounced off the hood and tumbled into the windshield as the car lurched to a halt.

Harris caught a glimpse of him in the glow of the streetlamp — a pale, round-faced man with a completely shaved head. Apparently, he was unhurt, because he jumped off the hood and hit the road in a full sprint.

Harris rolled down his window. *"Hey, come back! You should see a doctor!"* he shouted at the fleeing form. But the man was gone, barreling up the road that led away from the lake. He was in such a hurry that he probably never even noticed he'd nearly gotten himself killed.

That was when Harris heard the siren.

An ambulance screeched around the corner, its flashing lights playing across the ferry terminal like a disco ball. It raced up the road and stopped beside a white Mercedes.

Harris wheeled around and pulled even with the two vehicles. He nearly scrambled his brains against the Mini Cooper's door frame as he leaped out. But he recovered enough to flash his badge at the two paramedics. "Emmanuel Harris — FBI."

They were loading a thin olive-skinned teenager in a bloodstained T-shirt onto a stretcher.

"FBI?" The teen regarded the agent's lanky frame. "You look more like NBA."

"You're Reyes, right?" said Harris. "What happened?"

"I got shot. By some mean-looking bullet head straight out of some slasher flick."

"What about the Falconers?" the agent persisted. "A boy and a girl — they call themselves Eagleson — "

Miguel's jaw stiffened. "Don't know any eagles, falcons — no kinds of birds, yo."

The driver of the Mercedes spoke up. "It was two kids who flagged me down. They brought this one over, told me to call nine-one-one, and took off into the woods."

"How long ago?"

"Maybe ten minutes. They were in a real hurry to get out of here."

"He's lying!" rasped Miguel, determined to protect his friends. "I was alone, and some guy put a cap in me! If you cops spent less time hassling people, there wouldn't be so many wackos running around — "

"Quiet!" Harris snapped. Ten minutes! If those

bridges had been open . . . if the borders hadn't been so slow . . . if the ferries could have run . . .

If only he could have gotten here ten minutes sooner, those kids would be in custody right now. Instead of on the run, where anything could happen. Where they were risking their futures, their safety, their very *lives*, with every reckless footfall.

He was amazed at the depth of his emotions. Aiden and Margaret Falconer were not his problem. They weren't even his case. They were the responsibility of Adler and Juvenile Corrections, not the FBI.

Their *parents* had been Harris's case — case closed, and a job well done, too. The trial of the new millennium, two dangerous traitors behind bars.

And what did Harris get? A promotion, a pat on the back, and something else, too. Something agents weren't supposed to have.

A deep, nagging suspicion that the wrong people were in prison. And that two innocent children might be fugitives because of the government's haste to bring someone — *anyone* — to justice.

Well, at least that part would be over soon. With a sigh, he pulled out his cell phone and dialed the Colchester police. Ten minutes wasn't much of a head start when you were traveling on foot.

They wouldn't get far.

The ATV was a quad, with four fat wheels and an engine that might have been built for a jumbo jet. The speedometer said they were doing better than fifty over rugged terrain, bouncing like riders on a mechanical bull. Aiden had all but epoxied himself to the handlebars; Meg was clamped around his mid-section with force enough to collapse his rib cage. The onslaught of wind and rain threatened to hurl them off the speeding contraption at any moment.

The roar should have been enough to attract every cop in Vermont. But that was the advantage of the ATV. They were cutting across farms and fields, far from any roads or highways.

Another crime — was there such a thing as "grand theft dune buggy"? The scary part was not so much that they'd stolen it; Aiden had lost track of the number of times they had broken the law by now. It was the fact that they never thought twice about taking the quad from that garage.

We had to get out of town. And even more important: *We had to get away from Hairless Joe.*

Yesterday, Aiden couldn't have imagined their predicament getting any worse. But the close call with the monstrous bald stranger had ratcheted their fear up to a new, soul-shaking level. Before, the worst thing that could have happened to them was getting caught.

Now somebody wants us dead.

But who? Why? And how had he found them at the lake house?

They had been in full flight for a couple of hours when the old barn appeared in the ATV's single headlamp. It came up so suddenly that they almost crashed through the rotted plank walls. Aiden yanked the handlebars around. For an awful instant, he thought the speeding vehicle would roll. But the huge wheels bit into the turf, and Aiden and Meg whiplashed to a halt six inches in front of an ancient rusted tractor.

Aiden aimed the quad's light into the barn, and they hurried inside to shelter from the elements. The storm had brought down the temperature, so they were both soaked to the skin and shivering.

"I can't stop shaking," Aiden managed, teeth

chattering. "Is summer over already? What's it going to be like being a fugitive in January?"

"I'd still be shaking in a sauna," Meg said feelingly. "Who was that guy, and why was he trying to kill us?"

Aiden shrugged. "The whole country hates our parents. I guess it was only a matter of time before somebody tried to take it out on us."

"How do you know it wasn't just bad luck?" Meg suggested hopefully. "You know, a crazy person who picked a house at random."

Aiden shook his head. "He was gunning for us. He even said, 'Where's your sister?' when he thought Miguel was me."

"Miguel." She nodded sadly. "I hope he's okay."

"He got hit in the shoulder, which means the bullet missed the vital organs." Aiden paused, suddenly thoughtful. "I hated that kid more than I hated Sunnydale. More than what happened to us, almost. Now I feel like I've lost a brother. I mean, he's not dead, but he's caught. He's going back into the system."

After the frantic commotion at the house and the clamor of the ATV, the quiet between them was as jarring as a sonic boom. Both knew what "back into the system" represented for Miguel. Not another place like Sunnydale, but real jail, with bars and armed guards and inmates who could teach Miguel the true meaning of tough.

At last, Meg put an arm around her brother's shoulders. "We're still kicking, bro. That's the important thing. What's our next move?"

Carefully, Aiden pulled the soggy, partially crumpled photograph out of his pocket. It seemed even more bizarre in this setting — to be huddled in the headlamp of a stolen ATV in an abandoned barn, studying a nine-year-old image of two strangers sunbathing.

Uncle Frank, who could straighten everything out. The key to it all.

The despair was completely unexpected. One minute he was examining the photograph; the next, he was staring into a bottomless pit of desolation.

I was nuts to think this picture could somehow help our parents. I don't recognize this guy, and even if I did, so what? Does he even look like this today?

Aiden felt completely deflated. What did he expect? That one glance at this snapshot would tell him how to get in touch with the man who held the family's fate in his hands? Did he imagine Lindenauer would be holding up a sign with his contact information on it — WWW.CALLUNCLEFRANK.COM?

I must have been out of my mind to risk our lives crossing the entire country for a dumb old picture that doesn't give the slightest clue —

And then he saw it.

Above the reclining figures, almost out of frame, a life preserver was mounted on the slats of the pool area fence. Printed on the white plastic ring, small but clear, was:

RED JACKET BEACH MOTOR LODGE
MALLET'S BAY, VERMONT

Meg noticed it, too. "It's only the name of the hotel," she pointed out.

Aiden's heart began to pound "Yeah, but hotels have computers. They keep records. Addresses, phone numbers . . . "

"It's a clue," she agreed grudgingly.

At that moment, Aiden realized that he and his sister were not ordinary fugitives. Fugitives ran *away* from justice. The Falconers were running *toward* it.

As long as there was a place to start, a lead to follow, a stone left unturned in the quest to prove their parents' innocence, then there was hope.

He peered out of the barn. In the blinding light of the headlamp, everything else appeared dark.

Somewhere, he thought, *in that vast blackness between here and the end of the earth, is Frank Lindenauer.*

They would find him.

Goosebumps®

WELCOME TO DEAD HOUSE

R.L. STINE

24 23 22 21 20 19 18 17 16 15 14 13   5 6 7 8/0

Printed in the U.S.A.   40

First Scholastic printing, July 1992

Josh and I hated our new house.

Sure, it was big. It looked like a mansion compared to our old house. It was a tall redbrick house with a sloping black roof and rows of windows framed by black shutters.

It's so dark, I thought, studying it from the street. The whole house was covered in darkness, as if it were hiding in the shadows of the gnarled, old trees that bent over it.

It was the middle of July, but dead brown leaves blanketed the front yard. Our sneakers crunched over them as we trudged up the gravel driveway.

Tall weeds poked up everywhere through the dead leaves. Thick clumps of weeds had completely overgrown an old flower bed beside the front porch.

This house is creepy, I thought unhappily.

Josh must have been thinking the same thing. Looking up at the old house, we both groaned loudly.

Mr. Dawes, the friendly young man from the local real estate office, stopped near the front walk and turned around.

"Everything okay?" he asked, staring first at Josh, then at me, with his crinkly blue eyes.

"Josh and Amanda aren't happy about moving," Dad explained, tucking his shirttail in. Dad is a little overweight, and his shirts always seem to be coming untucked.

"It's hard for kids," my mother added, smiling at Mr. Dawes, her hands shoved into her jeans pockets as she continued up to the front door. "You know. Leaving all of their friends behind. Moving to a strange new place."

"Strange is right," Josh said, shaking his head. "This house is gross."

Mr. Dawes chuckled. "It's an old house, that's for sure," he said, patting Josh on the shoulder.

"It just needs some work, Josh," Dad said, smiling at Mr. Dawes. "No one has lived in it for a while, so it'll take some fixing up."

"Look how big it is," Mom added, smoothing back her straight black hair and smiling at Josh. "We'll have room for a den and maybe a rec room, too. You'd like that — wouldn't you, Amanda?"

I shrugged. A cold breeze made me shiver. It was actually a beautiful, hot summer day. But the closer we got to the house, the colder I felt.

I guessed it was because of all the tall, old trees.

I was wearing white tennis shorts and a sleeveless blue T-shirt. It had been hot in the car. But now I was freezing. Maybe it'll be warmer in the house, I thought.

"How old are they?" Mr. Dawes asked Mom, stepping onto the front porch.

"Amanda is twelve," Mom answered. "And Josh turned eleven last month."

"They look so much alike," Mr. Dawes told Mom.

I couldn't decide if that was a compliment or not. I guess it's true. Josh and I are both tall and thin and have curly brown hair like Dad's, and dark brown eyes. Everyone says we have "serious" faces.

"I really want to go home," Josh said, his voice cracking. "I hate this place."

My brother is the most impatient kid in the world. And when he makes up his mind about something, that's it. He's a little spoiled. At least, I think so. Whenever he makes a big fuss about something, he usually gets his way.

We may look alike, but we're really not that similar. I'm a lot more patient than Josh is. A lot more sensible. Probably because I'm older and because I'm a girl.

Josh had hold of Dad's hand and was trying to pull him back to the car. "Let's go. Come on, Dad. Let's go."

I knew this was one time Josh wouldn't get his way. We were moving to this house. No doubt

159

about it. After all, the house was absolutely free. A great-uncle of Dad's, a man we didn't even know, had died and left the house to Dad in his will.

I'll never forget the look on Dad's face when he got the letter from the lawyer. He let out a loud whoop and began dancing around the living room. Josh and I thought he'd flipped or something.

"My Great-Uncle Charles has left us a house in his will," Dad explained, reading and rereading the letter. "It's in a town called Dark Falls."

"Huh?" Josh and I cried. "Where's Dark Falls?"

Dad shrugged.

"I don't remember your Uncle Charles," Mom said, moving behind Dad to read the letter over his shoulder.

"Neither do I," admitted Dad. "But he must've been a great guy! Wow! This sounds like an incredible house!" He grabbed Mom's hands and began dancing happily with her across the living room.

Dad sure was excited. He'd been looking for an excuse to quit his boring office job and devote all of his time to his writing career. This house — absolutely free — would be just the excuse he needed.

And now, a week later, here we were in Dark Falls, a four-hour drive from our home, seeing our new house for the first time. We hadn't even gone inside, and Josh was trying to drag Dad back to the car.

"Josh — stop pulling me," Dad snapped impatiently, trying to tug his hand out of Josh's grasp.

Dad glanced helplessly at Mr. Dawes. I could see that he was embarrassed by how Josh was carrying on. I decided maybe I could help.

"Let go, Josh," I said quietly, grabbing Josh by the shoulder. "We promised we'd give Dark Falls a chance — remember?"

"I already gave it a chance," Josh whined, not letting go of Dad's hand. "This house is old and ugly and I hate it."

"You haven't even gone inside," Dad said angrily.

"Yes. Let's go in," Mr. Dawes urged, staring at Josh.

"I'm staying outside," Josh insisted.

He can be really stubborn sometimes. I felt just as unhappy as Josh looking at this dark, old house. But I'd never carry on the way Josh was.

"Josh, don't you want to pick out your own room?" Mom asked.

"No," Josh muttered.

He and I both glanced up to the second floor. There were two large bay windows side by side up there. They looked like two dark eyes staring back at us.

"How long have you lived in your present house?" Mr. Dawes asked Dad.

161

Dad had to think for a second. "About fourteen years," he answered. "The kids have lived there for their whole lives."

"Moving is always hard," Mr. Dawes said sympathetically, turning his gaze on me. "You know, Amanda, I moved here to Dark Falls just a few months ago. I didn't like it much either, at first. But now I wouldn't live anywhere else." He winked at me. He had a cute dimple in his chin when he smiled. "Let's go inside. It's really quite nice. You'll be surprised."

All of us followed Mr. Dawes, except Josh. "Are there other kids on this block?" Josh demanded. He made it sound more like a challenge than a question.

Mr. Dawes nodded. "The school's just two blocks away," he said, pointing up the street.

"See?" Mom quickly cut in. "A short walk to school. No more long bus rides every morning."

"I *liked* the bus," Josh insisted.

His mind was made up. He wasn't going to give my parents a break, even though we'd both promised to be open-minded about this move.

I don't know what Josh thought he had to gain by being such a pain. I mean, Dad already had plenty to worry about. For one thing, he hadn't been able to sell our old house yet.

I didn't like the idea of moving. But I knew that inheriting this big house was a great opportunity for us. We were so cramped in our little house.

And once Dad managed to sell the old place, we wouldn't have to worry at all about money anymore.

Josh should at least give it a chance. That's what I thought.

Suddenly, from our car at the foot of the driveway, we heard Petey barking and howling and making a fuss.

Petey is our dog, a white, curly-haired terrier, cute as a button, and usually well-behaved. He never minded being left in the car. But now he was yowling and yapping at full volume and scratching at the car window, desperate to get out.

"Petey — quiet! Quiet!" I shouted. Petey usually listened to me.

But not this time.

"I'm going to let him out!" Josh declared, and took off down the driveway toward the car.

"No. Wait — " Dad called.

But I don't think Josh could hear him over Petey's wails.

"Might as well let the dog explore," Mr. Dawes said. "It's going to be his house, too."

A few seconds later, Petey came charging across the lawn, kicking up brown leaves, yipping excitedly as he ran up to us. He jumped on all of us as if he hadn't seen us in weeks and then, to our surprise, he started growling menacingly and barking at Mr. Dawes.

"Petey — stop!" Mom yelled.

"He's never done this," Dad said apologetically. "Really. He's usually very friendly."

"He probably smells something on me. Another dog, maybe," Mr. Dawes said, loosening his striped tie, looking warily at our growling dog.

Finally, Josh grabbed Petey around the middle and lifted him away from Mr. Dawes. "Stop it, Petey," Josh scolded, holding the dog up close to his face so that they were nose-to-nose. "Mr. Dawes is our friend."

Petey whimpered and licked Josh's face. After a short while, Josh set him back down on the ground. Petey looked up at Mr. Dawes, then at me, then decided to go sniffing around the yard, letting his nose lead the way.

"Let's go inside," Mr. Dawes urged, moving a hand through his short blond hair. He unlocked the front door and pushed it open.

Mr. Dawes held the screen door open for us. I started to follow my parents into the house.

"I'll stay out here with Petey," Josh insisted from the walk.

Dad started to protest, but changed his mind. "Okay. Fine," he said, sighing and shaking his head. "I'm not going to argue with you. Don't come in. You can *live* outside if you want." He sounded really exasperated.

"I want to stay with Petey," Josh said again,

watching Petey nose his way through the dead flower bed.

Mr. Dawes followed us into the hallway, gently closing the screen door behind him, giving Josh a final glance. "He'll be fine," he said softly, smiling at Mom.

"He can be so stubborn sometimes," Mom said apologetically. She peeked into the living room. "I'm really sorry about Petey. I don't know what got into that dog."

"No problem. Let's start in the living room," Mr. Dawes said, leading the way. "I think you'll be pleasantly surprised by how spacious it is. Of course, it needs work."

He took us on a tour of every room in the house. I was beginning to get excited. The house was really kind of neat. There were so many rooms and so many closets. And my room was huge and had its own bathroom and an old-fashioned window seat where I could sit at the window and look down at the street.

I wished Josh had come inside with us. If he could see how great the house was inside, I knew he'd start to cheer up.

I couldn't believe how many rooms there were. Even a finished attic filled with old furniture and stacks of old, mysterious cartons we could explore.

We must have been inside for at least half an

hour. I didn't really keep track of the time. I think all three of us were feeling cheered up.

"Well, I think I've shown you everything," Mr. Dawes said, glancing at his watch. He led the way to the front door.

"Wait — I want to take one more look at my room," I told them excitedly. I started up the stairs, taking them two at a time. "I'll be down in a second."

"Hurry, dear. I'm sure Mr. Dawes has other appointments," Mom called after me.

I reached the second-floor landing and hurried down the narrow hallway and into my new room. "Wow!" I said aloud, and the word echoed faintly against the empty walls.

It was so big. And I loved the bay window with the window seat. I walked over to it and peered out. Through the trees, I could see our car in the driveway and, beyond it, a house that looked a lot like ours across the street.

I'm going to put my bed against that wall across from the window, I thought happily. And my desk can go over there. I'll have room for a computer now!

I took one more look at my closet, a long, walk-in closet with a light in the ceiling, and wide shelves against the back wall.

I was heading to the door, thinking about which of my posters I wanted to bring with me, when I saw the boy.

He stood in the doorway for just a second. And then he turned and disappeared down the hall.

"Josh?" I cried. "Hey — come look!"

With a shock, I realized it wasn't Josh.

For one thing, the boy had blond hair.

"Hey!" I called and ran to the hallway, stopping just outside my bedroom door, looking both ways. "Who's here?"

But the long hall was empty. All of the doors were closed.

"Whoa, Amanda," I said aloud.

Was I seeing things?

Mom and Dad were calling from downstairs. I took one last look down the dark corridor, then hurried to rejoin them.

"Hey, Mr. Dawes," I called as I ran down the stairs, "is this house haunted?"

He chuckled. The question seemed to strike him funny. "No. Sorry," he said, looking at me with those crinkly blue eyes. "No ghost included. A lot of old houses around here are said to be haunted. But I'm afraid this isn't one of them."

"I — I thought I saw something," I said, feeling a little foolish.

"Probably just shadows," Mom said. "With all the trees, this house is so dark."

"Why don't you run outside and tell Josh about the house," Dad suggested, tucking in the front of his shirt. "Your Mom and I have some things to talk over with Mr. Dawes."

"Yes, master," I said with a little bow, and obediently ran out to tell Josh all about what he had missed. "Hey, Josh," I called, eagerly searching the yard. "Josh?"

My heart sank.

Josh and Petey were gone.

2

"Josh! Josh!"

First I called Josh. Then I called Petey. But there was no sign of either of them.

I ran down to the bottom of the driveway and peered into the car, but they weren't there. Mom and Dad were still inside talking with Mr. Dawes. I looked along the street in both directions, but there was no sign of them.

"Josh! Hey, Josh!"

Finally, Mom and Dad came hurrying out the front door, looking alarmed. I guess they heard my shouts. "I can't find Josh or Petey!" I yelled up to them from the street.

"Maybe they're around back," Dad shouted down to me.

I headed up the driveway, kicking away dead leaves as I ran. It was sunny down on the street, but as soon as I entered our yard, I was back in the shade, and it was immediately cool again.

"Hey, Josh! Josh — where are you?"

Why did I feel so scared? It was perfectly natural for Josh to wander off. He did it all the time.

I ran full speed along the side of the house. Tall trees leaned over the house on this side, blocking out nearly all of the sunlight.

The backyard was bigger than I'd expected, a long rectangle that sloped gradually down to a wooden fence at the back. Just like the front, this yard was a mass of tall weeds, poking up through a thick covering of brown leaves. A stone birdbath had toppled onto its side. Beyond it, I could see the side of the garage, a dark, brick building that matched the house.

"Hey — Josh!"

He wasn't back here. I stopped and searched the ground for footprints or a sign that he had run through the thick leaves.

"Well?" Out of breath, Dad came jogging up to me.

"No sign of him," I said, surprised at how worried I felt.

"Did you check the car?" He sounded more angry than worried.

"Yes. It's the first place I looked." I gave the backyard a last quick search. "I don't believe Josh would just take off."

"I do," Dad said, rolling his eyes. "You know your brother when he doesn't get his way. Maybe he wants us to think he's run away from home." He frowned.

"Where is he?" Mom asked as we returned to the front of the house.

Dad and I both shrugged. "Maybe he made a friend and wandered off," Dad said. He raised a hand and scratched his curly brown hair. I could tell that he was starting to worry, too.

"We've *got* to find him," Mom said, gazing down to the street. "He doesn't know this neighborhood at all. He probably wandered off and got lost."

Mr. Dawes locked the front door and stepped down off the porch, pocketing the keys. "He couldn't have gotten far," he said, giving Mom a reassuring smile. "Let's drive around the block. I'm sure we'll find him."

Mom shook her head and glanced nervously at Dad. "I'll kill him," she muttered. Dad patted her on the shoulder.

Mr. Dawes opened the trunk of the small Honda, pulled off his dark blazer, and tossed it inside. Then he took out a wide-brimmed, black cowboy hat and put it on his head.

"Hey — that's quite a hat," Dad said, climbing into the front passenger seat.

"Keeps the sun away," Mr. Dawes said, sliding behind the wheel and slamming the car door.

Mom and I got in back. Glancing over at her, I saw that Mom was as worried as I was.

We headed down the block in silence, all four of us staring out the car windows. The houses we passed all seemed old. Most of them were even bigger than our house. All of them seemed to be in better condition, nicely painted with neat, well-trimmed lawns.

I didn't see any people in the houses or yards, and there was no one on the street.

It certainly is a *quiet* neighborhood, I thought. And shady. The houses all seemed to be surrounded by tall, leafy trees. The front yards we drove slowly past all seemed to be bathed in shade. The street was the only sunny place, a narrow gold ribbon that ran through the shadows on both sides.

Maybe that's why it's called Dark Falls, I thought.

"Where is that son of mine?" Dad asked, staring hard out the windshield.

"I'll kill him. I really will," Mom muttered. It wasn't the first time she had said that about Josh.

We had gone around the block twice. No sign of him.

Mr. Dawes suggested we drive around the next few blocks, and Dad quickly agreed. "Hope I don't get lost. I'm new here, too," Mr. Dawes said, turning a corner. "Hey, there's the school," he announced, pointing out the window at a tall red-brick building. It looked very old-fashioned, with white columns on both sides of the double front doors. "Of course, it's closed now," Mr. Dawes added.

My eyes searched the fenced-in playground behind the school. It was empty. No one there.

"Could Josh have walked this far?" Mom asked, her voice tight and higher than usual.

"Josh doesn't walk," Dad said, rolling his eyes. "He runs."

"We'll find him," Mr. Dawes said confidently, tapping his fingers on the wheel as he steered.

We turned a corner onto another shady block. A street sign read "Cemetery Drive," and sure enough, a large cemetery rose up in front of us. Granite gravestones rolled along a low hill, which sloped down and then up again onto a large flat stretch, also marked with rows of low grave markers and monuments.

A few shrubs dotted the cemetery, but there weren't many trees. As we drove slowly past, the gravestones passing by in a blur on the left, I realized that this was the sunniest spot I had seen in the whole town.

"There's your son." Mr. Dawes, pointing out the window, stopped the car suddenly.

"Oh, thank goodness!" Mom exclaimed, leaning down to see out the window on my side of the car.

Sure enough, there was Josh, running wildly along a crooked row of low, white gravestones. "What's he doing *here*?" I asked, pushing open my car door.

I stepped down from the car, took a few steps onto the grass, and called to him. At first, he didn't react to my shouts. He seemed to be ducking and dodging through the tombstones. He would run in one direction, then cut to the side, then head in another direction.

Why was he doing that?

I took another few steps — and then stopped, gripped with fear.

I suddenly realized why Josh was darting and ducking like that, running so wildly through the tombstones. He was being chased.

Someone — or something — was after him.

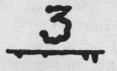

3

Then, as I took a few reluctant steps toward Josh, watching him bend low, then change directions, his arms outstretched as he ran, I realized I had it completely backward.

Josh wasn't being chased. Josh was *chasing*.

He was chasing after Petey.

Okay, okay. So sometimes my imagination runs away with me. Running through an old graveyard like this — even in bright daylight — it's only natural that a person might start to have weird thoughts.

I called to Josh again, and this time he heard me and turned around. He looked worried. "Amanda — come help me!" he cried.

"Josh, what's the matter?" I ran as fast as I could to catch up with him, but he kept darting through the gravestones, moving from row to row.

"Help!"

"Josh — what's wrong?" I turned and saw that

175

Mom and Dad were right behind me.

"It's Petey," Josh explained, out of breath. "I can't get him to stop. I caught him once, but he pulled away from me."

"Petey! Petey!" Dad started calling the dog. But Petey was moving from stone to stone, sniffing each one, then running to the next.

"How did you get all the way over here?" Dad asked as he caught up with my brother.

"I had to follow Petey," Josh explained, still looking very worried. "He just took off. One second he was sniffing around that dead flower bed in our front yard. The next second, he just started to run. He wouldn't stop when I called. Wouldn't even look back. He kept running till he got here. I had to follow. I was afraid he'd get lost."

Josh stopped and gratefully let Dad take over the chase. "I don't know what that dumb dog's problem is," he said to me. "He's just *weird*."

It took Dad a few tries, but he finally managed to grab Petey and pick him up off the ground. Our little terrier gave a halfhearted yelp of protest, then allowed himself to be carried away.

We all trooped back to the car on the side of the road. Mr. Dawes was waiting by the car. "Maybe you'd better get a leash for that dog," he said, looking very concerned.

"Petey's never been on a leash," Josh protested, wearily climbing into the backseat.

"Well, we might have to try one for a while,"

Dad said quietly. "Especially if he keeps running away." Dad tossed Petey into the backseat. The dog eagerly curled up in Josh's arms.

The rest of us piled into the car, and Mr. Dawes drove us back to his office, a tiny, white, flat-roofed building at the end of a row of small offices. As we rode, I reached over and stroked the back of Petey's head.

Why did the dog run away like that? I wondered. Petey had never done that before.

I guessed that Petey was also upset about our moving. After all, Petey had spent his whole life in our old house. He probably felt a lot like Josh and I did about having to pack up and move and never see the old neighborhood again.

The new house, the new streets, and all the new smells must have freaked the poor dog out. Josh wanted to run away from the whole idea. And so did Petey.

Anyway, that was my theory.

Mr. Dawes parked the car in front of his tiny office, shook Dad's hand, and gave him a business card. "You can come by next week," he told Mom and Dad. "I'll have all the legal work done by then. After you sign the papers, you can move in anytime."

He pushed open the car door and, giving us all a final smile, prepared to climb out.

"Compton Dawes," Mom said, reading the white business card over Dad's shoulder. "That's an unusual name. Is Compton an old family name?"

Mr. Dawes shook his head. "No," he said, "I'm the only Compton in my family. I have no idea where the name comes from. No idea at all. Maybe my parents didn't know how to spell Charlie!"

Chuckling at his terrible joke, he climbed out of the car, lowered the wide black Stetson hat on his head, pulled his blazer from the trunk, and disappeared into the small white building.

Dad climbed behind the wheel, moving the seat back to make room for his big stomach. Mom got up front, and we started the long drive home. "I guess you and Petey had quite an adventure today," Mom said to Josh, rolling up her window because Dad had turned on the air conditioner.

"I guess," Josh said without enthusiasm. Petey was sound asleep in his lap, snoring quietly.

"You're going to love your room," I told Josh. "The whole house is great. Really."

Josh stared at me thoughtfully, but didn't answer.

I poked him in the ribs with my elbow. "Say something. Did you hear what I said?"

But the weird, thoughtful look didn't fade from Josh's face.

The next couple of weeks seemed to crawl by. I walked around the house thinking about how I'd never see my room again, how I'd never eat breakfast in this kitchen again, how I'd never watch TV in the living room again. Morbid stuff like that.

I had this sick feeling when the movers came one afternoon and delivered a tall stack of cartons. Time to pack up. It was really happening. Even though it was the middle of the afternoon, I went up to my room and flopped down on my bed. I didn't nap or anything. I just stared at the ceiling for more than an hour, and all these wild, unconnected thoughts ran through my head, like a dream, only I was awake.

I wasn't the only one who was nervous about the move. Mom and Dad were snapping at each other over nothing at all. One morning they had a big fight over whether the bacon was too crispy or not.

In a way, it was funny to see them being so childish. Josh was acting really sullen all the time. He hardly spoke a word to anyone. And Petey sulked, too. That dumb dog wouldn't even pick himself up and come over to me when I had some table scraps for him.

I guess the hardest part about moving was saying good-bye to my friends. Carol and Amy were away at camp, so I had to write to them. But Kathy was home, and she was my oldest and best friend, and the hardest to say good-bye to.

I think some people were surprised that Kathy and I had stayed such good friends. For one thing, we look so different. I'm tall and thin and dark, and she's fair-skinned, with long blonde hair, and a little chubby. But we've been friends since pre-school, and best best friends since fourth grade.

When she came over the night before the move, we were both terribly awkward. "Kathy, you shouldn't be nervous," I told her. "You're not the one who's moving away forever."

"It's not like you're moving to China or something," she answered, chewing hard on her bubble gum. "Dark Falls is only four hours away, Amanda. We'll see each other a lot."

"Yeah, I guess," I said. But I didn't believe it. Four hours away was as bad as being in China, as far as I was concerned. "I guess we can still talk on the phone," I said glumly.

She blew a small green bubble, then sucked it back into her mouth. "Yeah. Sure," she said, pretending to be enthusiastic. "You're lucky, you know. Moving out of this crummy neighborhood to a big house."

"It's *not* a crummy neighborhood," I insisted. I don't know why I was defending the neighborhood. I never had before. One of our favorite pastimes was thinking of places we'd rather be growing up.

"School won't be the same without you," she sighed, curling her legs under her on the chair. "Who's going to slip me the answers in math?"

I laughed. "I always slipped you the *wrong* answers."

"But it was the thought that counted," Kathy said. And then she groaned. "Ugh. Junior high. Is your new junior high part of the high school or part of the elementary school?"

I made a disgusted face. "Everything's in one building. It's a small town, remember? There's no separate high school. At least, I didn't see one."

"Bummer," she said.

Bummer was right.

We chatted for hours. Until Kathy's mom called and said it was time for her to come home.

Then we hugged. I had made up my mind that I wouldn't cry, but I could feel the big, hot tears forming in the corners of my eyes. And then they were running down my cheeks.

"I'm so miserable!" I wailed.

I had planned to be really controlled and mature. But Kathy was my best friend, after all, and what could I do?

We made a promise that we'd always be together on our birthdays — no matter what. We'd force our parents to make sure we didn't miss each other's birthdays.

And then we hugged again. And Kathy said, "Don't worry. We'll see each other a lot. Really." And she had tears in her eyes, too.

She turned and ran out the door. The screen door slammed hard behind her. I stood there staring out into the darkness until Petey came scampering in, his toenails clicking across the linoleum, and started to lick my hand.

The next morning, moving day, was a rainy Saturday. Not a downpour. No thunder or lightning. But just enough rain and wind to make the long drive slow and unpleasant.

The sky seemed to get darker as we neared the new neighborhood. The heavy trees bent low over the street. "Slow down, Jack," Mom warned shrilly. "The street is really slick."

But Dad was in a hurry to get to the house before the moving van did. "They'll just put the stuff anywhere if we're not there to supervise," he explained.

Josh, beside me in the backseat, was being a real pain, as usual. He kept complaining that he was thirsty. When that didn't get results, he started whining that he was starving. But we had all had a big breakfast, so that didn't get any reaction, either.

He just wanted attention, of course. I kept trying to cheer him up by telling him how great the house was inside and how big his room was. He still hadn't seen it.

But he didn't want to be cheered up. He started wrestling with Petey, getting the poor dog all worked up, until Dad had to shout at him to stop.

"Let's all try really hard not to get on each other's nerves," Mom suggested.

Dad laughed. "Good idea, dear."

"Don't make fun of me," she snapped.

They started to argue about who was more exhausted from all the packing. Petey stood up on his hind legs and started to howl at the back window.

"Can't you shut him up?" Mom screamed.

I pulled Petey down, but he struggled back up and started howling again. "He's never done this before," I said.

"Just get him quiet!" Mom insisted.

I pulled Petey down by his hind legs, and Josh started to howl. Mom turned around and gave him a dirty look. Josh didn't stop howling, though. He thought he was a riot.

Finally, Dad pulled the car up the driveway of the new house. The tires crunched over the wet gravel. Rain pounded on the roof.

"Home sweet home," Mom said. I couldn't tell if she was being sarcastic or not. I think she was really glad the long car ride was over.

"At least we beat the movers," Dad said, glancing at his watch. Then his expression changed. "Hope they're not lost."

"It's as dark as night out there," Josh complained.

Petey was jumping up and down in my lap, desperate to get out of the car. He was usually a good traveler. But once the car stopped, he wanted out immediately.

I opened my car door and he leaped onto the driveway with a splash and started to run in a wild zigzag across the front yard.

"At least *someone's* glad to be here," Josh said quietly.

Dad ran up to the porch and, fumbling with the unfamiliar keys, managed to get the front door open. Then he motioned for us to come into the house.

Mom and Josh ran across the walk, eager to get in out of the rain. I closed the car door behind me and started to jog after them.

But something caught my eye. I stopped and looked up to the twin bay windows above the porch.

I held a hand over my eyebrows to shield my eyes and squinted through the rain.

Yes. I saw it.

A face. In the window on the left.

The boy.

The same boy was up there, staring down at me.

4

"Wipe your feet! Don't track mud on the nice clean floors!" Mom called. Her voice echoed against the bare walls of the empty living room.

I stepped into the hallway. The house smelled of paint. The painters had just finished on Thursday. It was hot in the house, much hotter than outside.

"This kitchen light won't go on," Dad called from the back. "Did the painters turn off the electricity or something?"

"How should I know?" Mom shouted back.

Their voices sounded so loud in the big, empty house.

"Mom — there's someone upstairs!" I cried, wiping my feet on the new welcome mat and hurrying into the living room.

She was at the window, staring out at the rain, looking for the movers probably. She spun around as I came in. "What?"

"There's a boy upstairs. I saw him in the window," I said, struggling to catch my breath.

Josh entered the room from the back hallway. He'd probably been with Dad. He laughed. "Is someone already living here?"

"There's no one upstairs," Mom said, rolling her eyes. "Are you two going to give me a break today, or what?"

"What did *I* do?" Josh whined.

"Listen, Amanda, we're all a little on edge today — " Mom started.

But I interrupted her. "I saw his face, Mom. In the window. I'm not crazy, you know."

"Says who?" Josh cracked.

"Amanda!" Mom bit her lower lip, the way she always did when she was really exasperated. "You saw a reflection of something. Of a tree probably." She turned back to the window. The rain was coming down in sheets now, the wind driving it noisily against the large picture window.

I ran to the stairway, cupped my hands over my mouth, and shouted up to the second floor, "Who's up there?"

No answer.

"Who's up there?" I called, a little louder.

Mom had her hands over her ears. "Amanda — please!"

Josh had disappeared through the dining room. He was finally exploring the house.

"There's someone up there," I insisted and, impulsively, I started up the wooden stairway, my sneakers thudding loudly on the bare steps.

"Amanda — " I heard Mom call after me.

But I was too angry to stop. Why didn't she believe me? Why did she have to say it was a reflection of a tree I saw up there?

I was curious. I had to know who was upstairs. I had to prove Mom wrong. I had to show her I hadn't seen a stupid reflection. I guess I can be pretty stubborn, too. Maybe it's a family trait.

The stairs squeaked and creaked under me as I climbed. I didn't feel at all scared until I reached the second-floor landing. Then I suddenly had this heavy feeling in the pit of my stomach.

I stopped, breathing hard, leaning on the banister.

Who could it be? A burglar? A bored neighborhood kid who had broken into an empty house for a thrill?

Maybe I shouldn't be up here alone, I realized.

Maybe the boy in the window was dangerous.

"Anybody up here?" I called, my voice suddenly trembly and weak.

Still leaning against the banister, I listened.

And I could hear footsteps scampering across the hallway.

No.

Not footsteps.

The rain. That's what it was. The patter of rain against the slate-shingled roof.

For some reason, the sound made me feel a little

187

calmer. I let go of the banister and stepped into the long, narrow hallway. It was dark up here, except for a rectangle of gray light from a small window at the other end.

I took a few steps, the old wooden floorboards creaking noisily beneath me. "Anybody up here?"

Again no answer.

I stepped up to the first doorway on my left. The door was closed. The smell of fresh paint was suffocating. There was a light switch on the wall near the door. Maybe it's for the hall light, I thought. I clicked it on. But nothing happened.

"Anybody here?"

My hand was trembling as I grabbed the doorknob. It felt warm in my hand. And damp.

I turned it and, taking a deep breath, pushed open the door.

I peered into the room. Gray light filtered in through the bay window. A flash of lightning made me jump back. The thunder that followed was a dull, distant roar.

Slowly, carefully, I took a step into the room. Then another.

No sign of anyone.

This was a guest bedroom. Or it could be Josh's room if he decided he liked it.

Another flash of lightning. The sky seemed to be darkening. It was pitch-black out there even though it was just after lunchtime.

I backed into the hall. The next room down was

going to be mine. It also had a bay window that looked down on the front yard.

Was the boy I saw staring down at me in *my* room?

I crept down the hall, letting my hand run along the wall for some reason, and stopped outside my door, which was also closed.

Taking a deep breath, I knocked on the door. "Who's in there?" I called.

I listened.

Silence.

Then a clap of thunder, closer than the last. I froze as if I were paralyzed, holding my breath. It was so hot up here, hot and damp. And the smell of paint was making me dizzy.

I grabbed the doorknob. "Anybody in there?"

I started to turn the knob — when the boy crept up from behind and grabbed my shoulder.

5

I couldn't breathe. I couldn't cry out.

My heart seemed to stop. My chest felt as if it were about to explode.

With a desperate, terrified effort, I spun a-round.

"Josh!" I shrieked. "You scared me to death! I thought — "

He let go of me and took a step back. "Gotcha!" he declared, and then started to laugh, a high-pitched laugh that echoed down the long, bare hallway.

My heart was pounding hard now. My forehead throbbed. "You're not funny," I said angrily. I shoved him against the wall. "You really scared me."

He laughed and rolled around on the floor. He's really a sicko. I tried to shove him again but missed.

Angrily, I turned away from him — just in time to see my bedroom door slowly swinging open.

I gasped in disbelief. And froze, gaping at the moving door.

Josh stopped laughing and stood up, immediately serious, his dark eyes wide with fright.

I could hear someone moving inside the room.

I could hear whispering.

Excited giggles.

"Who — who's there?" I managed to stammer in a high little voice I didn't recognize.

The door, creaking loudly, opened a bit more, then started to close.

"Who's there?" I demanded, a bit more forcefully.

Again, I could hear whispering, someone moving about.

Josh had backed up against the wall and was edging away, toward the stairs. He had an expression on his face I'd never seen before — sheer terror.

The door, creaking like a door in a movie haunted house, closed a little more.

Josh was nearly to the stairway. He was staring at me, violently motioning with his hand for me to follow.

But instead, I stepped forward, grabbed the doorknob, and pushed the door open hard.

It didn't resist.

I let go of the doorknob and stood blocking the doorway. "Who's there?"

The room was empty.

191

Thunder crashed.

It took me a few seconds to realize what was making the door move. The window on the opposite wall had been left open several inches. The gusting wind through the open window must have been opening and closing the door. I guessed that also explained the other sounds I heard inside the room, the sounds I thought were whispers.

Who had left the window open? The painters, probably.

I took a deep breath and let it out slowly, waiting for my pounding heart to settle down to normal.

Feeling a little foolish, I walked quickly to the window and pushed it shut.

"Amanda — are you all right?" Josh whispered from the hallway.

I started to answer him. But then I had a better idea.

He had practically scared me to death a few minutes before. Why not give *him* a little scare? He deserved it.

So I didn't answer him.

I could hear him take a few timid steps closer to my room. "Amanda? Amanda? You okay?"

I tiptoed over to my closet, pulled the door open a third of the way. Then I laid down flat on the floor, on my back, with my head and shoulders hidden inside the closet and the rest of me out in the room.

"Amanda?" Josh sounded very scared.

"Ohhhhh," I moaned loudly.

I knew when he saw me sprawled on the floor like this, he'd totally freak out!

"Amanda — what's happening?"

He was in the doorway now. He'd see me any second now, lying in the dark room, my head hidden from view, the lightning flashing impressively and the thunder cracking outside the old window.

I took a deep breath and held it to keep from giggling.

"Amanda?" he whispered. And then he must have seen me, because he uttered a loud "Huh?!" And I heard him gasp.

And then he screamed at the top of his lungs. I heard him running down the hall to the stairway, shrieking, "Mom! Dad!" And I heard his sneakers thudding down the wooden stairs, with him screaming and calling all the way down.

I snickered to myself. Then, before I could pull myself up, I felt a rough, warm tongue licking my face.

"Petey!"

He was licking my cheeks, licking my eyelids, licking me frantically, as if he were trying to revive me, or as if to let me know that everything was okay.

"Oh, Petey! Petey!" I cried, laughing and throwing my arms around the sweet dog. "Stop! You're getting me all sticky!"

But he wouldn't stop. He kept on licking fiercely.

The poor dog is nervous, too, I thought.

"Come on, Petey, shape up," I told him, holding his panting face away with both my hands. "There's nothing to be nervous about. This new place is going to be fun. You'll see."

6

That night, I was smiling to myself as I fluffed up my pillow and slid into bed. I was thinking about how terrified Josh had been that afternoon, how frightened he looked even after I came prancing down the stairs, perfectly okay. How angry he was that I'd fooled him.

Of course, Mom and Dad didn't think it was funny. They were both nervous and upset because the moving van had just arrived, an hour late. They forced Josh and me to call a truce. No more scaring each other.

"It's hard *not* to get scared in this creepy old place," Josh muttered. But we reluctantly agreed not to play any more jokes on each other, if we could possibly help it.

The men, complaining about the rain, started carrying in all of our furniture. Josh and I helped show them where we wanted stuff in our rooms. They dropped my dresser on the stairs, but it only got a small scratch.

The furniture looked strange and small in this big house. Josh and I tried to stay out of the way while Mom and Dad worked all day, arranging things, emptying cartons, putting clothes away. Mom even managed to get the curtains hung in my room.

What a day!

Now, a little after ten o'clock, trying to get to sleep for the first time in my new room, I turned onto my side, then onto my back. Even though this was my old bed, I couldn't get comfortable.

Everything seemed so different, so wrong. The bed didn't face the same direction as in my old bedroom. The walls were bare. I hadn't had time to hang any of my posters. The room seemed so large and empty. The shadows seemed so much darker.

My back started to itch, and then I suddenly felt itchy all over. The bed is filled with bugs! I thought, sitting up. But of course that was ridiculous. It was my same old bed with clean sheets.

I forced myself to settle back down and closed my eyes. Sometimes when I can't get to sleep, I count silently by twos, picturing each number in my mind as I think it. It usually helps to clear my mind so that I can drift off to sleep.

I tried it now, burying my face in the pillow, picturing the numbers rolling past . . . 4 . . . 6 . . . 8 . . .

I yawned loudly, still wide awake at two-twenty.

I'm going to be awake forever, I thought. I'm never going to be able to sleep in this new room.

But then I must have drifted off without realizing it. I don't know how long I slept. An hour or two at the most. It was a light, uncomfortable sleep. Then something woke me. I sat straight up, startled.

Despite the heat of the room, I felt cold all over. Looking down to the end of the bed, I saw that I had kicked off the sheet and light blanket. With a groan, I reached down for them, but then froze.

I heard whispers.

Someone was whispering across the room.

"Who — who's there?" My voice was a whisper, too, tiny and frightened.

I grabbed my covers and pulled them up to my chin.

I heard more whispers. The room came into focus as my eyes adjusted to the dim light.

The curtains. The long, sheer curtains from my old room that my mother had hung that afternoon were fluttering at the window.

So. That explained the whispers. The billowing curtains must have woken me up.

A soft, gray light floated in from outside. The curtains cast moving shadows onto the foot of my bed.

Yawning, I stretched and climbed out of bed. I felt chilled all over as I crept across the wooden floor to close the window.

As I came near, the curtains stopped billowing and floated back into place. I pushed them aside and reached out to close the window.

"Oh!"

I uttered a soft cry when I realized that the window *was* closed.

But how could the curtains flutter like that with the window closed? I stood there for a while, staring out at the grays of the night. There wasn't much of a draft. The window seemed pretty airtight.

Had I imagined the curtains billowing? Were my eyes playing tricks on me?

Yawning, I hurried back through the strange shadows to my bed and pulled the covers up as high as they would go. "Amanda, stop scaring yourself," I scolded.

When I fell back to sleep a few minutes later, I had the ugliest, most terrifying dream.

I dreamed that we were all dead. Mom, Dad, Josh, and me.

At first, I saw us sitting around the dinner table in the new dining room. The room was very bright, so bright I couldn't see our faces very well. They were just a bright, white blur.

But, then, slowly, slowly, everything came into focus, and I could see that beneath our hair, we had no faces. Our skin was gone, and only our gray-green skulls were left. Bits of flesh clung to my bony cheeks. There were only deep, black sockets where my eyes had been.

The four of us, all dead, sat eating in silence. Our dinner plates, I saw, were filled with small bones. A big platter in the center of the table was piled high with gray-green bones, human-looking bones.

And then, in this dream, our disgusting meal was interrupted by a loud knocking on the door, an insistent pounding that grew louder and louder. It was Kathy, my friend from back home. I could see her at our front door, pounding on it with both fists.

I wanted to go answer the door. I wanted to run from the dining room and pull open the door and greet Kathy. I wanted to talk to Kathy. I wanted to tell her what had happened to me, to explain that I was dead and that my face had fallen away.

I wanted to see Kathy *so* badly.

But I couldn't get up from the table. I tried and tried, but I couldn't get up.

The pounding on the door grew louder and louder, until it was deafening. But I just sat there with my gruesome family, picking up bones from my dinner plate and eating them.

I woke up with a start, the horror of the dream still with me. I could still hear the pounding in my ears. I shook my head, trying to chase the dream away.

It was morning. I could tell from the blue of the sky outside the window.

"Oh, no."

The curtains. They were billowing again, flapping noisily as they blew into the room.

I sat up and stared.

The window was still closed.

7

"I'll take a look at the window. There must be a draft or a leak or something," Dad said at breakfast. He shoveled in another mouthful of scrambled eggs and ham.

"But, Dad — it's so weird!" I insisted, still feeling scared. "The curtains were blowing like crazy, and the window was *closed*!"

"There might be a pane missing," Dad suggested.

"Amanda is a pain!" Josh cracked. His idea of a really witty joke.

"Don't start with your sister," Mom said, putting her plate down on the table and dropping into her chair. She looked tired. Her black hair, usually carefully pulled back, was disheveled. She tugged at the belt on her bathrobe. "Whew. I don't think I slept two hours last night."

"Neither did I," I said, sighing. "I kept thinking that boy would show up in my room again."

"Amanda — you've really got to stop this,"

Mom said sharply. "Boys in your room. Curtains blowing. You have to realize that you're nervous, and your imagination is working overtime."

"But, Mom — " I started.

"Maybe a ghost was behind the curtains," Josh said, teasing. He raised up his hands and made a ghostly "ooooooh" wail.

"Whoa." Mom put a hand on Josh's shoulder. "Remember what you promised about scaring each other?"

"It's going to be hard for all of us to adjust to this place," Dad said. "You may have dreamed about the curtains blowing, Amanda. You said you had bad dreams, right?"

The terrifying nightmare flashed back into my mind. Once again I saw the big platter of bones on the table. I shivered.

"It's so damp in here," Mom said.

"A little sunshine will help dry the place out," Dad said.

I peered out the window. The sky had turned solid gray. Trees seemed to spread darkness over our backyard. "Where's Petey?" I asked.

"Out back," Mom replied, swallowing a mouthful of eggs. "He got up early, too. Couldn't sleep, I guess. So I let him out."

"What are we doing today?" Josh asked. He always needed to know the plan for the day. Every detail. Mainly so he could argue about it.

"Your father and I still have a lot of unpacking

to do," Mom said, glancing to the back hallway, which was cluttered with unopened cartons. "You two can explore the neighborhood. See what you can find out. See if there are any other kids your age around."

"In other words, you want us to get lost!" I said.

Mom and Dad both laughed. "You're very smart, Amanda."

"But I want to help unpack *my* stuff," Josh whined. I knew he'd argue with the plan, just like always.

"Go get dressed and take a long walk," Dad said. "Take Petey with you, okay? And take a leash for him. I left one by the front stairs."

"What about our bikes? Why can't we ride our bikes?" Josh asked.

"They're buried in the back of the garage," Dad told him. "You'll never be able to get to them. Besides, you have a flat tire."

"If I can't ride my bike, I'm not going out," Josh insisted, crossing his arms in front of his chest.

Mom and Dad had to argue with him. Then threaten him. Finally, he agreed to go for "a short walk."

I finished my breakfast, thinking about Kathy and my other friends back home. I wondered what the kids were like in Dark Falls. I wondered if I'd be able to find new friends, real friends.

I volunteered to do the breakfast dishes since

Mom and Dad had so much work to do. The warm water felt soothing on my hands as I sponged the dishes clean. I guess maybe I'm weird. I like washing dishes.

Behind me, from somewhere in the front of the house, I could hear Josh arguing with Dad. I could just barely make out the words over the trickle of the tap water.

"Your basketball is packed in one of these cartons," Dad was saying. Then Josh said something. Then Dad said, "How should *I* know which one?" Then Josh said something. Then Dad said, "No, I don't have time to look now. Believe it or not, your basketball isn't at the top of my list."

I stacked the last dish onto the counter to drain, and looked for a dish towel to dry my hands. There was none in sight. I guess they hadn't been unpacked yet.

Wiping off my hands on the front of my robe, I headed for the stairs. "I'll be dressed in five minutes," I called to Josh, who was still arguing with Dad in the living room. "Then we can go out."

I started up the front stairs, and then stopped.

Above me on the landing stood a strange girl, about my age, with short black hair. She was smiling down at me, not a warm smile, not a friendly smile, but the coldest, most frightening smile I had ever seen.

8

A hand touched my shoulder.

I spun around.

It was Josh. "I'm not going for a walk unless I can take my basketball," he said.

"Josh — please!" I looked back up to the landing, and the girl was gone.

I felt cold all over. My legs were all trembly. I grabbed the banister.

"Dad! Come here — please!" I called.

Josh's face filled with alarm. "Hey, I didn't do anything!" he shouted.

"No — it's — it's not you," I said, and called Dad again.

"Amanda, I'm kind of busy," Dad said, appearing below at the foot of the stairs, already perspiring from uncrating living room stuff.

"Dad, I saw somebody," I told him. "Up there. A girl." I pointed.

"Amanda, please," he replied, making a face.

"Stop seeing things — okay? There's no one in this house except the four of us . . . . and maybe a few mice."

"Mice?" Josh asked with sudden interest. "Really? Where?"

"Dad, I didn't imagine it," I said, my voice cracking. I was really hurt that he didn't believe me.

"Amanda, look up there," Dad said, gazing up to the landing. "What do you see?"

I followed his gaze. There was a pile of my clothes on the landing. Mom must have just un-packed them.

"It's just clothes," Dad said impatiently. "It's not a girl. It's clothes." He rolled his eyes.

"Sorry," I said quietly. I repeated it as I started up the stairs. "Sorry."

But I didn't really feel sorry. I felt confused.

And still scared.

Was it possible that I thought a pile of clothes was a smiling girl?

No. I didn't think so.

I'm not crazy. And I have really good eye-sight.

So then, what was going on?

I opened the door to my room, turned on the ceiling light, and saw the curtains billowing in front of the bay window.

Oh, no. Not again, I thought.

I hurried over to them. This time, the window was open.

Who opened it?

Mom, I guessed.

Warm, wet air blew into the room. The sky was heavy and gray. It smelled like rain.

Turning to my bed, I had another shock.

Someone had laid out an outfit for me. A pair of faded jeans and a pale blue, sleeveless T-shirt. They were spread out side by side at the foot of the bed.

Who had put them there? Mom?

I stood at the doorway and called to her. "Mom? Mom? Did you pick out clothes for me?"

I could hear her shout something from downstairs, but I couldn't make out the words.

Calm down, Amanda, I told myself. Calm down.

Of *course* Mom pulled the clothes out. Of *course* Mom put them there.

From the doorway, I heard whispering in my closet.

Whispering and hushed giggling behind the closet door.

This was the last straw. "What's going on here?" I yelled at the top of my lungs.

I stormed over to the closet and pulled open the door.

Frantically, I pushed clothes out of the way. No one in there.

Mice? I thought. Had I heard the mice that Dad was talking about?

"I've got to get out of here," I said aloud.

The room, I realized, was driving me crazy.

No. I was driving *myself* crazy. Imagining all of these weird things.

There was a logical explanation for everything. Everything.

As I pulled up my jeans and fastened them, I said the word "logical" over and over in my mind. I said it so many times that it didn't sound like a real word anymore.

Calm down, Amanda. Calm down.

I took a deep breath and held it to ten.

"Boo!"

"Josh — cut it out. You didn't scare me," I told him, sounding more cross than I had meant to.

"Let's get out of here," he said, staring at me from the doorway. "This place gives me the creeps."

"Huh? You, too?" I exclaimed. "What's *your* problem?"

He started to say something, then stopped. He suddenly looked embarrassed. "Forget it," he muttered.

"No, tell me," I insisted. "What were you going to say?"

He kicked at the floor molding. "I had a really creepy dream last night," he finally admitted, looking past me to the fluttering curtains at the window.

"A dream?" I remembered my horrible dream.

"Yeah. There were these two boys in my room. And they were mean."

"What did they do?" I asked.

"I don't remember," Josh said, avoiding my eyes. "I just remember they were scary."

"And what happened?" I asked, turning to the mirror to brush my hair.

"I woke up," he said. And then added impatiently, "Come *on*. Let's go."

"Did the boys say anything to you?" I asked.

"No. I don't think so," he answered thoughtfully. "They just laughed."

"Laughed?"

"Well, giggled, sort of," Josh said. "I don't want to talk about it anymore," he snapped. "Are we going for this dumb walk, or not?"

"Okay. I'm ready," I said, putting down my brush, taking one last look in the mirror. "Let's go on this dumb walk."

I followed him down the hall. As we passed the stack of clothes on the landing, I thought about the girl I had seen standing there. And I thought about the boy in the window when we first arrived. And the two boys Josh had seen in his dream.

I decided it proved that Josh and I were both

really nervous about moving to this new place. Maybe Mom and Dad were right. We were letting our imaginations run away with us.

It had to be our imaginations.

I mean, what *else* could it be?

9

A few seconds later, we stepped into the backyard to get Petey. He was as glad to see us as ever, leaping on us with his muddy paws, yapping excitedly, running in frantic circles through the leaves. It cheered me up just to see him.

It was hot and muggy even though the sky was gray. There was no wind at all. The heavy, old trees stood as still as statues.

We headed down the gravel driveway toward the street, our sneakers kicking at the dead, brown leaves, Petey running in zigzags at our sides, first in front of us, then behind. "At least Dad hasn't asked us to rake all these old leaves," Josh said.

"He will," I warned. "I don't think he's unpacked the rake yet."

Josh made a face. We stood at the curb, looking up at our house, the two second-floor bay windows staring back at us like eyes.

The house next door, I noticed for the first time,

211

was about the same size as ours, except it was shingle instead of brick. The curtains in the living room were drawn shut. Some of the upstairs windows were shuttered. Tall trees cast the neighbors' house in darkness, too.

"Which way?" Josh asked, tossing a stick for Petey to chase.

I pointed up the street. "The school is up that way," I said. "Let's check it out."

The road sloped uphill. Josh picked up a small tree branch from the side of the road and used it as a walking stick. Petey kept trying to chew on it while Josh walked.

We didn't see anyone on the street or in any of the front yards we passed. No cars went by.

I was beginning to think the whole town was deserted, until the boy stepped out from behind the low ledge.

He popped out so suddenly, both Josh and I stopped in our tracks. "Hi," he said shyly, giving us a little wave.

"Hi," Josh and I answered at the same time.

Then, before we could pull him back, Petey ran up to the boy, sniffed his sneakers, and began snarling and barking. The boy stepped back and raised his hands as if he were protecting himself. He looked really frightened.

"Petey — stop!" I cried.

Josh grabbed the dog and picked him up, but he kept growling.

"He doesn't bite," I told the boy. "He usually doesn't bark, either. I'm sorry."

"That's okay," the boy said, staring at Petey, who was squirming to get out of Josh's arms. "He probably smells something on me."

"Petey, stop!" I shouted. The dog wouldn't stop squirming. "You don't want the leash — do you?"

The boy had short, wavy blond hair and very pale blue eyes. He had a funny turned-up nose that seemed out of place on his serious-looking face. He was wearing a maroon long-sleeved sweatshirt despite the mugginess of the day, and black straight-legged jeans. He had a blue baseball cap stuffed into the back pocket of his jeans.

"I'm Amanda Benson," I said. "And this is my brother Josh."

Josh hesitantly put Petey back on the ground. The dog yipped once, stared up at the boy, whimpered softly, then sat down on the street and began to scratch himself.

"I'm Ray Thurston," the boy said, stuffing his hands into his jeans pockets, still staring warily at Petey. He seemed to relax a little, though, seeing that the dog had lost interest in barking and growling at him.

I suddenly realized that Ray looked familiar. Where had I seen him before? Where? I stared hard at him until I remembered.

And then I gasped in sudden fright.

Ray was the boy, the boy in my room. The boy in the window.

"You — " I stammered accusingly. "You were in our house!"

He looked confused. "Huh?"

"You were in my room — right?" I insisted.

He laughed. "I don't get it," he said. "In your room?"

Petey raised his head and gave a low growl in Ray's direction. Then he went back to his serious scratching.

"I thought I saw you," I said, beginning to feel a little doubtful. Maybe it wasn't him. Maybe. . . .

"I haven't been in your house in a long time," Ray said, looking down warily at Petey.

"A long time?"

"Yeah. I used to live in your house," he replied.

"Huh?" Josh and I stared at him in surprise. "Our house?"

Ray nodded. "When we first moved here," he said. He picked up a flat pebble and heaved it down the street.

Petey growled, started to chase it, changed his mind, and plopped back down on the street, his stub of a tail wagging excitedly.

Heavy clouds lowered across the sky. It seemed to grow darker. "Where do you live now?" I asked.

Ray tossed another stone, then pointed up the road.

"Did you like our house?" Josh asked Ray.

"Yeah, it was okay," Ray told him. "Nice and shady."

"You liked it?" Josh cried. "I think it's gross. It's so dark and — "

Petey interrupted. He decided to start barking at Ray again, running up till he was a few inches in front of Ray, then backing away. Ray took a few cautious steps back to the edge of the curb.

Josh pulled the leash from the pocket of his shorts. "Sorry, Petey," he said. I held the growling dog while Josh attached the leash to his collar.

"He's never done this before. Really," I said, apologizing to Ray.

The leash seemed to confuse Petey. He tugged against it, pulling Josh across the street. But at least he stopped barking.

"Let's do something," Josh said impatiently.

"Like what?" Ray asked, relaxing again now that Petey was on the leash.

We all thought for a while.

"Maybe we could go to your house," Josh suggested to Ray.

Ray shook his head. "No. I don't think so," he said. "Not now anyway."

"Where is everyone?" I asked, looking up and down the empty street. "It's really dead around here, huh?"

He chuckled. "Yeah. I guess you could say

215

that," he said. "Want to go to the playground behind the school?"

"Yeah. Okay," I agreed.

The three of us headed up the street, Ray leading the way, me walking a few feet behind him, Josh holding his tree branch in one hand, the leash in the other, Petey running this way, then that, giving Josh a really hard time.

We didn't see the gang of kids till we turned the corner.

There were ten or twelve of them, mostly boys but a few girls, too. They were laughing and shouting, shoving each other playfully as they came toward us down the center of the street. Some of them, I saw, were about my age. The rest were teenagers. They were wearing jeans and dark T-shirts. One of the girls stood out because she had long, straight blonde hair and was wearing green spandex tights.

"Hey, look!" a tall boy with slicked-back black hair cried, pointing at us.

Seeing Ray, Josh, and me, they grew quiet but didn't stop moving toward us. A few of them giggled, as if they were enjoying some kind of private joke.

The three of us stopped and watched them approach. I smiled and waited to say hi. Petey was pulling at his leash and barking his head off.

"Hi, guys," the tall boy with the black hair said, grinning. The others thought this was very funny for some reason. They laughed. The girl in the green tights gave a short, red-haired boy a shove that almost sent him sprawling into me.

"How's it going, Ray?" a girl with short black hair asked, smiling at Ray.

"Not bad. Hi, guys," Ray answered. He turned to Josh and me. "These are some of my friends. They're all from the neighborhood."

"Hi," I said, feeling awkward. I wished Petey would stop barking and pulling at his leash like that. Poor Josh was having a terrible time holding onto him.

"This is George Carpenter," Ray said, pointing to the short, red-haired boy, who nodded. "And Jerry Franklin, Karen Somerset, Bill Gregory . . ." He went around the circle, naming each kid. I tried to remember all the names but, of course it was impossible.

"How do you like Dark Falls?" one of the girls asked me.

"I don't really know," I told her. "It's my first day here, really. It seems nice."

Some of the kids laughed at my answer, for some reason.

"What kind of dog is that?" George Carpenter asked Josh.

Josh, holding tight to the leash handle, told him. George stared hard at Petey, studying him, as if he had never seen a dog like Petey before.

Karen Somerset, a tall, pretty girl with short

blonde hair, came up to me while some of the other kids were admiring Petey. "You know, I used to live in your house," she said softly.

"What?" I wasn't sure I'd heard her correctly.

"Let's go to the playground," Ray said, interrupting.

No one responded to Ray's suggestion.

They grew quiet. Even Petey stopped barking.

Had Karen really said that she used to live in our house? I wanted to ask her, but she had stepped back into the circle of kids.

The circle.

My mouth dropped open as I realized they had formed a circle around Josh and me.

I felt a stab of fear. Was I imagining it? Was something going on?

They all suddenly looked different to me. They were smiling, but their faces were tense, watchful, as if they expected trouble.

Two of them, I noticed, were carrying baseball bats. The girl with the green tights stared at me, looking me up and down, checking me out.

No one said a word. The street was silent except for Petey, who was now whimpering softly.

I suddenly felt very afraid.

Why were they staring at us like that?

Or was my imagination running away with me again?

I turned to Ray, who was still beside me. He

didn't seem at all troubled. But he didn't return my gaze.

"Hey, guys — " I said. "What's going on?" I tried to keep it light, but my voice was a little shaky.

I looked over at Josh. He was busy soothing Petey and hadn't noticed that things had changed.

The two boys with baseball bats held them up waist high and moved forward.

I glanced around the circle, feeling the fear tighten my chest.

The circle tightened. The kids were closing in on us.

The black clouds overhead seemed to lower. The air felt heavy and damp.

Josh was fussing with Petey's collar and still didn't see what was happening. I wondered if Ray was going to say anything, if he was going to do anything to stop them. But he stayed frozen and expressionless beside me.

The circle grew smaller as the kids closed in.

I realized I'd been holding my breath. I took a deep breath and opened my mouth to cry out.

"Hey, kids — what's going on?"

It was a man's voice, calling from outside the circle.

Everyone turned to see Mr. Dawes coming quickly toward us, taking long strides as he crossed the street, his open blazer flapping behind him. He had a friendly smile on his face. "What's going on?" he asked again.

He didn't seem to realize that the gang of kids had been closing in on Josh and me.

220

"We're heading to the playground," George Carpenter told him, twirling the bat in his hand. "You know. To play softball."

"Good deal," Mr. Dawes said, pulling down his striped tie, which had blown over his shoulder. He looked up at the darkening sky. "Hope you don't get rained out."

Several of the kids had backed up. They were standing in small groups of two and three now. The circle had completely broken up.

"Is that bat for softball or hardball?" Mr. Dawes asked George.

"George doesn't know," another kid replied quickly. "He's never hit anything with it!"

The kids all laughed. George playfully menaced the kid, pretending to come at him with the bat.

Mr. Dawes gave a little wave and started to leave. But then he stopped, and his eyes opened wide with surprise. "Hey," he said, flashing me a friendly smile. "Josh. Amanda. I didn't see you there."

"Good morning," I muttered. I was feeling very confused. A moment ago, I'd felt terribly scared. Now everyone was laughing and kidding around.

Had I imagined that the kids were moving in on us? Ray and Josh hadn't seemed to notice anything peculiar. Was it just me and my overactive imagination?

What would have happened if Mr. Dawes hadn't come along?

221

"How are you two getting along in the new house?" Mr. Dawes asked, smoothing back his wavy blond hair.

"Okay," Josh and I answered together. Looking up at Mr. Dawes, Petey began to bark and pull at the leash.

Mr. Dawes put an exaggerated hurt expression on his face. "I'm crushed," he said. "Your dog still doesn't like me." He bent over Petey. "Hey, dog — lighten up."

Petey barked back angrily.

"He doesn't seem to like *anybody* today," I told Mr. Dawes apologetically.

Mr. Dawes stood back up and shrugged. "Can't win 'em all." He started back to his car, parked a few yards down the street. "I'm heading over to your house," he told Josh and me. "Just want to see if there's anything I can do to help your parents. Have fun, kids."

I watched him climb into his car and drive away.

"He's a nice guy," Ray said.

"Yeah," I agreed. I was still feeling uncomfortable, wondering what the kids would do now that Mr. Dawes was gone.

Would they form that frightening circle again?

No. Everyone started walking, heading down the block to the playground behind the school. They were kidding each other and talking normally, and pretty much ignored Josh and me.

I was starting to feel a little silly. It was obvious that they hadn't been trying to scare Josh and me. I must have made the whole thing up in my mind.

I must have.

At least, I told myself, I hadn't screamed or made a scene. At least I hadn't made a total fool of myself.

The playground was completely empty. I guessed that most kids had stayed inside because of the threatening sky. The playground was a large, flat grassy field, surrounded on all four sides by a tall metal fence. There were swings and slides at the end nearest the school building. There were two baseball diamonds on the other end. Beyond the fence, I could see a row of tennis courts, also deserted.

Josh tied Petey to the fence, then came running over to join the rest of us. The boy named Jerry Franklin made up the teams. Ray and I were on the same team. Josh was on the other.

As our team took the field, I felt excited and a little nervous. I'm not the best softball player in the world. I can hit the ball pretty well. But in the field, I'm a complete klutz. Luckily, Jerry sent me out to right field where not many balls are hit.

The clouds began to part a little and the sky got lighter. We played two full innings. The other team was winning, eight to two. I was having fun.

I had only messed up on one play. And I hit a double my first time at bat.

It was fun being with a whole new group of kids. They seemed really nice, especially the girl named Karen Somerset, who talked with me while we waited for our turn at bat. Karen had a great smile, even though she wore braces on all her teeth, up and down. She seemed very eager to be friends.

The sun was coming out as my team started to take the field for the beginning of the third inning. Suddenly, I heard a loud, shrill whistle. I looked around until I saw that it was Jerry Franklin, blowing a silver whistle.

Everyone came running up to him. "We'd better quit," he said, looking up at the brightening sky. "We promised our folks, remember, that we'd be home for lunch."

I glanced at my watch. It was only eleven-thirty. Still early.

But to my surprise, no one protested.

They all waved to each other and called out farewells, and then began to run. I couldn't believe how fast everyone left. It was as if they were racing or something.

Karen ran past me like the others, her head down, a serious expression on her pretty face. Then she stopped suddenly and turned around. "Nice meeting you, Amanda," she called back. "We should get together sometime."

"Great!" I called to her. "Do you know where I live?"

I couldn't hear her answer very well. She nodded, and I thought she said, "Yes. I know it. I used to live in your house."

But that *couldn't* have been what she said.

11

Several days went by. Josh and I were getting used to our new house and our new friends.

The kids we met every day at the playground weren't exactly friends yet. They talked with Josh and me, and let us on their teams. But it was really hard to get to know them.

In my room, I kept hearing whispers late at night, and soft giggling, but I forced myself to ignore it. One night, I thought I saw a girl dressed all in white at the end of the upstairs hall. But when I walked over to investigate, there was just a pile of dirty sheets and other bedclothes against the wall.

Josh and I were adjusting, but Petey was still acting really strange. We took him with us to the playground every day, but we had to leash him to the fence. Otherwise, he'd bark and snap at all the kids.

"He's still nervous being in a new place," I told Josh. "He'll calm down."

But Petey didn't calm down. And about two weeks later, we were finishing up a softball game with Ray, and Karen Somerset, and Jerry Franklin, and George Carpenter, and a bunch of other kids, when I looked over to the fence and saw that Petey was gone.

Somehow he had broken out of his leash and run away.

We looked for hours, calling "Petey!" wandering from block to block, searching front yards and backyards, empty lots and woods. Then, after circling the neighborhood twice, Josh and I suddenly realized we had no idea where we were.

The streets of Dark Falls looked the same. They were all lined with sprawling old brick or shingle houses, all filled with shady old trees.

"I don't believe it. We're lost," Josh said, leaning against a tree trunk, trying to catch his breath.

"That stupid dog," I muttered, my eyes searching up the street. "Why did he do this? He's never run away before."

"I don't know how he got loose," Josh said, shaking his head, then wiping his sweaty forehead with the sleeve of his T-shirt. "I tied him up really well."

"Hey — maybe he ran home," I said. The idea immediately cheered me up.

"Yeah!" Josh stepped away from the tree and headed back over to me. "I'll bet you're right,

Amanda. He's probably been home for hours. Wow. We've been stupid. We should've checked home first. Let's go!"

"Well," I said, looking around at the empty yards, "we just have to figure out which way is home."

I looked up and down the street, trying to figure out which way we'd turned when we left the school playground. I couldn't remember, so we just started walking.

Luckily, as we reached the next corner, the school came into sight. We had made a full circle. It was easy to find our way from there.

Passing the playground, I stared at the spot on the fence where Petey had been tied. That troublemaking dog. He'd been acting so badly ever since we came to Dark Falls.

Would he be home when we got there? I hoped so.

A few minutes later, Josh and I were running up the gravel driveway, calling the dog's name at the top of our lungs. The front door burst open and Mom, her hair tied in a red bandanna, the knees of her jeans covered with dust, leaned out. She and Dad had been painting the back porch. "Where have you two been? Lunchtime was two hours ago!"

Josh and I both answered at the same time. "Is Petey here?"

"We've been looking for Petey!"

"Is he here?"

Mom's face filled with confusion. "Petey? I thought he was with you."

My heart sank. Josh slumped to the driveway with a loud sigh, sprawling flat on his back in the gravel and leaves.

"You haven't seen him?" I asked, my trembling voice showing my disappointment. "He *was* with us. But he ran away."

"Oh. I'm sorry," Mom said, motioning for Josh to get up from the driveway. "He ran away? I thought you've been keeping him on a leash."

"You've got to help us find him," Josh pleaded, not budging from the ground. "Get the car. We've got to find him — right now!"

"I'm sure he hasn't gotten far," Mom said. "You must be starving. Come in and have some lunch and then we'll — "

"No. Right *now!*" Josh screamed.

"What's going on?" Dad, his face and hair covered with tiny flecks of white paint, joined Mom on the front porch. "Josh — what's all the yelling?"

We explained to Dad what had happened. He said he was too busy to drive around looking for Petey. Mom said she'd do it, but only after we had some lunch. I pulled Josh up by both arms and dragged him into the house.

We washed up and gulped down some peanut butter and jelly sandwiches. Then Mom took the car out of the garage, and we drove around and around the neighborhood searching for our lost pet.

With no luck.

No sign of him.

Josh and I were miserable. Heartbroken. Mom and Dad called the local police. Dad kept saying that Petey had a good sense of direction, that he'd show up any minute.

But we didn't really believe it.

Where was he?

The four of us ate dinner in silence. It was the longest, most horrible evening of my life. "I tied him up really good," Josh repeated, close to tears, his dinner plate still full.

"Dogs are great escape artists," Dad said, "Don't worry. He'll show up."

"Some night for a party," Mom said glumly.

I'd completely forgotten that they were going out. Some neighbors on the next block had invited them to a big potluck dinner party.

"I sure don't feel like partying, either," Dad said with a sigh. "I'm beat from painting all day. But I guess we have to be neighborly. Sure you kids will be okay here?"

"Yeah, I guess," I said, thinking about Petey. I kept listening for his bark, listening for scratching at the door.

But no. The hours dragged by. Petey still hadn't shown up by bedtime.

Josh and I both slinked upstairs. I felt really tired, weary from all the worrying, and the running around and searching for Petey, I guess. But I knew I'd never be able to get to sleep.

In the hall outside my bedroom door, I heard whispering from inside my room and quiet footsteps. The usual sounds my room made. I wasn't at all scared of them or surprised by them anymore.

Without hesitating, I stepped into my room and clicked on the light. The room was empty, as I knew it would be. The mysterious sounds disappeared. I glanced at the curtains, which lay straight and still.

Then I saw the clothes strewn all over my bed.

Several pairs of jeans. Several T-shirts. A couple of sweatshirts. My only dress-up skirt.

That's strange, I thought. Mom was such a neat freak. If she had washed these things, she surely would have hung them up or put them into dresser drawers.

Sighing wearily, I started to gather up the clothes and put them away. I figured that Mom simply had too much to do to be bothered. She had probably washed the stuff and then left it here for me to put away. Or she had put it all down, planning to come back later and put it away, and then got busy with other chores.

Half an hour later, I was tucked into my bed wide awake, staring at the shadows on the ceiling.

Some time after that — I lost track of the time — I was still wide awake, still thinking about Petey, thinking about the new kids I'd met, thinking about the new neighborhood, when I heard my bedroom door creak and swing open.

Footsteps on the creaking floorboards.

I sat up in the darkness as someone crept into my room.

"Amanda — ssshh — it's me."

Alarmed, it took me a few seconds to recognize the hushed whisper. "Josh! What do you want? What are you doing in here?"

I gasped as a blinding light forced me to cover my eyes. "Oops. Sorry," Josh said. "My flashlight. I didn't mean to — "

"Ow, that's bright," I said, blinking. He aimed the powerful beam of white light up at the ceiling.

"Yeah. It's a halogen flashlight," he said.

"Well, what do you want?" I asked irritably. I still couldn't see well. I rubbed my eyes, but it didn't help.

"I know where Petey is," Josh whispered, "and I'm going to go get him. Come with me?"

"Huh?" I looked at the little clock on my bed table. "It's after midnight, Josh."

"So? It won't take long. Really."

My eyes were nearly normal by now. Staring at Josh in the light from the halogen flashlight, I noticed for the first time that he was fully dressed in jeans and a long-sleeved T-shirt.

"I don't get it, Josh," I said, swinging around and putting my feet on the floor. "We looked everywhere. Where do you think Petey is?"

"In the cemetery," Josh answered. His eyes looked big and dark and serious in the white light.

"Huh?"

"That's where he ran the first time, remember? When we first came to Dark Falls? He ran to that cemetery just past the school."

"Now, wait a minute — " I started.

"We drove past it this afternoon, but we didn't look inside. He's there, Amanda. I know he is. And I'm going to go get him whether you come or not."

"Josh, calm down," I said, putting my hands on his narrow shoulders. I was surprised to discover that he was trembling. "There's no reason for Petey to be in that cemetery."

"That's where he went the first time," Josh insisted. "He was looking for something there that day. I could tell. I know he's there again, Amanda." He pulled away from me. "Are you coming or not?"

My brother has to be the stubbornest, most headstrong person in the world.

"Josh, you're really going to walk into a strange

233

cemetery so late at night?" I asked.

"I'm not afraid," he said, shining the bright light around my room.

For a brief second, I thought the light caught someone, lurking behind the curtains. I opened my mouth to cry out. But there was no one there.

"You coming or not?" he repeated impatiently.

I was going to say no. But then, glancing at the curtains, I thought, it's probably no more spooky out there in that cemetery than it is here in my own bedroom!

"Yeah. Okay," I said grudgingly. "Get out of here and let me get dressed."

"Okay," he whispered, turning off the flashlight, plunging us into blackness. "Meet me down at the end of the driveway."

"Josh — one quick look at the cemetery, then we hurry home. Got it?" I told him.

"Yeah. Right. We'll be home before Mom and Dad get back from that party." He crept out. I could hear him making his way quickly down the stairs.

This is the craziest idea ever, I told myself as I searched in the darkness for some clothes to pull on.

And it was also kind of exciting.

Josh was wrong. No doubt about it. Petey wouldn't be hanging around in that cemetery now. Why on earth should he?

But at least it wasn't a long walk. And it was an adventure. Something to write about to Kathy back home.

And if Josh happened to be right, and we did manage to find poor, lost Petey, well, that would be great, too.

A few minutes later, dressed in jeans and a sweatshirt, I crept out of the house and joined Josh at the bottom of the driveway. The night was still warm. A heavy blanket of clouds covered the moon. I realized for the first time that there were no streetlights on our block.

Josh had the halogen flashlight on, aimed down at our feet. "You ready?" he asked.

Dumb question. Would I be standing there if I weren't ready?

We crunched over dead leaves as we headed up the block, toward the school. From there, it was just two blocks to the cemetery.

"It's so dark," I whispered. The houses were black and silent. There was no breeze at all. It was as if we were all alone in the world.

"It's too quiet," I said, hurrying to keep up with Josh. "No crickets or anything. Are you sure you really want to go to the cemetery?"

"I'm sure," he said, his eyes following the circle of light from the flashlight as it bumped over the ground. "I really think Petey is there."

We walked in the street, keeping close to the curb. We had gone nearly two blocks. The school was just coming into sight on the next block when we heard the scraping steps behind us on the pavement.

Josh and I both stopped. He lowered the light.

We both heard the sounds. I wasn't imagining them.

Someone was following us.

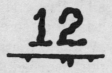

12

Josh was so startled, the flashlight tumbled from his hand and clattered onto the street. The light flickered but didn't go out.

By the time Josh had managed to pick it up, our pursuer had caught up to us. I spun around to face him, my heart pounding in my chest.

"Ray! What are *you* doing here?"

Josh aimed the light at Ray's face, but Ray shot his arms up to shield his face and ducked back into the darkness. "What are *you two* doing here?" he cried, sounding almost as startled as I did.

"You — you scared us," Josh said angrily, aiming the flashlight back down at our feet.

"Sorry," Ray said, "I would've called out, but I wasn't sure it was you."

"Josh has this crazy idea about where Petey might be," I told him, still struggling to catch my breath. "That's why we're out here."

"What about you?" Josh asked Ray.

237

"Well, sometimes I have trouble sleeping," Ray said softly.

"Don't your parents mind you being out so late?" I asked.

In the glow from the flashlight, I could see a wicked smile cross his face. "They don't know."

"Are we going to the cemetery or not?" Josh asked impatiently. Without waiting for an answer, he started jogging up the road, the light bobbing on the pavement in front of him. I turned and followed, wanting to stay close to the light.

"Where are you going?" Ray called, hurrying to catch up.

"The cemetery," I called back.

"No," Ray said. "You're not."

His voice was so low, so threatening, that I stopped. "What?"

"You're not going there," Ray repeated. I couldn't see his face. It was hidden in darkness. But his words sounded menacing.

"Hurry!" Josh called back to us. He hadn't slowed down. He didn't seem to notice the threat in Ray's words.

"Stop, Josh!" Ray called. It sounded more like an order than a request. "You can't go there!"

"Why not?" I demanded, suddenly afraid. Was Ray threatening Josh and me? Did he know something we didn't? Or was I making a big deal out of nothing once again?

I stared into the darkness, trying to see his face.

"You'd be nuts to go there at night!" he declared.

I began to think I had misjudged him. He was afraid to go there. That's why he was trying to stop us.

"Are you coming or not?" Josh demanded, getting farther and farther ahead of us.

"I don't think we should," Ray warned.

Yes, he's afraid, I decided. I only imagined that he was threatening us.

"You don't have to. But *we* do," Josh insisted, picking up his speed.

"No. Really," Ray said. "This is a bad idea." But now he and I were running side by side to catch up with Josh.

"Petey's there," Josh said, "I know he is."

We passed the dark, silent school. It seemed much bigger at night. Josh's light flashed through the low tree branches as we turned the corner onto Cemetery Drive.

"Wait — please," Ray pleaded. But Josh didn't slow down. Neither did I. I was eager to get there and get it over with.

I wiped my forehead with my sleeve. The air was hot and still. I wished I hadn't worn long sleeves. I felt my hair. It was dripping wet.

The clouds still covered the moon as we reached

the cemetery. We stepped through a gate in the low wall. In the darkness, I could see the crooked rows of gravestones.

Josh's light traveled from stone to stone, jumping up and down as he walked. "Petey!" he called suddenly, interrupting the silence.

He's disturbing the sleep of the dead, I thought, feeling a sudden chill of fear.

Don't be silly, Amanda. "Petey!" I called, too, forcing away my morbid thoughts.

"This is a very bad idea," Ray said, standing very close to me.

"Petey! Petey!" Josh called.

"I know it's a bad idea," I admitted to Ray. "But I didn't want Josh to come here by himself."

"But we shouldn't *be* here," Ray insisted.

I was beginning to wish he'd go away. No one had forced him to come. Why was he giving us such a hard time?

"Hey — look at this!" Josh called from several yards up ahead.

My sneakers crunching over the soft ground, I hurried between the rows of graves. I hadn't realized that we had already walked the entire length of the graveyard.

"Look," Josh said again, his flashlight playing over a strange structure built at the edge of the cemetery.

It took me a little while to figure out what it was in the small circle of light. It was so unexpected. It was some kind of theater. An amphitheater, I guess you'd call it, circular rows of bench seats dug into the ground, descending like stairs to a low stagelike platform at the bottom.

"What on earth!" I exclaimed.

I started forward to get a closer look.

"Amanda — wait. Let's go home," Ray called. He grabbed at my arm, but I hurried away, and he grabbed only air.

"Weird! Who would build an outdoor theater at the edge of a cemetery?" I asked.

I looked back to see if Josh and Ray were following me, and my sneaker caught against something. I stumbled to the ground, hitting my knee hard.

"Ow. What was that?"

Josh shone the light on it as I climbed slowly, painfully, to my feet. I had tripped over an enormous, upraised tree root.

In the flickering light, I followed the gnarled root over to a wide, old tree several yards away. The huge tree was bent over the strange belowground theater, leaning at such a low angle that it looked likely to topple over at any second. Big clumps of roots were raised up from the ground. Overhead, the tree's branches, heavy with leaves, seemed to lean to the ground.

"Timberrr!" Josh yelled.

"How weird!" I exclaimed. "Hey, Ray — what is this place?"

"It's a meeting place," Ray said quietly, standing close beside me, staring straight ahead at the leaning tree. "They use it sort of like a town hall. They have town meetings here."

"In the cemetery?" I cried, finding it hard to believe.

"Let's go," Ray urged, looking very nervous.

All three of us heard the footsteps. They were behind us, somewhere in the rows of graves. We turned around. Josh's light swept over the ground.

"Petey!"

There he was, standing between the nearest row of low, stone grave markers. I turned happily to Josh. "I don't believe it!" I cried. "You were right!"

"Petey! Petey!" Josh and I both started running toward our dog.

But Petey arched back on his hind legs as if he were getting ready to run away. He stared at us, his eyes red as jewels in the light of the flashlight.

"Petey! We found you!" I cried.

The dog lowered his head and started to trot away.

"Petey! Hey — come back! Don't you recognize us?"

With a burst of speed, Josh caught up with him

242

and grabbed him up off the ground. "Hey, Petey, what's the matter, fella?"

As I hurried over, Josh dropped Petey back to the ground and stepped back. "Ooh — he stinks!"

"What?" I cried.

"Petey — he stinks. He smells like a dead rat!" Josh held his nose.

Petey started to walk slowly away.

"Josh, he isn't glad to see us," I wailed. "He doesn't even seem to recognize us. Look at him!"

It was true. Petey walked to the next row of gravestones, then turned and glared at us.

I suddenly felt sick. What had happened to Petey? Why was he acting so differently? Why wasn't he glad to see us?

"I don't get it," Josh said, still making a face from the odor the dog gave off. "Usually, if we leave the room for thirty seconds, he goes nuts when we come back."

"We'd better go!" Ray called. He was still at the edge of the cemetery near the leaning tree.

"Petey — what's wrong with you?" I called to the dog. He didn't respond. "Don't you remember your name? Petey? Petey?"

"Yuck! What a stink!" Josh exclaimed.

"We've got to get him home and give him a bath," I said. My voice was shaking. I felt really sad. And frightened.

"Maybe this isn't Petey," Josh said thoughtfully. The dog's eyes again glared red in the beam of light.

"It's him all right," I said quietly. "Look. He's dragging the leash. Go get him, Josh — and let's go home."

"*You* get him!" Josh cried. "He smells too bad!"

"Just grab his leash. You don't have to pick him up," I said.

"No. *You.*"

Josh was being stubborn again. I could see that I had no choice. "Okay," I said. "I'll get him. But I'll need the light." I grabbed the flashlight from Josh's hand and started to run toward Petey.

"Sit, Petey. Sit!" I ordered. It was the only command Petey ever obeyed.

But he didn't obey it this time. Instead, he turned and trotted away, holding his head down low.

"Petey — stop! Petey, come on!" I yelled, exasperated. "Don't make me chase you."

"Don't let him get away!" Josh yelled, running up behind me.

I moved the flashlight from side to side along the ground. "Where is he?"

"Petey! Petey!" Josh called, sounding shrill and desperate.

I couldn't see him.

"Oh, no. Don't tell me we've lost him again!" I said.

We both started to call him. "What's *wrong* with that mutt?" I cried.

I moved the beam of light down one long row of gravestones, then, moving quickly, down the next. No sign of him. We both kept calling his name.

And then the circle of light came to rest on the front of a granite tombstone.

Reading the name on the stone, I stopped short.

And gasped.

"Josh — look!" I grabbed Josh's sleeve. I held on tight.

"Huh? What's wrong?" His face filled with confusion.

"Look! The name on the gravestone."

It was Karen Somerset.

Josh read the name. He stared at me, still confused.

"That's my new friend Karen. The one I talk to on the playground every day," I said.

"Huh? It must be her grandmother or something," Josh said, and then added impatiently, "Come on. Look for Petey."

"No. Look at the dates," I said to him.

We both read the dates under Karen Somerset's name. 1960–1972.

"It can't be her mother or grandmother," I said, keeping the beam of light on the stone despite my trembling hand. "This girl died when she was twelve. My age. And Karen is twelve, too. She told me."

"Amanda — " Josh scowled and looked away.

But I took a few steps and beamed the light onto the next gravestone. There was a name on it I'd never heard before. I moved on to the next stone. Another name I'd never heard.

"Amanda, come on!" Josh whined.

The next gravestone had the name George Carpenter on it. 1975–1988.

"Josh — look! It's George from the playground," I called.

"Amanda, we have to get Petey," he insisted.

But I couldn't pull myself away from the gravestones. I went from one to the next, moving the flashlight over the engraved letters.

To my growing horror, I found Jerry Franklin. And then Bill Gregory.

All the kids we had played softball with. They all had gravestones here.

My heart thudding, I moved down the crooked row, my sneakers sinking into the soft grass. I felt numb, numb with fear. I struggled to hold the light steady as I beamed it onto the last stone in the row.

RAY THURSTON. 1977–1988.

"Huh?"

I could hear Josh calling me, but I couldn't make out what he was saying.

The rest of the world seemed to fall away. I read the deeply etched inscription again:

RAY THURSTON. 1977–1988.

I stood there, staring at the letters and numbers. I stared at them till they didn't make sense anymore, until they were just a gray blur.

Suddenly, I realized that Ray had crept up beside the gravestone and was staring at me.

"Ray — " I managed to say, moving the light over the name on the stone. "Ray, this one is . . . *you!*"

His eyes flared, glowing like dying embers.

"Yes, it's me," he said softly, moving toward me. "I'm so sorry, Amanda."

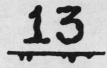

13

I took a step back, my sneakers sinking into the soft ground. The air was heavy and still. No one made a sound. Nothing moved.

Dead.

I'm surrounded by death, I thought.

Then, frozen to the spot, unable to breathe, the darkness swirling around me, the gravestones spinning in their own black shadows, I thought: What is he going to do to me?

"Ray — " I managed to call out. My voice sounded faint and far away. "Ray, are you really dead?"

"I'm sorry. You weren't supposed to find out yet," he said, his voice floating low and heavy on the stifling night air.

"But — how? I mean . . . I don't understand. . . ." I looked past him to the darting white light of the flashlight. Josh was several rows away, almost to the street, still searching for Petey.

"Petey!" I whispered, dread choking my throat, my stomach tightening in horror.

"Dogs always know," Ray said in a low, flat tone. "Dogs always recognize the living dead. That's why they have to go first. They always know."

"You mean — Petey's . . . dead?" I choked out the words.

Ray nodded. "They kill the dogs first."

"No!" I screamed and took another step back, nearly losing my balance as I bumped into a low marble gravestone. I jumped away from it.

"You weren't supposed to see this," Ray said, his narrow face expressionless except for his dark eyes, which revealed real sadness. "You weren't supposed to know. Not for another few weeks, anyway. I'm the watcher. I was supposed to watch, to make sure you didn't see until it was time."

He took a step toward me, his eyes lighting up red, burning into mine.

"Were you watching me from the window?" I cried. "Was that you in my room?"

Again he nodded yes. "I used to live in your house," he said, taking another step closer, forcing me back against the cold marble stone. "I'm the watcher."

I forced myself to look away, to stop staring into his glowing eyes. I wanted to scream to Josh to run and get help. But he was too far away. And I was frozen there, frozen with fear.

"We need fresh blood," Ray said.

"What?" I cried. "What are you saying?"

"The town — it can't survive without fresh blood. None of us can. You'll understand soon, Amanda. You'll understand why we had to invite you to the house, to the . . . Dead House."

In the darting, zigzagging beam of light, I could see Josh moving closer, heading our way.

Run, Josh, I thought. Run away. Fast. Get someone. Get *anyone*.

I could think the words. Why couldn't I scream them?

Ray's eyes glowed brighter. He was standing right in front of me now, his features set, hard and cold.

"Ray?" Even through my jeans, the marble gravestone felt cold against the back of my legs.

"I messed up," he whispered. "I was the watcher. But I messed up."

"Ray — what are you going to do?"

His red eyes flickered. "I'm really sorry."

He started to raise himself off the ground, to float over me.

I could feel myself start to choke. I couldn't breathe. I couldn't move. I opened my mouth to call out to Josh, but no sound came out.

Josh? Where was he?

I looked down the rows of gravestones but couldn't see his light.

Ray floated up a little higher. He hovered over me, choking me somehow, blinding me, suffocating me.

I'm dead, I thought. Dead.

Now I'm dead, too.

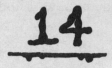

14

And then, suddenly, light broke through the darkness.

The light shone in Ray's face, the bright white halogen light.

"What's going on?" Josh asked, in a high-pitched, nervous voice. "Amanda — what's happening?"

Ray cried out and dropped back to the ground. "Turn that off! Turn it off!" he screeched, his voice a shrill whisper, like wind through a broken windowpane.

But Josh held the bright beam of light on Ray. "What's going on? What are you doing?"

I could breathe again. As I stared into the light, I struggled to stop my heart from pounding so hard.

Ray moved his arms to shield himself from the light. But I could see what was happening to him. The light had already done its damage.

Ray's skin seemed to be melting. His whole face

sagged, then fell, dropping off his skull.

I stared into the circle of white light, unable to look away, as Ray's skin folded and drooped and melted away. As the bone underneath was revealed, his eyeballs rolled out of their sockets and fell silently to the ground.

Josh, frozen in horror, somehow held the bright light steady, and we both stared at the grinning skull, its dark craters staring back at us.

"Oh!" I shrieked as Ray took a step toward me.

But then I realized that Ray wasn't walking. He was falling.

I jumped aside as he crumpled to the ground. And gasped as his skull hit the top of the marble gravestone, and cracked open with a sickening *splat*.

"Come on!" Josh shouted. "Amanda — come *on*!" He grabbed my hand and tried to pull me away.

But I couldn't stop staring down at Ray, now a pile of bones inside a puddle of crumpled clothes.

"Amanda, come on!"

Then, before I even realized it, I was running, running beside Josh as fast as I could down the long row of graves toward the street. The light flashed against the blur of gravestones as we ran, slipping on the soft, dew-covered grass, gasping in the still, hot air.

"We've got to tell Mom and Dad. Got to get *away* from here!" I cried.

"They — they won't believe it!" Josh said, as we reached the street. We kept running, our sneakers thudding hard against the pavement. "I'm not sure I believe it myself!"

"They've *got* to believe us!" I told him. "If they don't, we'll *drag* them out of that house."

The white beam of light pointed the way as we ran through the dark, silent streets. There were no streetlights, no lights on in the windows of the houses we passed, no car headlights.

Such a dark world we had entered.

And now it was time to get out.

We ran the rest of the way home. I kept looking back to see if we were being followed. But I didn't see anyone. The neighborhood was still and empty.

I had a sharp pain in my side as we reached home. But I forced myself to keep running, up the gravel driveway with its thick blanket of dead leaves, and onto the front porch.

I pushed open the door and both Josh and I started to scream. "Mom! Dad! Where are you?"

Silence.

We ran into the living room. The lights were all off.

"Mom? Dad? Are you here?"

Please be here, I thought, my heart racing, the pain in my side still sharp. Please be here.

We searched the house. They weren't home.

"The potluck party," Josh suddenly remembered. "Can they still be at that party?"

We were standing in the living room, both of us breathing hard. The pain in my side had let up just a bit. I had turned on all the lights, but the room still felt gloomy and menacing.

I glanced at the clock on the mantel. Nearly two in the morning.

"They should be home by now," I said, my voice shaky and weak.

"Where did they go? Did they leave a number?" Josh was already on his way to the kitchen.

I followed him, turning on lights as we went. We went right to the memo pad on the counter where Mom and Dad always leave us notes.

Nothing. The pad was blank.

"We've *got* to find them!" Josh cried. He sounded very frightened. His wide eyes reflected his fear. "We have to get away from here."

What if something has happened to them?

That's what I started to say. But I caught myself just in time. I didn't want to scare Josh any more than he was already.

Besides, he'd probably thought of that, too.

"Should we call the police?" he asked, as we walked back to the living room and peered out the front window into the darkness.

"I don't know," I said, pressing my hot forehead against the cool glass. "I just don't know *what* to do. I want them to be home. I want them here so we can all leave."

"What's your hurry?" a girl's voice said from behind me.

Josh and I both cried out and spun around.

Karen Somerset was standing in the center of the room, her arms crossed over her chest.

"But — you're *dead*!" I blurted out.

She smiled, a sad smile, a bitter smile.

And then two more kids stepped in from the hallway. One of them clicked off the lights. "Too bright in here," he said. They moved next to Karen.

And another kid, Jerry Franklin — another dead kid — appeared by the fireplace. And I saw the girl with short black hair, the one I had seen on the stairs, move beside me by the curtains.

They were all smiling, their eyes glowing dully in the dim light, all moving in on Josh and me.

"What do you *want*?" I screamed in a voice I didn't even recognize. "What are you going to do?"

"We used to live in your house," Karen said softly.

"Huh?" I cried.

"We used to live in your house," George said.

"And now, guess what?" Jerry added. *"Now we're dead in your house!"*

The others started to laugh, crackling, dry laughs, as they all closed in on Josh and me.

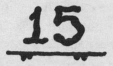

15

"They're going to kill us!" Josh cried.

I watched them move forward in silence. Josh and I had backed up to the window. I looked around the dark room for an escape route.

But there was nowhere to run.

"Karen — you seemed so nice," I said. The words just tumbled out. I hadn't thought before I said them.

Her eyes glowed a little brighter. "I *was* nice," she said in a glum monotone, "until I moved here."

"We were all nice," George Carpenter said in the same low monotone. "But now we're dead."

"Let us go!" Josh cried, raising his hands in front of him as if to shield himself. "Please — let us go."

They laughed again, the dry, hoarse laughter. Dead laughter.

"Don't be scared, Amanda," Karen said. "Soon you'll be with us. That's why they invited you to this house."

"Huh? I don't understand," I cried, my voice shaking.

"This is the Dead House. This is where everyone lives when they first arrive in Dark Falls. When they're still alive."

This seemed to strike the others as funny. They all snickered and laughed.

"But our great-uncle — " Josh started.

Karen shook her head, her eyes glowing with amusement. "No. Sorry, Josh. No great-uncle. It was just a trick to bring you here. Once every year, someone new has to move here. Other years, it was us. We lived in this house — until we died. This year, it's your turn."

"We need new blood," Jerry Franklin said, his eyes glowing red in the dim light. "Once a year, you see, we need new blood."

Moving forward in silence, they hovered over Josh and me.

I took a deep breath. A last breath, perhaps. And shut my eyes.

And then I heard the knock on the door.

A loud knock, repeated several times.

I opened my eyes. The ghostly kids all vanished. The air smelled sour.

Josh and I stared at each other, dazed, as the loud knocking started again.

"It's Mom and Dad!" Josh cried.

We both ran to the door. Josh stumbled over

the coffee table in the dark, so I got to the door first.

"Mom! Dad!" I cried, pulling open the door. "Where have you been?"

I reached out my arms to hug them both — and stopped with my arms in the air. My mouth dropped open and I uttered a silent cry.

"Mr. Dawes!" Josh exclaimed, coming up beside me. "We thought — "

"Oh, Mr. Dawes, I'm so glad to see you!" I cried happily, pushing open the screen door for him.

"Kids — you're okay?" he asked, eyeing us both, his handsome face tight with worry. "Oh, thank God!" he cried. "I got here in time!"

"Mr. Dawes — " I started, feeling so relieved, I had tears in my eyes. "I — "

He grabbed my arm. "There's no time to talk," he said, looking behind him to the street. I could see his car in the driveway. The engine was running. Only the parking lights were on. "I've got to get you kids out of here while there's still time."

Josh and I started to follow him, then hesitated. What if Mr. Dawes was one of them?

"Hurry," Mr. Dawes urged, holding open the screen door, gazing nervously out into the darkness. "I think we're in terrible danger."

"But — " I started, staring into his frightened eyes, trying to decide if we could trust him.

"I was at the party with your parents," Mr.

Dawes said. "All of a sudden, they formed a circle. Everyone. Around your parents and me. They — they started to close in on us."

Just like when the kids started to close in on Josh and me, I thought.

"We broke through them and ran," Mr. Dawes said, glancing to the driveway behind him. "Somehow the three of us got away. Hurry. We've all got to get away from here — *now!*"

"Josh, let's go," I urged. Then I turned to Mr. Dawes. "Where are Mom and Dad?"

"Come on. I'll show you. They're safe for now. But I don't know for how long."

We followed him out of the house and down the driveway to his car. The clouds had parted. A sliver of moon shone low in a pale, early morning sky.

"There's something wrong with this whole town," Mr. Dawes said, holding the front passenger door open for me as Josh climbed into the back.

I slumped gratefully into the seat, and he slammed the door shut. "I know," I said, as he slid behind the wheel. "Josh and I. We both — "

"We've got to get as far away as we can before they catch up with us," Mr. Dawes said, backing down the drive quickly, the tires sliding and squealing as he pulled onto the street.

"Yes," I agreed. "Thank goodness you came.

My house — it's filled with kids. Dead kids and — "

"So you've seen them," Mr. Dawes said softly, his eyes wide with fear. He pushed down harder on the gas pedal.

As I looked out into the purple darkness, a low, orange sun began to show over the green treetops. "Where are our parents?" I asked anxiously.

"There's a kind of outdoor theater next to the cemetery," Mr. Dawes said, staring straight ahead through the windshield, his eyes narrow, his expression tense. "It's built right into the ground, and it's hidden by a big tree. I left them there. I told them not to move. I think they'll be safe. I don't think anyone'll think to look there."

"We've seen it," Josh said. A bright light suddenly flashed on in the backseat.

"What's that?" Mr. Dawes asked, looking into the rearview mirror.

"My flashlight," Josh answered, clicking it off. "I brought it just in case. But the sun will be up soon. I probably won't need it."

Mr. Dawes hit the brake and pulled the car to the side of the road. We were at the edge of the cemetery. I climbed quickly out of the car, eager to see my parents.

The sky was still dark, streaked with violet now. The sun was a dark orange balloon just barely poking over the trees. Across the street, beyond the jagged rows of gravestones, I could see the dark outline of the leaning tree that hid the mysterious amphitheater.

"Hurry," Mr. Dawes urged, closing his car door quietly. "I'm sure your parents are desperate to see you."

We headed across the street, half-walking, half-jogging, Josh swinging the flashlight in one hand.

Suddenly, at the edge of the cemetery grass, Josh stopped. "Petey!" he cried.

I followed his gaze, and saw our white terrier walking slowly along a slope of gravestones.

"Petey!" Josh yelled again, and began running to the dog.

My heart sank. I hadn't had a chance to tell Josh what Ray had revealed to me about Petey. "No — Josh!" I called.

Mr. Dawes looked very alarmed. "We don't have time. We have to hurry," he said to me. Then he began shouting for Josh to come back.

"I'll go get him," I said, and took off, running as fast as I could along the rows of graves, calling to my brother. "Josh! Josh, wait up! Don't! Don't go after him! Josh — Petey is *dead*!"

Josh had been gaining on the dog, which was ambling along, sniffing the ground, not looking up, not paying any attention to Josh. Then suddenly, Josh tripped over a low grave marker.

He cried out as he fell, and the flashlight flew out of his hand and clattered against a gravestone.

I quickly caught up with him. "Josh — are you okay?"

He was lying on his stomach, staring straight ahead.

"Josh — answer me. Are you okay?"

I grabbed him by the shoulders and tried to pull him up, but he kept staring straight ahead, his mouth open, his eyes wide.

"Josh?"

"Look," he said finally.

I breathed a sigh of relief, knowing that Josh wasn't knocked out or something.

"Look," he repeated, and pointed to the gravestone he had tripped over.

I turned and squinted at the grave. I read the inscription, silently mouthing the words as I read:

COMPTON DAWES. R.I.P. 1950–1980.

My head began to spin. I felt dizzy. I steadied myself, holding onto Josh.

COMPTON DAWES.

It wasn't his father or his grandfather. He had told us he was the only Compton in his family.

So Mr. Dawes was dead, too.

Dead. Dead. Dead.

Dead as everyone else.

He was one of them. One of the dead ones.

Josh and I stared at each other in the purple darkness. Surrounded. Surrounded by the dead.

Now what? I asked myself.

Now what?

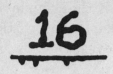

16

"Get up, Josh," I said, my voice a choked whisper. "We've got to get away from here."

But we were too late.

A hand grabbed me firmly by the shoulder.

I spun around to see Mr. Dawes, his eyes narrowing as he read the inscription on his own gravestone.

"Mr. Dawes — you, too!" I cried, so disappointed, so confused, so . . . scared.

"Me, too," he said, almost sadly. "All of us." His eyes burned into mine. "This was a normal town once. And we were normal people. Most of us worked in the plastics factory on the outskirts of town. Then there was an accident. Something escaped from the factory. A yellow gas. It floated over the town. So fast we didn't see it . . . didn't realize. And then, it was too late, and Dark Falls wasn't a normal town anymore. We were all dead, Amanda. Dead and buried. But we couldn't rest.

We couldn't sleep. Dark Falls was a town of living dead."

"What — what are you going to do to us?" I managed to ask. My knees were trembling so hard, I could barely stand. A dead man was squeezing my shoulder. A dead man was staring hard into my eyes.

Standing this close, I could smell his sour breath. I turned my head, but the smell already choked my nostrils.

"Where are Mom and Dad?" Josh asked, climbing to his feet and standing rigidly across from us, glaring accusingly at Mr. Dawes.

"Safe and sound," Mr. Dawes said with a faint smile. "Come with me. It's time for you to join them."

I tried to pull away from him, but his hand was locked on my shoulder. "Let go!" I shouted.

His smile grew wider. "Amanda, it doesn't hurt to die," he said softly, almost soothingly. "Come with me."

"No!" Josh shouted. And with sudden quickness, he dived to the ground and picked up his flashlight.

"Yes!" I cried. "Shine it on him, Josh!" The light could save us. The light could defeat Mr. Dawes, as it had Ray. The light could destroy him. "Quick — shine it on him!" I pleaded.

Josh fumbled with the flashlight, then pointed

it toward Mr. Dawes's startled face, and clicked it on.

Nothing.

No light.

"It — it's broken," Josh said. "I guess when it hit the gravestone. . . ."

My heart pounding, I looked back at Mr. Dawes. The smile on his face was a smile of victory.

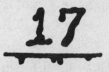

17

"Nice try," Mr. Dawes said to Josh. The smile faded quickly from his face.

Close up, he didn't look so young and handsome. His skin, I could see, was dry and peeling and hung loosely beneath his eyes.

"Let's go, kids," he said, giving me a shove. He glanced up at the brightening sky. The sun was raising itself over the treetops.

Josh hesitated.

"I *said* let's go," Mr. Dawes snapped impatiently. He loosened his grip on my shoulder and took a menacing step toward Josh.

Josh glanced down at the worthless flashlight. Then he pulled his arm back and heaved the flashlight at Mr. Dawes's head.

The flashlight hit its target with a sickening *crack*. It hit Mr. Dawes in the center of his forehead, splitting a large hole in the skin.

Mr. Dawes uttered a low cry. His eyes widened in surprise. Dazed, he reached a hand up to the hole where a few inches of gray skull poked through.

"Run, Josh!" I cried.

But there was no need to tell him that. He was already zigzagging through the rows of graves, his head ducked low. I followed him, running as fast as I could.

Glancing back, I saw Mr. Dawes stagger after us, still holding his ripped forehead. He took several steps, then abruptly stopped, staring up at the sky.

It's too bright for him, I realized. He has to stay in the shade.

Josh had ducked down behind a tall marble monument, old and slightly tilted, cracked down the middle. I slid down beside him, gasping for breath.

Leaning on the cool marble, we both peered around the sides of the monument. Mr. Dawes, a scowl on his face, was heading back toward the amphitheater, keeping in the shadows of the trees.

"He — he's not chasing us," Josh whispered, his chest heaving as he struggled to catch his breath and stifle his fear. "He's going back."

"The sun is too bright for him," I said, holding onto the side of the monument. "He must be going to get Mom and Dad."

"That stupid flashlight," Josh cried.

"Never mind that," I said, watching Mr. Dawes

until he disappeared behind the big leaning tree. "What are we going to do now? I don't know — "

"Shhh. Look!" Josh poked me hard on the shoulder, and pointed. "Who's that?"

I followed his stare and saw several dark figures hurrying through the rows of tombstones. They seemed to have appeared from out of nowhere.

Did they rise out of the graves?

Walking quickly, seeming to float over the green, sloping ground, they headed into the shadows. All were walking in silence, their eyes straight ahead. They didn't stop to greet one another. They strode purposefully toward the hidden amphitheater, as if they were being drawn there, as if they were puppets being pulled by hidden strings.

"Whoa. Look at them all!" Josh whispered, ducking his head back behind the marble monument.

The dark, moving forms made all the shadows ripple. It looked as if the trees, the gravestones, the entire cemetery had come to life, had started toward the hidden seats of the amphitheater.

"There goes Karen," I whispered, pointing. "And George. And all the rest of them."

The kids from our house were moving quickly in twos and threes, following the other shadows, as silent and businesslike as everyone else.

Everyone was here except Ray, I thought.

Because we killed Ray.

We killed someone who was already dead.

"Do you think Mom and Dad are really down in that weird theater?" Josh asked, interrupting my morbid thoughts, his eyes on the moving shadows.

"Come on," I said, taking Josh's hand and pulling him away from the monument. "We've got to find out."

We watched the last of the dark figures float past the enormous leaning tree. The shadows stopped moving. The cemetery was still and silent. A solitary crow floated high above in the clear blue, cloudless sky.

Slowly, Josh and I edged our way toward the amphitheater, ducking behind gravestones, keeping low to the ground.

It was a struggle to move. I felt as if I weighed five hundred pounds. The weight of my fear, I guess.

I was desperate to see if Mom and Dad were there.

But at the same time, I didn't want to see.

I didn't want to see them being held prisoner by Mr. Dawes and the others.

I didn't want to see them . . . killed.

The thought made me stop. I reached out an arm and halted Josh.

We were standing behind the leaning tree, hidden by its enormous clump of upraised roots. Beyond the tree, down in the theater below, I could hear the low murmur of voices.

"Are Mom and Dad there?" Josh whispered. He started to poke his head around the side of the bent tree trunk, but I cautiously pulled him back.

"Be careful," I whispered. "Don't let them see you. They're practically right beneath us."

"But I've *got* to know if Mom and Dad are really here," he whispered, his eyes frightened, pleading.

"Me, too," I agreed.

We both leaned over the massive trunk. The bark felt smooth under my hands as I gazed into the deep shadows cast by the tree.

And then I saw them.

Mom and Dad. They were tied up, back-to-back, standing in the center of the floor at the bottom of the amphitheater in front of everyone.

They looked so uncomfortable, so terrified. Their arms were tied tightly down at their sides. Dad's face was bright red. Mom's hair was all messed up, hanging wildly down over her forehead, her head bowed.

Squinting into the darkness cast by the tree, I saw Mr. Dawes standing beside them along with another, older man. And I saw that the rows of long benches built into the ground were filled with people. Not a single empty space.

Everyone in town must be here, I realized.

271

Everyone except Josh and me.

"They're going to kill Mom and Dad," Josh whispered, grabbing my arm, squeezing it in fear. "They're going to make Mom and Dad just like them."

"Then they'll come after us," I said, thinking out loud, staring through the shadows at my poor parents. Both of them had their heads bowed now as they stood before the silent crowd. Both of them were awaiting their fates.

"What are we going to do?" Josh whispered.

"Huh?" I was staring so hard at Mom and Dad, I guess I momentarily blanked out.

"What are we going to do?" Josh repeated urgently, still holding desperately to my arm. "We can't just stand here and — "

I suddenly knew what we were going to do.

It just came to me. I didn't even have to think hard.

"Maybe we can save them," I whispered, backing away from the tree. "Maybe we *can* do something."

Josh let go of my arm. He stared at me eagerly.

"We're going to push this tree over," I whispered with so much confidence that I surprised myself. "We're going to push the tree over so the sunlight will fill the amphitheater."

"Yes!" Josh cried immediately. "Look at this tree. It's practically down already. We can do it!"

I *knew* we could do it. I don't know where my confidence came from. But I *knew* we could do it.

And I knew we had to do it fast.

Peering over the top of the trunk again, struggling to see through the shadows, I could see that everyone in the theater had stood up. They were all starting to move forward, down toward Mom and Dad.

"Come on, Josh," I whispered. "We'll take a running jump, and push the tree over. Come on!"

Without another word, we both took several steps back.

We just had to give the trunk a good, hard push, and the tree would topple right over. The roots were already almost entirely up out of the ground, after all.

One hard push. That's all it would take. And the sunlight would pour into the theater. Beautiful, golden sunlight. Bright, bright sunlight.

The dead people would all crumble.

And Mom and Dad would be saved.

All four of us would be saved.

"Come on, Josh," I whispered. "Ready?"

He nodded, his face solemn, his eyes frightened.

"Okay. Let's *go!*" I cried.

We both ran forward, digging our sneakers into the ground, moving as fast as we could, our arms outstretched and ready.

In a second, we hit the tree trunk and pushed with all of our strength, shoving it with our hands and then moving our shoulders into it, pushing . . . pushing . . . pushing . . .

It didn't budge.

18

"Push!" I cried. "Push it again!"

Josh let out an exasperated, defeated sigh. "I can't, Amanda. I can't move it."

"Josh — " I glared at him.

He backed up to try again.

Below, I could hear startled voices, angry voices.

"Quick!" I yelled. "*Push!*"

We hurtled into the tree trunk with our shoulders, both of us grunting from the effort, our muscles straining, our faces bright red.

"Push! Keep pushing!"

The veins at my temples felt about to pop.

Was the tree moving?

No.

It gave a little, but bounced right back.

The voices from below were getting louder.

"We can't do it!" I cried, so disappointed, so frustrated, so terrified. "We can't move it!"

Defeated, I slumped over onto the tree trunk,

and started to bury my face in my hands.

I pulled back with a gasp when I heard the soft cracking sound. The cracking sound grew louder until it was a rumble, then a roar. It sounded as if the ground were ripping apart.

The old tree fell quickly. It didn't have far to fall. But it hit with a thundering crash that seemed to shake the ground.

I grabbed Josh and we both stood in amazement and disbelief as bright sunlight poured into the amphitheater.

The cries went up instantly. Horrified cries. Angry cries. Frantic cries.

The cries became howls. Howls of pain, of agony.

The people in the amphitheater, the living dead caught in the golden light, began scrambling over one another, screeching, pulling, climbing, pushing, trying to claw their way to shade.

But it was too late.

Their skin began to drop off their bones and, as I stared open-mouthed, they crumbled to powder and dissolved to the ground, their clothes disintegrating along with them.

The painful cries continued to ring out as the bodies fell apart, the skin melted away, the dry bones collapsed. I saw Karen Somerset staggering across the floor. I saw her hair fall to the ground in a heap, revealing the dark skull underneath. She cast a glance up at me, a longing look, a look of regret. And then her eyeballs rolled out of their sockets, and she opened her toothless mouth, and she cried, "Thank you, Amanda! Thank you!" and collapsed.

Josh and I covered our ears to shut out the ghastly cries. We both looked away, unable to keep watching the entire town fall in agony and crumble to powder, destroyed by the sun, the clear, warm sun.

When we looked back, they had all disappeared.

Mom and Dad were standing right where they had been, tied back-to-back, their expressions a mixture of horror and disbelief.

"Mom! Dad!" I cried.

I'll never forget their smiles as Josh and I ran forward to free them.

It didn't take our parents long to get us packed up and to arrange for the movers to take us back to our old neighborhood and our old house. "I guess it's lucky after all that we couldn't sell the old place," Dad said, as we eagerly piled into the car to leave.

Dad backed down the driveway and started to roar away.

"Stop!" I cried suddenly. I'm not sure why, but I had a sudden, powerful urge to take one last look at the old house.

As both of my parents called out to me in confusion, I pushed open the door and jogged back to the driveway. Standing in the middle of the yard, I stared up at the house, silent, empty, still covered in thick layers of blue-gray shadows.

I found myself gazing up at the old house as if I were hypnotized. I don't know how long I stood there.

The crunch of tires on the gravel driveway snapped me out of my spell. Startled, I turned to see a red station wagon parked in the driveway.

Two boys about Josh's age jumped out of the back. Their parents followed. Staring up at the house, they didn't seem to notice me.

"Here we are, kids," the mother said, smiling at them. "Our new house."

"It doesn't look new. It looks old," one of the boys said.

And then his brother's eyes widened as he noticed me. "Who are *you*?" he demanded.

The other members of his family turned to stare at me.

"Oh. I . . . uh . . ." His question caught me by surprise. I could hear my dad honking his horn impatiently down on the street. "I . . . uh . . . used to live in your house," I found myself answering.

And then I turned and ran full speed down to the street.

Wasn't that Mr. Dawes standing at the porch, clipboard in hand? I wondered, catching a glimpse of a dark figure as I ran to the car.

No, it couldn't be Mr. Dawes up there waiting for them, I decided.

It just couldn't be.

I didn't look back. I slammed the car door behind me, and we sped away.

About the Author

R.L. STINE is the author of the series *Fear Street*, *Nightmare Room*, *Give Yourself Goosebumps*, and the phenomenally successful *Goosebumps*. His thrilling teen titles have sold more than 250 million copies internationally — enough to earn him a spot in the *Guinness Book of World Records*! Mr. Stine lives in New York City with his wife, Jane, and his son, Matt.

ANIMORPHS ®

The Encounter

K.A. Applegate

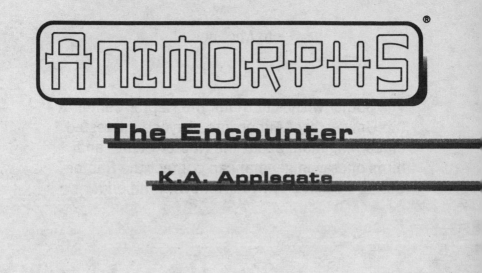

Even the book morphs!
Flip the pages
and check it out!

To Michael

The author wishes to thank the Raptor Center at the University of Minnesota. Anyone interested in learning more about the Raptor Center and birds of prey in general can contact the Raptor Center web site: www.raptor.cvm.umn.edu.

ISBN 0-590-62979-4

24   4 5 6 7 8 9/0

Printed in the U.S.A.   40

First Scholastic printing, August 1996

CHAPTER 1

My name is Tobias. A freak of nature. One of a kind.

I won't tell you my last name. I *can't* tell you my last name. Or the name of the city where I live.

I want to tell you everything, but I can't give any clues to my true identity. Or the identity of the others. Everything I will tell you is true. I know it's going to seem unbelievable, but believe it anyway.

I am Tobias. I'm a normal kid, I guess. Or used to be. I used to do okay in school. Not great, but not bad either. Just okay.

I guess I was a dweeb, kind of. Big, but not big enough to keep from getting picked on. I had blond hair, kind of wild because I could never get it to look right. My eyes were . . . what color were my eyes? It's only been a few weeks, and already I'm forgetting things about being human.

I guess it doesn't matter, anyway. My eyes now are gold and brown. I have eyes that look fierce and angry all the time. I'm not always fierce or angry, but I look that way.

One afternoon, I was riding the thermals, the upswelling hot air. I rode them way up into the sky. The bottoms of low clouds, heavy with moisture, scudded just a few feet above me.

I looked down and focused my laserlike eyes. My fierce eyes. I could still read — I hadn't forgotten how to do that. I could see the big red-and-white sign that said: DEALIN' DAN HAWKE'S USED CARS.

I pressed my wings back, closer to my body, and began to fall.

Down, down, down! Faster. Faster!

I fell through the warm, early evening air like a rock. Like an artillery shell falling toward its target.

All was silent except for the sound of the air rushing over the tops of my wings. The ground came up at me. It came up like it was trying to hit me.

I saw the cage. It was no more than three feet on each side. In the cage was a hawk. A red-tail.

Like me.

The man was close by. I recognized him because I had seen him on his TV commercials. He was Dealin' Dan Hawke. He owned the car dealership.

He was the one holding the hawk prisoner.

She was a mascot. On the commercials he called her Price-Cut Polly. It made me sick. It made me furious.

I saw the camera. There were three guys standing around. They would be shooting a live commercial soon. I didn't care.

Dealin' Dan went to the hawk's cage to feed her. It was locked with a bike-style combination lock. Four numbers. I could see them as he turned the combination. 8-1-2-5.

I was two hundred yards up, plummeting to earth at seventy miles an hour. But I could see the numbers as he turned them. And the human part of me, Tobias, could remember.

He opened the cage and tossed in some food. Then he closed it again and spun the lock.

Brilliant lights came on. He was starting the commercial. It would be live on TV all over the area.

What I was planning was insane. That's what Marco would have said. It was one of his favorite words. Insane.

I didn't care.

285

A hawk was in a tiny cage, being used as a prop for some lowlife car dealer. That wasn't going to go on. Not if I could help it.

"Tseeeeeeeer!" I screamed.

Twenty feet from the ground, I opened my wings. The strain was terrible. I absorbed most of the momentum and used the rest for speed. I shot across the parked cars to the cage.

I landed on the bars and grabbed on with my talons.

I used the hook of my deadly sharp beak to click the first number into place.

"Hey! What the — " someone yelled.

The bright TV light focused right on me.

"Well, ladies and gentlemen in TV-land," Dealin' Dan yapped in surprise, "I guess we have a bird trying to break into our Price-Cut Polly's cage. Boys, you better shoo him away."

Yeah, right. Shoo me, I thought.

I clicked the second number. There were people coming for me. I saw a mechanic swinging a long steel wrench. But I wasn't going to leave without freeing this bird.

Hawks do not belong in cages. Hawks belong in the sky.

But they were all around me.

"Get him, Earl! Hit the thing!"

"Look out for that beak of his!"

"Maybe he's got rabies!"

WHAM!

The mechanic swung the wrench! It barely missed my head. I was dead if I didn't get some help. Fast.

<Rachel?> I cried silently with my mind. <Rachel? *Now* would be a good time!>

<Sorry! I missed the first bus. I just got here!> Her voice was in my head. We call it thought-speak. It's something we can do when we morph.

I breathed a sigh of relief. Help was on the way.

"HhhuuuurrHHHHEEEEEAAAAH!"

"What in the world was — " the mechanic cried.

I knew what it was. It was Rachel. Pretty, blond Rachel. Although right at the moment she wasn't pretty — impressive, but not pretty.

BOOM! Cr-u-u-u-nch!

"Oh. My. Lord," Dealin' Dan gasped. "Forget the bird! There's an elephant stomping over the convertibles!"

I would have smiled. If I'd had a mouth.

I finished turning the lock. I yanked open the cage door.

The hawk was wary. She was a true hawk, with only a hawk's mind and instincts to guide her. But she did know an open path to the sky when she saw one.

287

Out she came, in a rush of gray and brown and white feathers. She didn't know that I had freed her. That kind of concept was beyond her thinking. And she felt no gratitude.

But she flapped her wings and rose into the air.

Free.

And right then I had the strangest feeling. Like I should go with her. Like I should be with her.

<Can we get out of here now?> Rachel asked.

She was bellowing loudly, tossing her big trunk around and stomping various cars. Having a very good time, by elephant standards. But it was time for us to leave. For Rachel to resume her human form.

I looked up again. I saw the sunlight shine through the hawk's red tail. She flew toward the setting sun.

CHAPTER 2

<I hear sirens,> I said urgently.

<I hear them, too,> Rachel snapped. <I have ears the size of quilts. You think I can't *hear* them? I'm morphing as fast as I can.>

<I just hope it's *real* cops. Not Controllers.>

We had reached a patch of woods behind Dealin' Dan's car dealership. It was really just a few scruffy trees between the car place and a convenience store.

I watched from a low tree branch as Rachel morphed back to human again. If you've never seen someone morph, you have no idea just how incredibly weird it is.

When she began, she was a full-grown African elephant. Ten feet tall. Almost twice that from

289

head to tail. She weighed at least six thousand pounds. I say "at least" because we've never exactly tried to stick her on the bathroom scale.

She had two curved tusks, each about as long as a child. And a trunk that dragged the ground when she walked and could pick up a big slashing, yelling, dangerously angry Hork-Bajir warrior and throw him twenty feet.

I'd seen her do it.

<Tobias, you could at least have waited till he was done broadcasting that commercial. Thousands of people saw that on TV! Thousands!>

<Most people will figure it was some kind of a stunt or a trick,> I said.

<Most people, maybe. But not Controllers. Any Controllers who happened to be watching will guess right away that we were not just animals.>

Controllers. There's a word you need to know. A Controller is anyone with a Yeerk in his head. Yeerks are alien parasites. They are evil little slugs who live in the bodies of other species and enslave them. All the Hork-Bajir are Controllers. So are the Taxxons.

So are more and more humans. Human-Controllers.

As I watched, Rachel began to shrink. The ropy tail was sucked up like a piece of spaghetti. Her trunk grew smaller.

Blond hair began to sprout from her massive gray forehead. Her eyes wandered across her face toward the middle. The vast leathery ears became pink and small and perfectly formed.

<The others are going to ream us out big time, aren't they?> I said.

<Oh, yes. I think we can count on that.>

<It was my idea. I'll take the blame.>

<Oh, shut up, Tobias. Stop being all noble. Besides, it was amazing fun stomping those cars!>

She was small enough now that she could stand on her hind legs. As she did, her front legs grew smooth and human. Her back legs lost their clunkiness and became her own long, coltish legs.

Her morphing clothes, a skintight black leotard, emerged.

The tusks *shlooped* back into her mouth and divided into sparkling teeth. She was a very pretty girl, beautiful even, except that she still had a two-foot-long gray nose.

At last the trunk seemed to roll up and became a regular nose.

She was a girl again. Barefoot, because no one had figured out how to morph shoes. Her mouth was back to normal. She spoke in her normal voice, no longer in my head. Thought-speech is only for morphs.

"Okay, I'm back. Let's bail!"

The siren sounds were coming ever closer. <Head for the convenience store. I'll go up and look around.>

"I hope they have some flip-flops for sale in there," Rachel grumbled. "This shoe situation is a pain."

The elephant was gone. The girl had emerged.

See? I told you it would be hard to believe.

It began at a deserted construction site, when we found the crashed spaceship of an Andalite prince. He was the last surviving Andalite in our solar system. He and his fellow Andalites had fought a great battle to drive away the Yeerk mother ship.

They fought and lost.

And now the Yeerks are among us. And they are now trying to enslave the human race.

Before he died at the hands of the Yeerk leader, a terrible creature called Visser Three, the Andalite gave us a great gift — and a great curse.

The gift was the power to morph. To absorb the DNA of any living animal and to become that animal. Never before had anyone but the Andalites themselves been given the power to morph.

It meant a life of secrets. Of terrible danger.

The Yeerks think we are a small band of escaped Andalites. They know that morphs had attacked their Yeerk pool. They know that morphs had even infiltrated the home of one of their most important Controllers — Chapman.

But they don't know that we are just five normal human kids who'd been walking home from the mall one night.

Visser Three wants us caught or dead. Visser Three usually gets what he wants.

But I was glad to fight the Yeerks. Maybe I just had less to lose than the others. Or maybe something about the lonely, defeated, yet courageous Andalite prince touched me so deeply that I could never regret fighting to settle the score.

But there has been a price to pay. You see, there is a limit on the power to morph. You must never remain in a morph for more than two hours. If you do, you are trapped.

Forever.

And that is the curse of the Andalite's gift.

That is why, when Rachel returned to her human body, I didn't.

It would take Rachel a while to get home on the bus. I traveled a little faster. So I had time to waste.

The sun was setting, and in my mind I could still picture the freed hawk heading into the sun.

I hoped she had found a nice patch of forest to spend the night. That's what a red-tail likes: a nice tree branch with a clear view of a meadow full of little mice and rats and shrews and voles as they scurry below. That's how we . . . they . . . hunt.

I headed toward the tall buildings of downtown. I caught a beautiful thermal that billowed up the face of some skyscrapers. A thermal is like a big bubble of warm air. It rises beneath your wings and makes it effortless to just go soaring up and up.

I caught the thermal and went shooting up the side of the skyscraper like I was riding an elevator.

A lot of the offices were empty, since it was Saturday. But around the sixtieth floor I saw an old man looking out the window. Maybe he was some big, important businessman, I don't know.

But when he saw me he smiled. He watched me soar up and away. And I knew he was jealous.

I was half a mile up when I finally turned away from the sun and headed toward Rachel's house.

The sun was going down. The moon just peeked over the rim of the world.

Then, I felt . . . I don't know how to describe it. It was in the air above me. Huge. Vast! Bigger than any jet.

I looked up. But there was nothing there.

And yet, I felt it in my heart. I knew it was up

there. Coming toward me, but perhaps a mile higher than me.

I focused all the power of my hawk's eyes on the sky.

A ripple!

That's what it was. A ripple. Like the ripple you make throwing a stone into a calm pond. The faint twilight stars flickered as it passed by. The sun's light bent. And for just a split second I was sure I could see . . . something.

But no. No. It was gone.

If it had ever really been there.

I tried to follow the hole in the sky, but it was moving too fast. I tried to see which way it was going. And where it had come from. It seemed to be moving away from the mountains and picking up speed.

But I lost it over the suburbs as it accelerated away.

I flew on to Rachel's house. I watched as she got off the bus far below me. The others, Jake, Marco, and Cassie, were all up in her room, waiting for us. I was not surprised.

<Hey, Rachel,> I said, floating above her.

She could only wave up at me. You can "hear" thought-speak when you're human, but you can't make thought-speech.

<I predict Marco's first words will be "Are you insane?"> I told Rachel.

She gave me a little wink.

Rachel went in through the front door. I flew in an open window. There we were, all together, the five of us: the Animorphs.

The other three of us must have seen the commercial and were not at all happy.

Marco started the conversation.

"Are you INSANE?!!" he said.

CHAPTER 3

Marco yelled for a while. Jake made us promise never to do something that stupid again. And Cassie, being Cassie, got everyone to make up and be friends again.

"We aren't supposed to be rescuing animals," Marco said. "We're *supposed* to be rescuing the entire human race from being enslaved by the Yeerks."

<I thought you didn't want to save the world, Marco,> I pointed out.

He scowled at me. But there's no point in scowling at me. With my face I can out-scowl anyone.

"You're right," Marco said. "But since all of you guys think you have to save the world, and since you're all my friends, more or less, I figure someone has to keep you from being *total* idiots."

Marco is the most reluctant of the Animorphs. Although actually he's the one who came up with the word "Animorph." And he's been in with us from the start. Marco just thinks we should look out for ourselves and our own families.

Marco and I will probably never be very close. He's a typical smart-aleck kind of guy. Always confident. Always has some funny or sarcastic thing to say. He's short, or at least he's not very tall. I guess girls think he's cute because he has this long brown hair and dark eyes.

Jake grinned at Marco. "So you're the one who has to rescue all of us from being idiots?"

"Boy, if Marco's the sensible one, we're all in serious trouble," Rachel said.

Everyone laughed.

Jake gave Marco an affectionate punch in the shoulder. "Just the same, it's nice of you to want to save us all. It's almost *sweet*."

Marco made a face and grabbed one of Rachel's pillows to throw at Jake.

Marco and Jake are absolute opposites, although they've been buds forever. Jake is big. Not football-player big, but solid. Jake is one of those people who are natural leaders. If you were ever trapped in a burning building, you would turn to Jake and ask, "What do we do?" And he would have an answer, too.

You can tell he and Rachel are cousins. They're both kind of determined people.

"I have to get going," Cassie said. "I have horses to feed and birdcages to clean."

"Don't say the word 'cage' around Tobias," Marco said. "He'll do some guerrilla-commando-Ninja-SWAT-team-hawk-from-hell attack on the Center. And he'll talk Rachel into stomping your house flat."

Everyone laughed, because we all knew why Cassie had birdcages. Her father and mother are both veterinarians. Her mom works for The Gardens, which is this huge zoo and amusement park.

Her dad runs the Wildlife Rehabilitation Center in the barn on their family farm. The Center takes in wild animals that are sick or hurt and cares for them.

The cages Cassie had to get home to clean were filled with sparrows with broken wings and eagles who'd been shot and seagulls who'd gotten tangled in trash.

Cassie is our expert on animals. She also gets us access to animals to morph. She's a gentle person. She can also morph better than any of us.

Everyone stood up and started to go.

"You coming, Tobias?" Jake asked me.

<No, not right away. I think I'll fly around. It's a nice night.>

"Cool," he said. "I'll put some food up in your attic for you in case you get home late. I don't want anything getting at it, though. Can you open one of those Rubbermaid things?"

I saw the way the others kind of looked away when Jake mentioned the attic. They feel sorry for me.

<I can get it open,> I said. <Just be careful. You know — Tom.>

Tom is Jake's big brother. Tom is one of *them*.

Everyone said good night. I saw Cassie and Jake touch their hands together in a way that could almost have been accidental. Then they were all gone. All but me and Rachel.

"I don't like thinking of you living in a cold attic," Rachel said.

<I'm okay,> I said. I wondered if I should tell her what I had seen, the darkness within darkness, the hole in the sky. But the truth was, even I didn't know what it was.

It would just worry her. And she worried about me too much.

<Good night,> I said.

"Yeah. Take care of yourself, Tobias."

I flew out through her window into the night. Rachel's sad eyes seemed to follow me. I hated the way they all felt sorry for me. All they could see was that I was not what I used to be. All they saw was that I had no home.

But they didn't really understand. I hadn't had a real home since my parents died. I was used to being alone.

And I had the sky.

CHAPTER 4

The next day I decided to go back to where I had seen — or not seen — the big thing in the sky.

I had a feeling about it. A bad feeling.

I flew up over the same area, rising as high as I could on the thermals.

Hawks are not quite as good at soaring as eagles or some buzzards are. (Man, you should see the way a turkey buzzard can work those thermals! Awesome.) And actually, the red-tail hawk in my head would be just as happy perched patiently on the branch of a tree, waiting to see its next meal go scurrying past.

But I didn't eat like a hawk. I ate food that

Jake gave me. I didn't hunt. Although sometimes the urge to hunt was pretty strong.

I could just hear Marco making some smart crack about me eating mice. Or roadkill.

When you're in a morph, it's hard to resist the animal's instincts. Jake found that out when he became a lizard. He glomped down a live spider before he got control of the lizard's instincts.

I hadn't done that. Yet. I was afraid if I did it once, I'd never be able to stop.

I soared high above the city, over the area I'd been through the day before. But nothing. Nothing moved in the air above me.

Then it occurred to me: Whatever it was, maybe it only happened at certain times of day. It had been almost sunset when I'd felt its presence last.

I decided to come back around sunset. Which meant I had the whole day ahead of me with nothing special to do. This did not make me happy. See, the fact is, a hawk spends almost all its time hunting food.

As for me, Tobias, when I hadn't been in school, I used to spend most of my free time watching TV, hanging out at the mall, doing homework, reading . . . all things it was difficult for me to do, now.

I missed school. Even though I had constantly

been picked on by bullies. I didn't really miss my home, though. See, when my parents died, there was no one who really wanted me. I ended up getting shunted back and forth between an uncle here and an aunt across the country.

Neither of them really cared about me. I don't think they even missed me. I had arranged for Jake to leave a message with my uncle. We told him I had gone to stay with my aunt. Each of them, my uncle and my aunt, thought I was staying with the other.

I had no idea how long that trick would hold up before one of them figured out I wasn't in either place.

I guess when they realize it they'll call the cops and report me as a runaway. Or maybe they won't even bother.

So. What was I going to do with my day? I'd been floating up here in the high air, just below the clouds, for a couple of hours. It was time to give it up and try again another time.

I tilted my wings and adjusted my tail, turning toward Rachel's house. Maybe she would be hanging around the house, bored.

Then it happened.

A mile or more above me, the ripple passed through the air. An emptiness, a hole where no hole could be.

I reacted instantly. I had to get closer.

I flapped till my chest and shoulders were sore. But it was moving too fast, and it was too high.

It pulled away from me, a wave of air, a rippling of the fabric of the sky. It was moving in a different direction, though. It was moving *toward* the mountains.

Then . . . a flight of geese on the move in a tight V-formation.

There were maybe a dozen of the big, determined geese, moving along at an amazing rate, powering their way through the air like they always do. Geese always seem to be on a mission. Like, "Get out of our way, we're geese and we're coming through."

The geese were aimed straight for the disturbance.

Suddenly, the lead goose folded like it had been hit by a truck. Its wings collapsed. But it did not fall.

The crippled goose slid through the air. It slid horizontally, rolling and flopping like it was passing over the top of a racing train.

Most of the other geese suffered the same fate. One or two peeled away in time, but geese are not real agile.

The invisible wave smacked into the flight, and the geese were crushed. They were rolling and sliding along some unseen but solid surface.

And everywhere the geese hit, I could catch little glimpses of steel-gray metal.

The wave passed by. The geese fell in its wake, dead or crippled.

It flew on, unconcerned. But then, why should the Yeerks care about a handful of geese?

And that's what they were, I was certain. Yeerks.

What I had seen, or not quite seen, was a Yeerk ship.

CHAPTER 5

"It figures," Marco said thoughtfully. "The Yeerks would have to have some kind of cloaking ability. Like 'stealth' technology, only much better."

We are all in Cassie's barn. Her dad was away for the afternoon. And it's one of the few places where I can go and not look out of place.

It's a regular old-fashioned barn, but with rows of clean cages and fluorescent lights. There are partitions keeping the birds away from the horses, and more partitions keeping the raccoons and opossums and the occasional coyote away from the skittish horses. The floor of the barn is usually strewn with hoses and buckets and scattered hay. There are charts on each cage showing

307

the condition of the animal and what treatment it's getting.

It's usually a pretty noisy place, what with various birds chirping or cooing, horses snuffling, and raccoons fussing with their food.

I looked over a little nervously at a pair of wolves, one male, one female. One had been shot. The other had eaten poison left out by a farmer. Wolves were new in the area. Wildlife experts had brought some back to the nearby forest.

Wolves make hawks a little edgy.

"We were always able to see Yeerk ships," Rachel pointed out. "We saw the Bug fighters and the Blade ship." She was leaning against a cage that housed an injured mourning dove. The dove was watching me suspiciously.

"Yeah, but every Yeerk ship we've ever dealt with has been either on the ground or about to land," Jake said. "Maybe the cloaking ability doesn't work when they get close to land. But if you think about it, Marco is right. They would have to be able to avoid being picked up by radar. Maybe they also have the ability to avoid being seen."

<It was a Yeerk ship,> I said flatly.

"How can you be so sure?" Cassie asked. She was working as we talked, cleaning an empty cage with a brush and a bucket of sudsy water.

<It just was,> I said stubbornly. <I . . . I just got this feeling from it. Also, it seemed huge. Far bigger than even the biggest jet. This was huge. More like a real ship, you know, like an ocean liner.>

"The question is, what do we do about it?" Jake asked. Of course, I knew he'd already made up his mind to do *something*. But Jake doesn't like to act like the one in charge, even though that's how I think of him. He lets everyone have their say first.

<I want to find out what it's doing,> I said. <The first time, I had the feeling it was heading away from the mountains. The second time, it was doing just the opposite. It was flying too low to make it *over* the mountains. So I'm guessing it was doing something *in* the mountains.>

Rachel nodded. "That makes sense."

Marco rolled his eyes. "The mountains? Have you suburb-dwellers ever been to the mountains? We're talking about a large area. No matter how big this ship is, it could hide in a thousand places in the mountains."

"Then we'd better start looking right away," Rachel said brightly.

Jake looked at Cassie. "Cass? What do you think?"

Cassie shrugged. "I halfway feel like we've done enough. You know? We attacked the Yeerk pool. We barely got out alive. We infiltrated Chapman's house and Rachel was captured. Again, we barely got out alive. I guess the question is, how many risks are we going to take? How many more times are we going to barely escape?"

I could see that Marco was surprised. Suddenly it sounded like Cassie was on his side. "Exactly! Exactly! Just what I've been saying. Why is it our job to get killed?"

But then Cassie went and blew it all for him.

"I mean, as far as I'm concerned, I can't just do *nothing* while people are enslaved by the Yeerks," Cassie said. "Maybe it's just me . . ." She shrugged. "The thing is, I have these powers." She shrugged again. "I can't just do nothing."

"Look, these aren't people we know," Marco argued. "They aren't my friends. Or my family." He shot a guilty look at Jake. "And we did everything we could for Tom. So why should I get killed for strangers? We can't stay lucky forever. Don't you people understand that? Sooner or later, we'll slip up. Sooner or later we'll be standing around here crying because Jake or Rachel or Cassie or Tobias is gone."

"You know something?" Rachel exploded. "I'm tired of trying to talk you into this, Marco. You want out? Fine, you're OUT!"

"Hey, Rachel, you're not just doing this to

help save the human race," Marco yelled back. "You get off on the danger. That's why you went with Tobias to free that bird. That wasn't about saving the world. That was about rescuing some stupid bird."

Marco realized he'd gone too far. He fell silent. The others all looked guiltily at me. Rachel shot Marco a look of pure anger.

<As of right now,> I said, <as of today, only one of us has been hurt. Me. But I'm not going to give up. I'm not anyone's leader. But what I am going to do is go to the mountains tomorrow morning. What the rest of you do is your business.>

"I'll be with you," Rachel said instantly.

Cassie nodded.

Jake made a wry smile. "You say you're not a leader, but I'll go with you."

Marco shook his head. "No," he said.

"Your choice," Rachel said.

"That's not what I meant," Marco said angrily. "I meant no, not in the morning. Tomorrow's a school day. If all of us skip school on the same day and later there's some trouble with the Yeerks, don't you think Chapman might put two and two together?"

Jake raised an eyebrow. "Marco's right. After school." He looked at the others and nodded.

It bothered me that Marco was right. But he

311

was. Marco might be a pain in the butt. But he's a very smart guy.

It worried me a little. It made me wonder. Was he right about other things as well?

How many risks could we take before we lost? How long till the five of us were four? Or two? Or none?

CHAPTER 6

Jake had a peregrine falcon morph we'd used before. Marco and Cassie had morphed ospreys. Rachel had been a bald eagle. So we all should have been able to fly up to the mountains.

But there are millions of bird-watchers in this country. They're very cool people because they never hurt a bird. They don't hunt. They just get pleasure out of watching birds fly or nest.

Bird-watchers would think it was very, very weird if they saw a red-tail hawk, a bald eagle, a falcon, and two ospreys all flying together as if they were on a mission.

And some of those gentle bird-watchers might be not-so-gentle Controllers.

"Bird-watchers!" Marco snorted as he tramped over the carpet of pine needles deeper into the woods. "We could fly, but no. No, we have to walk. Twenty miles, probably!"

Cassie's farm has a lot of open grass areas, and it borders on a national forest. The national forest goes on forever. It stretches from the edge of town all the way up into the mountains. It's all pines and oaks and elms and birches. Wilderness, really. Thousands of square acres of it.

"Oh, come on, Marco," Cassie chided gently. "It's an opportunity to try out a new morph!"

"Yeah," Jake chided. "Instead of being home doing math homework, you get to turn into a wolf. Are you going to tell me you'd rather be doing equations?"

"Let's see," Marco considered. "Math? Or becoming a wolf and going off to find aliens? Maybe I should ask the school counselor what she thinks. It's such a common problem. I'm sure she'd have some good advice."

Since it wasn't a good idea for us all to travel to the mountains as birds, the others needed a morph that could travel far and fast through woods. And there were the two injured wolves in Cassie's barn . . .

Jake stopped, looked around, and announced, "This is good." We were a few hundred yards into the woods. I came to rest on a low branch of a huge oak tree. The hawk in me took note of a squirrel a few branches up. He started chittering and shrieking his little squirrel warning: Danger! Danger!

Hawk! Hawk!

I gave him a look. He twitched, stuck the acorn he was holding into his cheek, and took off at full speed.

"What I don't get is why I have to be a girl wolf," Marco grumbled.

"We had one male and one female," Cassie explained for the tenth time. "If two of us morphed into the male, we'd have two males. Two male wolves might decide they had to fight for dominance."

"I could control it," Marco said.

"Marco, you and Jake *already* fight for dominance, and you're just ordinary guys," Rachel pointed out.

"She's right," Cassie said sadly. "I'm afraid your primitive male behavior might slow us down."

"Hey, when I morphed into a gorilla, I handled that gorilla brain okay, didn't I?" Marco demanded.

"Sure, Marco," Rachel said. She batted her eyes. "But that was different. You and the gorilla were already so much alike."

Cassie and Rachel gave each other discreet high-fives.

"Hugely funny," Marco said.

"We flipped a coin, fair and square," Jake said. "I got to be the male. You're one of the females. Get over it."

"Let me see that coin again," Marco said suspiciously.

Jake just smiled. "Let's just do this. Cassie, you want to go first, to see what it's like?"

We had learned from hard experience that morphing can be extremely disturbing. Jake had morphed into a lizard and been almost overpowered by the animal's fearful brain. The same had happened to Rachel when she'd morphed a shrew. She still had nightmares about the shrew experience — its fear and, worse, its hunger for bugs and rotting flesh.

On the other hand, Jake had morphed into a flea, and according to him it was kind of a big nothing. Like being trapped inside a very old, very bad video game where you could barely see anything. The flea brain had been too simple to make trouble.

"Okay. I'll let you know." Cassie closed her eyes and concentrated. Then she opened them again. "Wait. Let me get down to my morph suit first. I don't want to get tangled up in my clothes."

She removed everything but a leotard, kicked

off her shoes, and stood barefoot on the pine needles.

The first change was her hair. It went from very short black to shaggy silver in just a few seconds. It traveled down from her head, down her neck, over her shoulders, around her neck. Long, shaggy fur.

Then her nose bulged out.

I shuddered. You never really get used to seeing people morph. It is something straight out of a nightmare. Even though Cassie seems to have some kind of talent for it. She's never quite as gross as the others. I guess it's because she's so close to so many animals. Maybe she just has a special feel for them.

Still, as the wolf snout began to push out from her face, it was not a pleasant sight.

Her ears grew furry and pointed. Then they slid straight up the side of her head till they almost touched on top.

Her eyes went from brown-black to golden brown.

All over her body, the fur replaced the bright pinks and greens of her leotard. A tail suddenly shot out from behind. I could hear the grinding of her bones as they rearranged. Her upper arms shortened. Her lower arms grew longer. Fingers shriveled and disappeared, leaving behind only stubby black nails.

317

There was a sickening crunch as her knees changed direction. Her legs shrank and thinned and grew fur.

Suddenly she fell forward, no longer able to stand erect.

It had taken about two minutes.

Cassie was now a wolf.

"How is it?" Jake asked.

Cassie jerked suddenly at the sound of his voice and spun around to face him. She bared her teeth and snarled a warning that would have made a Taxxon back up.

She had very impressive teeth.

"Let's all stand really still," Jake said.

"Good idea," Marco agreed. "Really, really still. Because those are really, really big teeth."

Everyone stood motionless. They had all been through similar experiences. We knew what was happening. Inside the wolf's head, Cassie was fighting to gain control of the wolf's wild instincts.

<Sorry,> she thought-spoke at last. <I have it now.>

"Are you sure?" Rachel asked warily.

<Yes, it's fine. I'm fine. In fact . . . it's really kind of wonderful! The sense of hearing. Wow! And my nose. Whoa, that's incredible. I've never morphed an animal with such a strong sense of smell.>

"Then I'm extra glad I put on deodorant," Marco joked.

<Who had bacon for breakfast?> Cassie turned her wolf head this way and that. <Rachel? Bacon? I thought you were going to go vegetarian!>

Marco laughed at the guilty look on Rachel's face. "Oooh, busted by Cassie the wonder-nose."

"Let's get busy," Jake said. "The two-hour clock is now running. Tick-tock."

One by one they each stole a glance at me. I'm the handy reminder of what happens if you stay in a morph for too long.

CHAPTER 7

I was jealous.

I mean, okay, if you ever have to be stuck as an animal, I think being a hawk is the coolest choice of all.

But still, I was jealous. My friends were really enjoying being wolves. I guess it was a strange experience for them.

I flew above the forest, skimming the tree-tops, while down below they ran. They moved so fast it wasn't always easy for me to keep up. Not that their actual speed was so great. It's just that they never stopped. Never rested. They just moved at a constant twenty miles an hour or so. Over fallen logs. Between trees. Under bushes. Nothing even slowed them down.

Well, actually, that's not completely true. Two things slowed them down a little.

One was Jake. He was the dominant male. In wolf packs that's called an "alpha." So he had a special wolf job to perform.

<Jake, just how many more times are you going to pee?> Rachel demanded after his fifth stop.

<I . . . I don't know. I kind of have to do it a lot,> he admitted.

<Why? Did you drink too much soda before we left?>

<I don't know,> he admitted. <I just keep getting this urge to pee.>

<You're scent marking,> Cassie explained. <You're marking out a territory.>

<I am?>

<Yes, you are. It's normal. For a dominant wolf. At least that's what my wolf book said. Although it's a little gross for the rest of us to have to watch.>

The other thing that slowed them down was when they stopped once and started to howl. It was Jake who started it. It caught everyone by surprise. Including Jake himself.

"OWWW-OOOOOOO-yow-yow-OOOOOO."

<What the — > Marco started to say, but then he was doing it, too. "Yow-yow-OOWWOOOOO!"

Cassie and Rachel weren't far behind.

321

"OOOOO-yowww-OWW-OOOOOOO!"

I heard the yowling, of course, so I took a quick turn around a tree and headed back to them. <What are you people doing?> I demanded. <We're in a hurry here. You guys can only stay in morph for two hours. Why are you wasting time howling?>

<I don't know,> Jake admitted sheepishly. <I just suddenly felt like it would be a good idea.>

<Once he started I . . . I kind of felt like I should join in,> Rachel said.

<I think it's a way to warn all the other wolves that we're here, so we don't run into any other packs and get in fights,> Cassie suggested. Which sounded perfectly reasonable. Until you saw that "Cassie" had her head tilted back and her snout pointed at the sky and was yodeling like an idiot.

I flapped my wings and broke out from under the trees. The city and the suburbs were far behind me now. We had traveled pretty far in an hour's time. It was about the same time of day as my second sighting of the invisible ship. The time when it had been heading toward the mountains.

I swooped back down into the trees. <You guys keep moving. I'm going up top to look around.>

<Be careful,> Rachel said.

I banked left around a tree, then flapped my way back up into the sun. I climbed hard and fast, using a lot of energy. The exercise helped distract me. It's hard feeling sorry for yourself when you're working out big time.

After a while I was able to catch a nice thermal and get some easy altitude. I could still see the little wolf pack, moving like it had a single mind, flowing around the trees, swift and sure.

I tried to imagine what it must be like to be a wolf. The amazing sense of smell. The incredible hearing. All that confident power, those ripping teeth, the cool intelligence.

Maybe later I would ask Jake or Rachel about it.

Then you could ask them what it was like to be human. Maybe they can tell me about that, too, I thought bitterly.

Stop it, Tobias, I ordered myself. *Stop it.*

I guess I felt that if I ever started to feel really sorry for myself, I might never stop.

I kept a sharp eye out on the sky above, but it was probably still too early for the ship to come. If it even came. There was no reason to think it kept some kind of schedule.

Then, down below, I saw something that caught my attention. There was a convoy of trucks and Jeeps moving along a narrow, snaking dirt road. Maybe five vehicles. They had the markings of the Park Service. But they seemed to be in a big hurry.

They drove to a lake that I had just glimpsed up ahead. By the shore of the lake, they pulled off the road. Then, to my surprise, several dozen uniformed men jumped from the trucks and began to fan out through the woods.

They were carrying guns. But not rifles or even pistols. I could see them clearly. They were carrying automatic weapons.

Suddenly, movement in the sky! What the —

To my left I spotted a pair of helicopters. They zipped just inches above the trees. They began to circle the lake. These also had Park Service markings.

This is all wrong, I told myself. *These guys don't act or move like Park Rangers. These guys move like an army.*

And as I watched, half a dozen of the armed men surrounded a small patch of bright yellow. It was a tent.

Two people — they looked like college types — were cooking over a little fire outside the tent.

I could see the expressions of total amazement and fear when they suddenly realized they were surrounded by six men with automatic weapons.

The two campers were marched back to the nearest truck and driven away at high speed.

I don't know what story the two campers were told. Maybe the Park Rangers told them there was a dangerous fugitive in the area. Or maybe they said there was a forest fire. I don't know. I just know those two campers were out of there before they knew what hit them.

The two choppers circled the lake. Then they landed in a small clearing at the far side of the lake at the same time.

It was more than a mile away. Far, even for my hawk's eyes, in the slanting light of afternoon. But I could still see what came out of those helicopters.

Out they leaped, one after another.

Seven feet tall. The most dangerous-looking creatures you'll ever want to see. Foot-long, razor-sharp blades raked forward from their snake heads. More blades at their elbows, wrists, and knees. Feet like Tyrannosaurus rex.

The shock troops of the Yeerks.

Hork-Bajir warriors.

CHAPTER 8

<**H**ork-Bajir!>

The first time I'd seen them was at the construction site. I was still fully human then. It was while Visser Three was taunting the fallen Andalite. The five of us had been cowering behind a low wall. A Hork-Bajir had been within a few feet of us.

The Andalite told us they had once been a good people, the Hork-Bajir. That despite their fearsome appearance, they were a gentle race.

But the Hork-Bajir were all Controllers now. They all carried the Yeerk slug in their brains. And they were no longer gentle.

I made a sharp turn back. I had to warn the

others. I passed over a group of the Park Rangers, and swooped low enough to read one man's watch. My friends had been in morph for more than an hour.

Great. Low on time, and the Hork-Bajir are here.

I soon spotted the wolf pack, still trotting along resolutely, never tiring. Pausing only for Jake to pee.

I dived toward them. Just over their heads I pulled up suddenly.

"Yowl! Yip! Rrawr!"

They yelped and scampered around. Jake bared his fangs at me.

I came to rest on a decayed log.

Instantly, as if on command, the others started fanning out around me, encircling me. The five of them were acting like a wolf pack surrounding prey. In their own way they kind of reminded me of Hork-Bajir.

<Hey, it's just me, relax,> I said.

No answer. Jake snarled a brief command at one of the others.

Wait a minute. *Five?* Five wolves?

Jake, who wasn't really Jake, leaped at me.

Whoa!

Wolves don't usually hurt humans, but they will definitely eat a bird when they're hungry enough. And one thing you don't ever want to see is a hungry wolf, yellowed fangs bared, gold-brown eyes glaring, fur bristling, coming at you.

I flapped my wings hard.

The big male wolf went shooting past. Barely. But the rest were all around me!

I flapped again and got airborne, but just a few inches. I was skimming wildly over the pine-needle carpet, flapping for all I was worth, with five determined wolves hot on my tail.

SWOOOOM! I caught the tiniest headwind, but it was all I needed.

I was up! Up and out of there, while the wolves yowled and snapped their powerful jaws in frustration below me.

Ten minutes later I found a second wolf pack. This time I counted. *Four* wolves.

Still, I was cautious. <Is that you guys?>

<Who else would it be?> Marco asked.

<Don't ask,> I said. <Look, we have trouble.> I flapped down to a low branch and rested my wings. I was still a little shaken up from my close call with the wrong wolves.

<There's a lake just a little way ahead. It's crawling with Park Rangers who aren't really Park Rangers.>

<Yeah, I thought I smelled water. And humans,> Cassie said.

<How do you know they aren't real Park Rangers?> Jake asked.

<Because real Park Rangers don't carry machine guns,> I said. <Plus, they don't hang around with Hork-Bajir.>

<Hork-Bajir?> Cassie asked shakily. <You're sure?>

<Oh yeah,> I said. <It's kind of hard to confuse them with anything else. The Park Rangers are clearing out the area around the lake. They hustled some campers out of there real fast. At gunpoint.>

<Hork-Bajir,> Marco said with distaste. <I really don't like those guys.>

Rachel asked, <This lake, it's in the same direction your big invisible ship was moving?>

<It's in a perfectly straight line,> I said. <Whatever that ship was, I'd bet anything it was heading for that lake.>

<And judging by the way you say these Park-Ranger Controllers and Hork-Bajir are acting, it's on its way again,> Marco said thoughtfully.

<I'll tell you one thing,> I said. <These guys all looked like they'd done this many times before. You know what I mean? Like this was a real common routine. They had it down.>

<We don't have a lot of time left in morph,> Jake said. <But it would be a shame to miss the chance to find out what this is all about.>

<I say go for it,> Rachel said.

<You *always* say go for it,> Marco muttered.

<If just once you would say, 'Hey, let's *not* do this,' it would make me so happy.>

<You have about forty minutes left,> I told them. <The lake is about five minutes away.>

<Okay. Let's go. But in and out fast,> Jake warned. <Just enough to see what's going on.> They took off, with Jake in the lead. <Remember, just act like wolves.>

<Yeah, so if anyone sees the Three Little Pigs, don't forget to huff and puff,> Marco said.

I went airborne again, but this time I stayed close by.

<Park Rangers just ahead,> I said.

<Yeah, I can definitely smell them now,> Rachel replied. <And hear them, too.>

<Okay, look, wolves would try to steer clear of humans,> Cassie advised. <So a little slinking would be perfectly normal.>

They moved in a cautious circle around the phony Park Rangers. But I could see that the Rangers had spotted them. They tensed up, then relaxed when they saw it was just a wolf pack minding its own business.

I decided to get some altitude. Unfortunately, since there were no convenient thermals, I had to flap my way up. I was a few thousand yards high, able to see my friends and the lake, when I felt its presence again.

I looked up.

The invisible wave. The slight ripple in the fabric of the sky. It was there. It was moving slowly overhead. Even more slowly than before.

And then, as I watched, it was invisible no more.

CHAPTER 9

<Don't act suspicious or freak,> I called down to the others. <But look up.>

<Oh my God,> Rachel gasped.

<It's . . . it's huge!> Cassie cried.

It was huge. But the word huge doesn't really begin to describe it.

Have you ever seen a picture of an oil tanker? Or maybe an aircraft carrier? That's what I mean by huge. Compared to this thing, the biggest jumbo jet ever built was a toy.

It was shaped like a manta ray. There was a bulging, fat portion in the middle, with swooped, curvy wings, one either side. On top of the wings were huge scoops, like air intakes on a fighter jet, but much bigger. You could suck a fleet of buses in through those scoops.

The only windows were in a small bulge at the top. The bridge, I realized. Focusing on it, I could see the shadowy shapes of Taxxons inside.

But mostly that ship was just big. Really big. As in, it blocked out the sun, it was so big.

Suddenly, out from behind the ship, a pair of Bug fighters zipped into view. We had seen them before. They are small, for spaceships. You couldn't park one in your garage, but you could land it on your front lawn. They look like metal cockroaches with two serrated spearlike protrusions pointed forward on either side.

<I have Bug fighters up here,> I called down to the others. <A pair.>

<Who cares about Bug fighters?> Marco asked. <They're nothing compared to that . . . that whale!>

<The Bug fighters are circling the lake. I guess they're looking around for trouble.>

<Try not to look like trouble,> Jake advised dryly.

I did my best to look like a normal, harmless hawk. Doing normal hawk things. But the main ship was unbelievably intimidating. I mean, nothing that big should be floating in the air.

Suddenly one of the Bug fighters went shooting right past me, low and slow. I could see in the window. Inside was the usual crew: one Hork-Bajir and one Taxxon.

The Taxxons are the second most common type of Controller. Imagine a very big centipede. Now imagine it even bigger, twice as long as a man. So big around, you couldn't get your arms around it if you wanted to give it a hug.

Not that you'd ever want to give it a hug. Taxxons are gross, disgusting creatures. Unlike the Hork-Bajir, who were enslaved against their will, Taxxons chose to turn their minds over to the Yeerk parasites. They are allies of the Yeerks. I don't know why, and I probably don't want to.

The Bug fighter shot past, not interested in me.

The huge main ship sank slowly down toward the surface of the lake. <Are you guys seeing this? It looks like it's going to land on the lake.>

<Are we seeing it? No. We've totally missed the fact that a spaceship the size of Delaware is hovering in midair.>

Marco, of course.

<It's incredible,> Rachel said. <Incredible.>

<You know, I hate to be a pessimist,> Marco said, <but when I look at that thing I get a bad feeling about our chances. Four hounds and a bird versus a ship the size of Idaho!>

<A minute ago it was just the size of Delaware,> Cassie pointed out mildly.

<What's it doing here? That's what I want to know,> Jake said.

They had reached the shore of the lake and were prowling along, looking like wolves should look. But they were also glancing regularly up at the massive ship. I worried a little that some Controller, human or Hork-Bajir, would notice that they were paying a little too much attention.

<You guys? Watch how you act. The Yeerks will be looking for any animals that act strangely,> I said. <They're on the lookout for Andalites who can morph.>

<He's right,> Marco agreed. <Jake? Start peeing on things again.>

<Very funny,> Jake said.

Then something began to happen. <Hey. Look!>

From the belly of the ship, a pipe began to lower into the water. Then a second pipe, and a third.

<They're like straws,> Cassie said. <They're *drinking*!>

I could hear the sucking sound. Thousands, maybe millions of gallons of water being sucked up into the ship.

<That's why it's so big,> Marco said. He laughed. <Well, well, well. What do you know? We have just discovered that the Yeerks have a great big weakness.>

<A weakness?> Rachel demanded. <You can look at that ship and talk about *weakness*?>

But I understood what Marco meant. <It means they need something,> I said.

<Exactly,> Marco said. <Those big scoops on the sides? I think those are for air. That's why they fly so far through the atmosphere when they come down. They're scooping up oxygen. And now they are sucking up water.>

<It's a truck!> Cassie cried. <That whole huge ship is really just a truck!>

<Yeah,> I said. <It carries air and water up to the Yeerk mother ship in orbit. I guess they need Earth to supply them.>

<So. It's not like *Star Trek*, where they can just make their own air and water,> Marco mused. <As long as they are up there in orbit, the Yeerks need the planet to supply them with air and water. Well, well. I think that's the first hopeful sign yet.>

<We're running low on time,> Cassie reminded everyone. <Time to get out of here.>

<Okay, but everyone be cool about it,> Jake advised. <We act like we're just sauntering off to go kill a moose — or whatever it is wolves saunter off to do.>

They drifted back from the shore of the lake. I stayed behind. I no longer have a time limit to worry about.

The Yeerk ship was creating a warm updraft, so I spread my wings wide and rode it up. The two Bug fighters were still circling low and slow. On the shore all around the lake, the bogus Park Rangers and the few Hork-Bajir kept up their patrols.

Then I saw her.

I know to human eyes, every hawk looks pretty much alike. But I knew right away it was her — the hawk I had freed from the car dealer.

She, too, was riding the thermal, a thousand yards higher than me. Without even really thinking about it, I adjusted the angle of my wings and soared up toward her.

She saw me, I was sure of that. Hawks don't miss much of what goes on around them. She knew I was coming toward her, and she waited.

It wasn't like we were friends. Hawks don't know what "friend" means. And she certainly did not feel any gratitude toward me for saving her from captivity. Hawks don't have that sort of emotion, either. In fact, in her mind there may have been no connection between me and her freedom.

Still, I soared up to her. I don't know why. I really don't. All we shared was the same outer body. We both had wings. We both had talons. We both had feathers.

Suddenly I was afraid. I was afraid of her. And

it was insane, because there I was, floating above an alien spaceship so big it could have been turned into a mall.

But it was the hawk that frightened me.

Or maybe not the hawk herself. Maybe it was the feeling I had, rising up to meet her in the sky.

The feeling of recognition. The feeling of going home. The feeling that I belonged with her.

It hit me in a wave of disgust and horror.

No. NO!

I was Tobias. A human. A human being, not a bird!

I banked sharply away from her.

I was *human*. I was a boy named Tobias. A boy with blond hair that was always a mess. A boy with human friends. Human interests.

But part of me kept saying, "It's a lie. It's a lie. You are the hawk. The hawk is you. And Tobias is dead."

I plummeted toward the ground. I folded my wings back and welcomed the sheer speed. Faster! Faster!

Then, with eyes that Tobias never had, I saw the wolf pack below. And I saw the danger before them.

CHAPTER 10

My four friends stood stock still. They were staring with deadly focus at five other wolves.

The two packs had run into each other. Between them lay a dead rabbit. It was the other pack's kill. My friends had stumbled into them. Now the two alpha males were locked in a deadly dominance battle.

One of those alpha males was Jake.

The other was an actual wolf.

Jake had human intelligence on his side. But if it came to a fight, the other wolf had more experience. He hadn't gotten to be the head wolf in his pack by losing fights.

I would have laughed if I could. It was ridiculous! But at least it took my mind off the female

339

hawk. Off the feeling that drew me to her, that called out to me, even while Yeerk ships zipped in a deadly dance through the air.

Then it hit me with a shock: The time! They'd been low on time when they'd left the shore and started back. How much time had elapsed?

I swooped down low. <What are you guys doing?> I demanded.

<Shut up, Tobias,> Jake snapped tersely. <We're in a situation here.>

<Yeah, I can see that. Back away from them.>

<I can't. If I back off, I lose.>

<Lose *what*?> I yelled. <You're not a wolf. He's a wolf. Let him be *boss* wolf. You guys are way low on time!>

<It's not that simple,> Cassie said. <If Jake looks weak, the other alpha may attack. We screwed up. We're in their territory. And they think we're trying to steal their kill.>

Suddenly the other big male snarled and took a step forward. Instantly Jake bared his teeth still further and stood his ground.

The dead rabbit lay between them, only a few feet from the vicious teeth on either side.

<This fight's over the rabbit, right?> I said.

No answer. Everyone was so tense they were quivering. At any second this would explode into all-out gang warfare of the wolf variety.

I knew what I should do. But it went against every instinct in the hawk's brain.

And Tobias the human wasn't exactly thrilled, either.

I flapped up to gain a little height. I would need the speed. Then I locked my eyes on that rabbit and prayed that I was as fast as I thought I was.

<Oh, maaaaaan!>

Down I shot. My talons came forward.

"Tseeeeer!" I screamed.

Zoom!

A wolf on each side.

A dead rabbit.

Thwack! My talons hit the dead animal and snatched at the fur.

I flapped once, twice. The rabbit came off the ground.

The big wolf lunged. I could feel his teeth rake my tail.

I flapped for all I was worth, scooting along the ground, half-carrying, half-dragging the dead rabbit, with the wolf racing just inches behind me.

<Tobias!> Rachel cried.

<Get out of here!> I yelled. <I have to drop this thing. It's too heavy!>

Fortunately, when he isn't being an idiot wolf,

Jake is quick and decisive. <Let's go while we can!>

I dropped the rabbit just as the wolf caught up to me.

SNAP!

Jaws that could kill a moose scissored the air a tenth of an inch from me. I'm telling you, he was close enough for me to count his molars.

I felt the tiniest bit of a breeze. It was enough. I opened my wings and let the breeze lift me up and away.

<Oh, that was really not fun,> I said.

<Are you okay?>

<I think I lost some tail feathers,> I said. Tail feathers grow back.

I caught up with the others. They were moving as fast as wolves can move. Time was running short. I didn't know exactly how much time. It was one of the continuing problems of morphing. Even if you *could* wear a watch, you wouldn't want to. A wolf or a hawk with a watch looks slightly suspicious.

<I'll see if I can get a time reading,> I said. I was tired. Very tired, after the long flight here and not one but two close calls involving wolves. The hawk in me just wanted to find a nice branch with a view of an open field and take a rest. But I knew I couldn't.

I gained a little altitude, not too much. Just

enough to spot one of the Park Service trucks. The Controllers were off somewhere, but there was a clock in the dashboard.

I stared at the number in disbelief.

It had to be wrong! It had to be!

CHAPTER 11

I wasn't tired anymore.

At top speed, I raced back to my friends. I felt sick. I felt like my heart was going to burst.

They had missed the deadline! It was too late. Too late, and they would all be trapped. Like me. Forever.

<MORPH!> I screamed as I closed   on them.

Thought-speak is like regular speech. It gets harder to hear the farther away you are.

<Morph back! Now!> Maybe the clock in the truck was off. Maybe five minutes one way or the other wouldn't matter.

There! I saw them. Four wolves moving relentlessly toward the distant city.

<Morph! Now!> I screamed as I shot like a bullet over their heads.

<How much time do we have?!> Marco demanded.

<None.>

That got them going. I landed, exhausted, on a branch.

Cassie was the first to begin the change. Her fur grew short. Her snout flattened into a nose. Long, human legs swelled and burst from the thin dog legs.

Her tail sucked back in and disappeared. She was already more than half human by the time the first changes began to appear on the others.

<Come on, hurry,> I urged them.

<What time is it?> Jake demanded.

<You have about two minutes,> I said. It was a lie. According to the clock, they were already seven minutes too late.

Too late.

And yet Cassie was continuing to emerge from her wolf body. Skin was replacing fur. Her leotard covered her legs.

But the others were not so lucky.

<*Ahhhh!*> I heard Rachel cry in my mind. Her morph was going all wrong. Her human hands appeared at the end of her wolf legs. But nothing else seemed to be changing.

I looked, horrified, at Marco. His normal head

345

emerged with startling suddenness from his wolf body. But the rest of him had not changed. He looked down at himself and cried out in terror. "Helowl. Yipmeahhh!" It was an awful sound, half human, half wolf.

This was worse than I had feared. I figured they could be trapped as wolves, like I had been trapped as a hawk. But they were emerging as half-human freaks of nature.

They were living nightmares.

Cassie ran from one to the next. "Come on, Jake, concentrate! Focus! Rachel, bear down, girl. Picture yourself human. See yourself like you're looking in the mirror. Fight the fear, Marco!"

I saw Marco roll his human eyes up and stare at me. His gaze locked on me. It was like he hated me. Or feared me. Both, maybe.

I didn't move. If Marco needed me to concentrate, that was fine.

But it sent a shiver of disgust through me. I suddenly saw myself as they all must see me: as something frightening. A freak. An accident. A sickening, pitiable creature.

Slowly, slowly, Marco began to emerge. Slowly, slowly, the human body appeared.

Rachel, too, and Jake. They were winning their battle.

"That's it, Jake," Cassie urged. She held his hand tight between both of hers. "Come back to me, Jake. Come all the way back."

I watched Rachel. She still had a small, shrinking tail. Her mouth still protruded. Her blond hair was still more like gray fur. But she was going to make it. The clock must have been fast. A matter of five minutes one way or the other had determined their fates.

I was glad they had made it. They were all human again.

"We did it," Jake gasped weakly. He lay on his back on the pine needles. "We made it."

"That was close," Rachel said. "That was way too close. It was so hard. It was like trying to climb up out of a pool of molasses."

"I'm human again," Marco muttered. "Human! Toes. Hands. Arms and shoulders." He checked himself all over.

"Ha ha! That was *close*!" Cassie exulted. She gave Jake a hug. Then I guess she felt self-conscious, because she ran over and hugged Rachel and Marco.

They were all laughing, all giggling with relief.

"We're okay," Jake sighed.

I was happy for them. Really I was. But suddenly I didn't want to be there.

Suddenly I desperately didn't want to be

there. I felt an awful, gaping black hole open up all around me. I was sick. Sick with the feeling of being trapped.

Trapped.

Forever!

I looked at my talons. They would never be feet again.

I looked at my wing. It would never be an arm. It would never again end in a hand. I would never touch. I would never touch anything . . . any*one* . . . again.

I dropped from the branch and opened my wings.

"Tobias!" Jake shouted after me.

But I couldn't stay. I flapped like a demon, no longer caring that I was tired. I had to fly. I had to get away.

"Tobias, no! Come back!" Rachel cried.

I caught a blessed breeze and soared up and away, my own silent, voiceless scream echoing in my head.

CHAPTER 12

It was late when I returned to what was now my home.

After I was first trapped in my hawk body, Jake had removed an outside panel that led into the attic of his house. I flew in through the opening. It was a typical attic. There were some dusty old cardboard boxes full of Jake and Tom's old baby clothes. There were open boxes of Christmas lights and decorations. There was a chest of drawers with a top that had been scarred by something or other.

Jake had opened one of the drawers in the chest and packed it with an old blanket.

It was nice of him. Jake has always been a decent guy. In the old days he used to protect me from the punks at school who liked to beat me up.

The old days. When I still went to school. How long ago had it been? A few weeks? A month? Not even.

There was a Rubbermaid dish in a corner where no one was likely to see it. I was hungry. I clutched the dish with my left talon and pried the lid off with my hooked beak.

Meat and potatoes and green beans. The meat was hamburger. I don't know how he arranged to get the food. His mom probably thought he was sneaking scraps to his dog, Homer.

I hadn't told him yet, but I couldn't eat the vegetables or the potatoes. My system couldn't deal with much except meat. I . . . the hawk . . . was a predator. In the wild, hawks live on rat and squirrel and rabbit.

I ate some of the hamburger. It was cold. It was dead. It made me feel bad to be eating it, but it filled me up.

But it wasn't dead meat that I wanted. I wanted *live* meat. I wanted living, breathing, scurrying prey. I wanted to swoop down on it and grab it with my razor talons and tear into it.

That's what I wanted. What the hawk wanted. And when it came to food, it was hard to deny the hawk brain in my head. The hunger I felt was the hunger of the hawk.

I flopped and hopped up into my drawer. But it was soft. And what my hawk body wanted was not the warmth and comfort of the blanket.

Hawks make nests of sticks. Hawks spend their nights on a friendly branch, feeling the breeze, hearing the nervous chittering of prey, watching the owls hunt.

I hopped up out of the drawer. I couldn't stay there. I was so tired I was past being able to rest. I was restless.

I flew back out into the night. Hawks are not usually nocturnal. The night belongs to other hunters. But I wasn't ready to rest.

I flew aimlessly for a while, but I knew in my heart where I was going.

Rachel's bedroom light was still on. I fluttered down and landed on a birdhouse she had deliberately nailed out there for me to land on when I came over.

I rustled my wing softly against the glass. I scratched with one talon. <Rachel?>

A moment later the window slid up. She was there, wearing a bathrobe and fuzzy slippers.

"Hi," she said. "I was worried about you!"

<Why?> I asked. But I knew the answer.

"We weren't very sensitive this afternoon," she said. She spoke in a whisper. We couldn't let

351

her mother or one of her little sisters overhear her having a one-sided conversation with no one.

<Don't be silly,> I said. <You guys barely escaped being . . . you know.>

"Come inside. I have my bedroom door locked."

I hopped in through the window and fluttered over to her dresser.

Suddenly I realized something was behind me. I turned my head around. It was a mirror. I was looking at myself.

I had a reddish tail of long straight feathers. The rest of my back was mottled dark brown. I had big shoulders that looked kind of hunched, like I was a football lineman ready for the snap. My head was streamlined. My brown eyes were fierce as I stared over the deadly weapon of my beak.

I turned my head forward, looking away from my reflection. <I don't know what's happening to me, Rachel.>

"What do you mean, Tobias?"

I wish I could have smiled. She looked so worried. I wish I could have smiled, just a little, to make her feel better.

<Rachel. I think I'm losing myself.>

"Wh — What . . . How do you mean?" she asked. She bit her lip and tried not to let me see. But of course, hawk eyes miss nothing.

<Today the hawk we freed . . . she was there. At the lake. I wanted to go with her. I felt like I belonged with her.>

"You belong with us," Rachel said firmly. "You are a human being, Tobias."

<How can you be so sure?> I asked her.

"Because what counts is what is in your head and in your heart," she said with sudden passion. "A person isn't his body. A person isn't what's on the outside."

<Rachel . . . I don't even remember what I looked like.>

I could see that she wanted to cry. But Rachel is a person with strength that runs all the way through her. Maybe that's why I came to see her. I needed someone to be sure. I wanted someone to let me borrow a little of their strength.

She went over to her nightstand and opened the drawer. She rummaged for a minute, then came back to me. She was holding a small photograph. She turned it so I could see.

It was me. The me I used to be.

<I didn't know you had a picture of me,> I said.

She nodded. "It's not a great picture. In real life you look better."

<In real life,> I echoed.

"Tobias, someday the Andalites will return. If they don't, we're all lost, all the human race. If

353

they do come back, I know they'll have some way to return you to your own body."

<I wish I was sure,> I said.

"I am sure," she said. She put every ounce of faith into those three words. She wanted me to believe. But I could see the tears that were threatening to well up in her eyes as she lied.

Like I said, hawks don't miss much.

CHAPTER 13

Talking to Rachel helped. A little, anyway. I spent the night in my little drawer in Jake's attic.

I spent the next day flying around, waiting for my friends to get out of school. In some ways, I realized, my situation wasn't all bad. For one thing, I had no homework. For another, I could fly. How many average kids can hit forty miles per hour in level flight and break eighty in a stoop — a dive?

I went to the beach and rode the thermals there. It was best where the cliffs pressed right up against the blue ocean.

I saw some prey, some mice and voles in the grass along the top of the cliff, but I ignored them. I was Tobias. I was human.

Jake had called a meeting for all of us for that evening in his room. Tom, Jake's brother, would be away at a meeting of The Sharing.

The Sharing is a "front" for the Yeerks. They pretend it's just some kind of Boy Scouts or whatever, but its real purpose is to recruit voluntary hosts for the Yeerks.

I've gotten into the habit of checking people's watches from up in the air. Also, you know how banks sometimes will have a big sign showing the time and temperature? Those are helpful, too.

It's strange the things you miss when you lose your human body. Like showers. Like really sleeping, all the way, totally passed out. Or like knowing what time it is.

In the afternoon I flew back to the school. I drifted around overhead till it let out. Then I waited till I saw Jake, Rachel, Cassie, and Marco come out. They came out separately. Marco had pointed out that it was bad security for them to be seen together all the time.

I followed the bus with Jake and Rachel in it. They lived closest, just a few blocks away from each other. Marco lived in some apartments on the other side of the boulevard. He lived with just his dad, since his mom drowned a few years ago.

Cassie had to travel farthest, out to the farm, which was about a mile from the others. For me it was about a three-minute flight.

Like I say, there are some good things about having wings. I guess really it's okay most of the time. Really.

I floated on a nice thermal above Jake's house, waiting for him to get home. I saw him get off the bus and go inside. I couldn't see Rachel from where I was because there were trees in the way, but I did see Marco for just a second or two.

I concentrated on watching my friends. That way I didn't notice the squirrels in the trees as much. Or the mice that poked their little noses from their holes and sniffed the air.

After a while I saw Tom leave Jake's house.

Tom looks just like Jake, only he's bigger and has shorter hair. I'd never really known Tom well. But it was during the doomed attempt to rescue him from the Yeerk pool that I was trapped.

He headed down the street, acting nonchalant. Then, a block away, a car pulled up and opened a door. He jumped in.

Off to his meeting of The Sharing.

After a while, I saw the others start to head for Jake's house. I could identify Rachel easily. She was practicing for her gymnastics as she walked. She would walk along the edges of curbs, pretending they were balance beams.

I flew in Jake's window once everyone was there. I didn't want it to look like I'd been hanging around all that time with nothing to do.

357

"About time," Marco said. "We've all been waiting here for like an hour."

They'd been there for about two minutes. <I'm a busy bird,> I said. <I lost track of time.>

"We better make this kind of quick," Cassie said. "Ms. Lambert gave us papers to write by day after tomorrow, and I promised my dad I'd help him release this great horned owl. He was a mess. He'd landed on a power line and got fried. But he's ready to go now. We have a habitat picked out."

"Friend of yours, Tobias?" Marco teased me.

The others all shot him nasty looks. But the truth was, it made me feel okay to be teased by Marco. Marco teased everyone.

<We hawks don't hang with owls,> I said. <They do nights, we mostly do days.>

"He's a beautiful animal," Cassie said.

<I see them sometimes at night,> I said. <They're amazing. So cool. Totally silent. Their wings don't make a sound. One can fly an inch in front of your face and you won't hear it.>

"Um, okay, look, if Cassie has to get going, maybe we better deal with business," Jake said.

"Yeah, if you two are done with the bird-talk part of the meeting," Marco added.

"I have to get going soon, too," Rachel said. She looked a little embarrassed. "My gymnastics class is putting on an exhibition at the mall."

"Oh, I'm *there*," Marco crowed.

"No, you are *not* there," Rachel snapped. "None of you is going near that place. You know how I feel about having to put on stupid exhibitions."

Rachel is not one of those people who like to perform in front of a crowd.

"We have learned how the Yeerks get their air and water," Jake said, trying to get down to business. "And we even know where they do it. And we more or less know when. There ought to be some way for us to use this information. Any ideas?"

Rachel shrugged. "We try and find a way to destroy the ship."

Marco raised his hand like he was in class. "How about if we, um, go back to talking about birds?"

Rachel ignored him, as she usually did. "Look, we find some way to destroy that ship and maybe the Yeerks will run out of air and water. Maybe that will even mean that they have to give up and go home."

"Maybe," Cassie said. "Or they may have a dozen more of those ships in different places all over the earth. We don't know how many ships they have."

"This one would be all we need if — " Marco began to say. Then I guess he realized he was about to suggest something dangerous. "I mean . . . nothing."

"What?" Jake asked him. "What were you going to say?"

Marco looked trapped. He shrugged. "Okay, look, what if that ship didn't get blown up or disintegrated or whatever. What if it was flying over the city and suddenly the cloaking device was turned off?"

We were all silent while we thought about that image. Suddenly a million people would look up in the sky and see a ship the size of a skyscraper.

"People would probably notice it," Jake said.

"Oh yeah, they would notice it," Rachel agreed. "Radar would see it, too. A million eyewitnesses. The Controllers would never be able to cover it up!"

<People would videotape it,> I said. <They would take pictures. There would be radar tapes.>

Jake grinned. "The whole world would see. The entire human race would realize what was happening." He was getting excited now. "And *then* we could go to the authorities. The Controllers wouldn't be able to stop us! We could tell all we know!"

Rachel's eyes were gleaming. "We could tell them about The Sharing. We could turn in Chapman!"

"And you figure Visser Three and his pals are

just going to sit around and do nothing?" Marco asked. "Like you said, we have no idea how many ships they have. Or how much power."

Jake looked a little disappointed.

<They don't have enough power to attack Earth openly,> I said.

"And how do you know that?" Marco asked.

<Because they are going to a lot of trouble to keep themselves a big secret. You don't hide if you're tough enough to come out and kick butt in a fair fight.>

I expected Marco to have some smart comeback. But he just nodded. "Yeah, you're right."

"This could be our big chance," Rachel said. "Uncloak that ship, so the whole world can see."

"I hate to ask this," Marco said with a groan, "but how do you think you're going to do that?"

It was Jake who answered. "We'll have to get inside that ship." He winked at Marco. "Want to know how?"

Marco shook his head. "Not really."

"Through the water pipes. As fish."

Marco sighed. "Jake, I just *told* you I didn't want to know."

CHAPTER 14

Rachel and Cassie took off, heading in different directions.

"Have a good show," Cassie called to Rachel.

"Yeah, right," Rachel said grumpily.

"I'll be there soon," Marco told Rachel. "Don't fall off any balance beams until I get there."

Rachel shot Marco one of her "you're a dead man if you mess with me" looks and disappeared, leaving just Marco, Jake, and me.

"She really kind of likes me," Marco said, with a wink at Jake and me.

"Uh-uh," Jake commented dryly. "Look, Tobias, if we're going to do this mission, it can't be till the weekend."

<Why?>

"The timing. We have to morph to travel up there. There are no buses and we can't walk that far in human bodies. Even as wolves, though, it takes time. It took more than an hour last time. It just seemed to me that we might want to get up there in the morning, camp out somewhere hidden, and then be ready by afternoon when the Yeerks show up."

"And this time we may want to travel *around* that other wolf pack's territory," Marco pointed out. "I don't want to get into it with them again."

It made sense. <I guess you're right. So if you're going to camp early in the day, you need a Saturday.>

"Anyway, it might be a good idea if we had as much information about the area as we can get." Jake gave me a thoughtful look. "So I was thinking — "

<Yeah,> I interrupted. <I'll spy out the situation. I'll look for someplace you can hide. I have a lot of time on my hands. No hands, exactly, but lots of time.>

Marco and Jake both laughed. I think Marco was surprised that I could make a joke about myself.

I saw an intense look in Jake's eyes. He was wondering if I was okay.

<I'm cool,> I thought-spoke privately to him, so Marco couldn't hear. <I was just a little

363

weirded-out by watching you all struggle to get out of those wolf morphs.>

He raised an eyebrow and nodded. He had been upset, too. I could imagine. I suspected there had been a lot of nightmares over that mess.

"Okay, so now what?" Marco asked. "Do I sneak into the mall without Rachel being able to see me, or do we all sit around and play Doom?"

"I have homework," Jake said. "And trust me, Marco, if Rachel sees you at the mall making faces while she's on the balance beam, she will turn into an elephant and stomp you."

Marco winced. "Remember the good old days when all a girl could do to you was call you names?"

I flew off, leaving them to play video games or do homework, or however they ended up killing time. Either way, it wasn't something I could participate in.

It's kind of a shame, really. With my eyesight and the reaction time I have, I could probably be major competition in Doom.

But joysticks and control pads aren't made for talons.

I swooped out into the cool afternoon.

I drifted around for a while. I checked out Chapman's house. Chapman is our assistant principal. He's also one of the highest-ranking Controllers.

When we first learned Chapman was one of *them*, he was ordering a Hork-Bajir to kill any of us who were caught. He told the Hork-Bajir to save our heads for identification. Not the kind of thing you expect to hear.

Even from an assistant principal.

But it turned out things were more complicated than we thought. Chapman had joined the Yeerks. But he had done it in part to save his daughter, Melissa.

Melissa would be at the gymnastics thing with Rachel. At the mall.

Remembering the mall made me sad. It was just another one of the places I couldn't go anymore. There was a long list: school, movie theaters, amusement parks . . .

Wait a minute. I *could* go to the amusement park. And I wouldn't even have to pay admission.

The thought made me happy. I don't know why. It wasn't like I could ride the roller coaster. But still, the idea kind of perked me up.

I could bust right into The Gardens any time I wanted. Come to think of it, I could also watch any football or baseball game I ever wanted to see, too, as long as it was outdoors.

And concerts!

Whoa! Big stadium concerts, no problem. No tickets needed.

That's the way I needed to be thinking. There were millions of things I could do as a bird that I couldn't do as a human.

But not right now. I turned and headed toward the mountains. I had a job to do. It was another good thing about being me. I was the ultimate airborne spy.

There was a long line of towering clouds running to the mountains. Perfect weather for me. Thermals are what push those clouds up so high.

I just let myself get into it. It wasn't a bad life. Not really.

I was flying. Back when I was in my old body, I used to look up in the sky and wish I could fly. Now I could. I figured there were probably kids down on the ground right now looking up at me and thinking, "Wow, that would be so cool."

If only I had something to eat. I was feeling a little hungry. Should have asked Jake to grab me a snack.

It happened before I really even had time to think about it. I guess it was because I was feeling good. Feeling relaxed.

I was above the woods, just a half mile or so beyond Cassie's farm. The trees opened up to form a little meadow. This is what red-tails love. A little meadow.

It was full of prey. Squirrels scouring the ground for nuts. Hopping, then sitting up on their hind legs to look around nervously. Mice that scurried from hole to hole. Rabbits.

A rat.

My eyes focused on it with absolute intensity. I sort of shrugged one shoulder, turned sharply in midair, and plummeted toward the earth in a stoop.

My wings were back. My head low. My talons tucked back for maximum speed.

Sudden flare! I opened my wings. The shock of the air. Talons raked forward. Eyes never moving even a millimeter from the rat.

Focus!

I struck!

An incredible rush of excitement surged through me. I was ecstatic! Ecstatic! That's the only word for it. It was intense beyond anything I had ever experienced.

Talons hit warm flesh. My razor claws squeezed. The rat squirmed in my grip. But it was helpless! Helpless!

I was in a frenzy.

I hooded my wings around my kill, shielding it from any other predator that might try to steal it away.

<NO! NO! NO! NO! **NO!**>

I fell back.

367

I looked down at my talons. They were red with blood.

Rat meat dripped from my beak.

In my panic, I forgot what I was. I tried to run away. But I no longer had legs and feet to run with. I had killing talons. Bloody talons.

I fell in the dirt.

No, I cried voicelessly. But I could still see the dead rat. And I could taste it. And no matter how many times I said "no," it would always be "yes."

CHAPTER 15

I flew.

I flew as fast and as hard as I could. I wanted to go so fast that the memory of killing and eating the rat would be left way behind me.

But not even I can fly that fast.

Human! I am human! I am Tobias!

I don't know why it was Rachel I wanted to see right at that moment. Maybe she was just the closest thing I had to a real friend. Maybe it was the way she had seemed so sure of who and what I was.

I needed someone to be sure.

Down below I saw the huge, irregular rectangles of the mall. I saw a glass door. People streamed in and out. Rachel. That's where she was.

"Tseeeeer!"

I screamed in rage and frustration and terror as I stooped. I shot toward the door like I'd shot toward the rat.

But I wasn't going to stop. I wasn't going to slow down. I was just going to end this right now. I would hit the glass at full speed and maybe that would awaken me from this nightmare.

The speed just kept building. The door rushed up at me. The earth itself was jumping up to hit me.

A guy, dark hair, short, stepped to the door. He opened it.

Shwoooop!

I must have been doing eighty as I hurtled through the open door.

A second set of doors, but these were open, too.

No impact.

No awakening.

Colors and bright lights all around me. Like a high-speed kaleidoscope.

The Gap. Express. The Body Shop. Easy Spirit. Mrs. Fields.

Zoom!

I was a bullet, blazing inches over the heads

of the shoppers. I heard screams. I heard cries of amazement.

I didn't care. I wanted to hit something. I wanted to wake up. I wanted to fall to the ground because my wings had disappeared and been replaced by clumsy legs and flailing arms.

I wanted to be me again.

I am human! I am human! I am Tobias!

Nine West. Radio Shack. B. Dalton. Benetton. A world I knew. A world where I belonged. Places I had been. Foods I had eaten. The world of human beings.

Zoom!

Suddenly, in seconds, I was at the center of the mall.

A crowd was standing around in a circle. In the middle of the circle blue mats were on the floor. Girls in leotards were doing midair flips and graceful backbends. People on the upper level were crowded around the railing to look down.

Rachel was on the balance beam. She was just raising one leg, balancing on the other.

I was a brown and gold and red missile shooting past her.

"Tobias!" she cried.

Straight ahead, a wall. A blank wall where they were going to put a new shop. I was still moving fast. I could still hit it and wake myself up from the nightmare.

"No!" Rachel cried.

I flared and shot straight up. The wall scraped my stomach. The ceiling was glass, a skylight. I was there! A last-second turn, almost too late. My shoulder hit the glass. I bounced off and began to fall down toward upraised faces staring at me with horror and amazement and pity.

I saw Rachel's face in that crowd. Her eyes pleaded silently. No, she mouthed. No. .

I fell, stunned and dazed. Rachel, still balanced on the beam, caught me as I dropped. She fell off and the two of us tumbled onto the mat.

"You have to get out of here!" she muttered tersely.

<I killed,> I cried. <You don't understand, Rachel. I'm lost. I *killed*!>

"No. As long as you have me and the others, you aren't lost, Tobias."

Helping hands were clawing, trying to save Rachel from the crazed, out-of-control bird. She gave me a heave. Just enough to get me into the air. Anyone watching would have thought she was trying to get me off her.

I flapped up, just out of reach of a dozen hands that clawed the air trying to grab me. Someone threw a shopping bag at me. I dodged.

But there was no escape. Overhead I saw the skylight. Blue sky.

The hawk in my head wanted the sky. It knew safety was up in the high blue. The hawk powered straight up. Straight up at the glass that he didn't understand. The glass that would be like a brick wall.

But I couldn't fight it anymore. The hawk had won. I had killed. I had killed and eaten. And I had loved it. The ecstasy of the hunt.

Ecstasy!

In a second it would all be over. One more stroke of my powerful wings and the glass . . .

Out of the corner of my eye I saw a familiar face on the upper level. Suddenly, something shot past me. Small, white, stitched.

CRASH!

The baseball hit the glass just inches ahead of my beak. Just where Marco had aimed it. Glass shards fell around me. I shot through the hole.

Sky!

The hawk flew fast and straight.

I let it go. I surrendered.

Tobias, a boy whose face I could no longer remember, no longer existed.

373

CHAPTER 16

The next few days were like a long, slow dream. I stayed away from Jake's house. I did not communicate with my friends. I disappeared.

I found a place for myself. It was perfect red-tail territory — the place where I had made my first kill. A nice meadow surrounded by trees. Not far off there was a marshy area that was good, too. Although there was another red-tail who had a territory over there, so I couldn't hunt there often.

I spent my days hunting. Sometimes I would ride the high hot winds and watch the meadow. Sometimes I would sit in a tree and watch till some unwary creature ventured out. Then I would swoop down on it, snatch it up, kill it. Eat it while the blood was still warm.

Days were easier than nights. During the day I was hunting almost all the time. It keeps you busy, because most of the time you miss. It can take quite a few tries before you make a kill.

Nights were worse. I couldn't hunt at night. The nights belong to other predators, mostly the owls. At night my human mind would surface.

The human in my head would show me memories. Pictures of human life. Pictures of his friends. The human in my head was sad. Lonely.

But the human Tobias really just wanted to sleep. He wanted to disappear and let the hawk rule. He wanted to accept that he was no longer human.

Still, at night, as I sat on my familiar branch and watched the owls do their silent, deadly work, the human memories would play in my head.

But other memories were there, too. I remembered the female hawk. The one who had been in the cage. I knew where her territory was. Near a clear lake in the mountains.

So one day I flew there. To the mountain lake.

I saw her down on a tree branch. She was watching a baby raccoon, preparing to go for a kill. She would have to be very hungry to go for a raccoon, no matter how small. Raccoons are very tough, very violent creatures.

As I watched, unnoticed by her, she swooped.

375

The raccoon spotted her. A quick dodge left, and the hawk sailed harmlessly past. The baby raccoon ran for the edge of the woods. His mother was there.

No hawk was crazy enough to go after a full-grown raccoon. That was not a fight the hawk was going to win.

She settled back on her branch.

I floated overhead, waiting to see if she would spot me. And waiting to see what she would do when she did notice me. I had to be cautious. She was a female, and females are a third bigger, on average, than males.

Suddenly I saw fast movement in the woods. A chase!

It was always kind of exciting watching a kill, even by another species. It heightened my own hunting edge.

The prey was running awkwardly on its two legs. Running and threading its way through the underbrush. It stumbled and hit the ground hard. It seemed very slow to get up. It ran again.

I could hear gasping breath. It was weakening. The prey was squealing. Loud, yelping vocalizations.

Prey often squeal.

The predator moved on two legs also. But these legs were built for greater speed. It had blades growing from its arms. It used the blades to slash the bushes and weeds. It cleared its way through them like a lawn mower chopping down tall grass.

Lawn mower?

No. Something else. Salad Shooter. Yes, that's what Marco called them.

Marco? The image came to my mind. Short. Dark hair. Human.

It hit me like a lightning bolt. Suddenly I realized: This prey was a *human*.

Why should I care? It was prey. That was the way it worked: Predator killed prey.

NO! It was a human being.

"Help! Help!" That was the vocalization. It meant something. "Help! Help me!"

The predator was very close. In a few seconds he would make his kill. The predator was powerful. The predator was swift.

Hork-Bajir.

"Help me, someone help!"

I don't know how to describe what happened next. It was like my entire world flipped over. Like one minute it was one thing, one way, then, boom, it was something totally different. It was like opening your eyes after a dream.

The prey was a human being. The predator was a Hork-Bajir. This was wrong. Wrong! It had to be stopped.

I stopped.

A few seconds earlier I was thinking that no sane hawk would go after a full-grown raccoon. Now I was going after a Hork-Bajir. Hork-Bajir compare to raccoons like a nuclear bomb compares to a bow and arrow.

It would have to be the eyes. The eyes were the only weak spot.

"Tseeeeer!"

I rocketed toward the Hork-Bajir. The human slipped and fell again.

Talons forward. The Hork-Bajir was totally focused on his prey. I hit him fast and hard and sailed past.

"Gurrawwwrr!" the Hork-Bajir yelled. He clutched at his eyes.

The human was up and running again.

"Gurr gafrasch! To me! Getting away! Hilch nahurrn!" the Hork-Bajir yelled, in the strange combination of human and alien speech that they use when working with humans.

He was calling for help. I used my momentum to soar up over the tops of the trees. He had plenty of help available. Another Hork-Bajir about a thousand yards off. And two of the bogus Park Rangers were nearer.

It was all coming back to me. The fake Park Rangers. The Hork-Bajir enforcers. This was the lake. A Yeerk supply ship must be on its way in.

Yeerks. Andalites.

My friends, the Animorphs.

Yes, my *friends*. I remembered now. But this human was not one of them. This human prey was older. A stranger.

The freed hawk was watching me. I could almost feel her drawing me toward her. It was like a magnet. She was my kind. She was like me.

But the Park Rangers were in hot pursuit of the human now. The human was nothing like me. Poor, clumsy ground runner that he was. He was just prey.

And yet, for some reason, I couldn't let him be prey.

I couldn't. *Me.*

Tobias.

CHAPTER 17

I landed on the perch outside Rachel's window. It was night. But she wasn't asleep. She was reading a book in bed, propped up by several pillows.

I fluttered a wing against the glass.

<Rachel?>

She started. The book went flying. She jumped up and ran to the window, throwing it open.

"Tobias?"

<More or less,> I said wryly.

She started to hug me, to put her arms around me. But then she realized that wasn't possible. Birds aren't exactly made for hugging.

"Are you okay? We've all been terrified. Cassie said maybe you were killed or something.

There are all kinds of things that can happen. Jake is so depressed."

<I'm okay,> I said. I flapped over to her dresser.

Now that she was sure I was safe, she started getting mad. It made me smile inwardly. That was Rachel for you.

"Tobias, what is the deal with you? Why would you just disappear and leave us all worrying for days?"

<It's hard to explain,> I said. <I guess . . . the hawk sort of won out over me. Not that it's really that way. I mean, the hawk instincts . . . they're strong.> I told her about my first kill. About how much it horrified me.

I don't know how I expected her to react. She tried to look sympathetic, but I could see it bothered her.

<I lost control,> I admitted. <For the last couple of days I've been living like a hawk. All the way, like a hawk. I think I was starting to forget . . . me. I was starting to lose touch with humans. Then something happened.>

"What?" She went to check her door and make sure neither of her sisters was nearby. I could hear that the house was quiet. "What happened?"

I told her about going to the lake. I told her about the guy being chased by Hork-Bajir.

<Fortunately, I can see the terrain better than the Hork-Bajir or those human-Controller Park Rangers. I led him away from them. I told him when to hide and when to run.>

"You talked to him?"

<I thought-spoke, yes. There was no alternative. I couldn't let them catch him. He had seen a Hork-Bajir. They would never have let him live.>

Rachel looked stunned. "But now he knows about you! And he knows about the Hork-Bajir."

<What's he going to do? Go tell people he was chased through the woods by an alien monster, and rescued by a telepathic bird?>

Rachel laughed. "Yeah, good point. People would just think he was insane. Besides, if he started talking openly about the Yeerks, they would find him and silence him."

<Exactly what I explained to him. I think he'll probably keep quiet. He'll try to forget it ever happened.>

"You saved him," Rachel said.

<I almost didn't,> I admitted. <At first I just saw another predator and his prey. No different from watching the owls at night. No different from what I do myself. Kill to eat.>

Rachel thought about that for a moment. "The Yeerks and their slaves aren't killing to eat," she said. "They are killing to control and dominate. Killing because it's the only way you can eat, because that's the way nature designed you, that's one thing. Killing because you want power or control is evil."

<I guess you're right,> I said. <I hadn't thought about it that way.>

"What you did . . . eating . . . you know, whatever. Well, that's natural for the hawk. Nothing a Hork-Bajir does is natural. They aren't even in control of their own bodies or minds. They are tools of the Yeerks. And the Yeerks only want power and domination."

<I know,> I said. But I wasn't totally convinced. Still, it was comforting to be talking to Rachel.

"You are *human*, Tobias," she told me softly.

<Yeah. Maybe. I don't know. Sometimes I just feel so trapped. I want to move my fingers, but I don't have any. I want to speak out loud, but I have a mouth that's only good for ripping and tearing.>

Rachel looked like she might start crying. It was alarming to me, because Rachel isn't a girl who bursts out in tears, ever.

<Anyway, look, I'm sorry I ruined your exhibition at the mall the other day.>

She smiled. "What do you mean? It was perfect. I was just starting my routine, and you know how much I hate to have to do public shows like that. You put an end to the whole thing real fast."

I laughed silently. <I can imagine. I hope no one was hurt by the falling glass.>

"No, everyone was fine. But what were you going to do if Marco had missed with that baseball? You would have hit the glass awfully hard."

I didn't know what to say.

Rachel came closer and stroked my crest with her hand. It made the hawk in me uncomfortable. But at the same time, it was similar to preening, which is kind of pleasurable.

"What I told you the other day, Tobias . . . remember? You're not lost as long as you have Jake and Cassie and me. Even Marco. He came through for you, big time. We're your friends. You're not alone."

I think I would have cried then. But hawks can't cry.

"And someday, the Andalites will come. . . ."

<Someday,> I said, trying to sound confident. <Well, I better go see Jake. The mission is supposed to begin tomorrow.>

"We don't have to go through with that," Rachel said.

<Yes, we do,> I said. <More than ever, I understand that. See . . . there are human beings all over, trapped in bodies controlled by Yeerks.

Trapped. Unable to escape. Rachel, I know how they feel. Maybe I can't escape. Maybe I am trapped forever. But if we can free some of those others. Maybe . . . I don't know. Maybe that's what I need to do to stay human.>

CHAPTER 18

The next day, we went ahead with the mission. I flew cover overhead while four gray wolves ran beneath me. We timed it so we would arrive in the area very early in the morning, many hours before the Yeerks would arrive to hunt intruders.

<So, let me get this straight, Tobias,> Marco said. <You're taking us to a bear cave? As in big grizzly bears? And this is a good thing?>

<Not grizzlies,> Cassie interrupted. <Not in this area. We'd be talking black bears. They're much smaller.>

<Swell. I am totally reassured. Just a *small* bear cave.>

<The bears are long gone,> I said. <There are

just a few bears around, and this cave is empty. Trust me. I spied it out yesterday. I've seen raccoons and skunks running in and out of there. They wouldn't be doing that if there were bears.>

<Excuse me. Jake? Did Tobias just say 'skunks'? I must have heard wrong, because only an idiot would think hanging out with skunks is a good idea.>

<We're not going to hang out with skunks,> Jake said patiently.

<The skunks don't live there,> I said. <They just run in there to get away from predators.>

I didn't have to explain any more. I think everyone guessed how I knew that skunks ran in there to get away from predators.

<Look, it's close to the lake but I don't think the Yeerks know about it,> I said. <Sorry, but there wasn't a convenient Marriott hotel where I could get you a room for the night.>

<So, that means no room service, either?> Marco asked. <Well, okay. As long as this cave gets cable. The big game's on ESPN tonight.>

I was carrying a tiny nylon pouch that Rachel had put together. It was tan in color, so a casual observer wouldn't notice it and wonder why a red-tail hawk was carrying luggage.

In the sack was a small watch. It weighed almost nothing. There were also some fish hooks, fishing line, and a small lighter. All together it only weighed about two ounces. But it did slow me down a little.

We reached the cave with plenty of time to spare on the two-hour deadline.

<Oh, this looks lovely,> Marco said, looking at the thorns and a scrub brush around the cave entrance.

<I haven't really been inside,> I admitted.

I landed outside the entrance. The opening to the cave was no more than two feet across and about four feet high. It was easy for Jake and Rachel, in their wolf morphs, to leap nimbly through. Unless there really was a bear inside, they would scare off whatever might be in there.

<Empty,> Rachel reported. <Nothing in here but a couple of spiders and a scared mouse.>

I decided to try a joke. <Chase him out here. I'm hungry.>

Only Marco laughed. The others all acted like I'd said something embarrassing. Maybe I had.

<Let's morph back,> Marco suggested. <One close call with being trapped as a wolf is plenty for me.>

<I'll go look around,> I said. Sometimes I didn't like being there when they morphed.

A few minutes later they all came out. Marco was complaining, as usual. "You know, we really have to figure out how to deal with the shoe situation," he muttered. "Thorns and no shoes. Not a good combination."

The four of them were barefoot and dressed only in their morphing outfits: leotards for the girls, bike shorts and tight T-shirts for Jake and Marco.

"We need to gather firewood," Jake said, with his hands on his hips. "It wouldn't hurt to warm that cave up a little before the Yeerks get here."

"Don't you love it when Jake's all masterful like that?" Rachel teased.

"I'm just trying to get us organized," Jake said defensively.

"We'd better get started fishing," Cassie pointed out. "If we don't catch a fish, we're pretty much wasting our time."

The plan was to morph into fish to enter the Yeerk ship's water pipes. Of course, in order to morph into something, you first have to "acquire" it. Which means being able to touch it.

"Shouldn't be any big problem," Jake said confidently.

"Uh-huh," Cassie said dryly. "And how many times have you gone fishing?"

"Counting this time? Once." He laughed.

Cassie rolled her eyes. "Typical suburban boy," she said affectionately. "It isn't all that easy."

<Then you guys better get started,> I advised. <I'll go look around.>

"Take care of yourself, Tobias," Rachel called out as I took wing.

I watched from on high as they made one failed attempt after another to convince a fish to bite one of our hooks.

It seemed ridiculous, but the entire plan was hanging on the question of whether or not we could catch a fish. And time was running out. The day wore on. Still no fish.

Jake was getting edgy. Rachel was downright cranky. And Marco? Forget Marco. "This is ridiculous!" he raged. "We're four — I mean, five — fairly intelligent human beings. And we can't outsmart one fish that probably has an IQ of four?"

Cassie was the only one remaining calm. "Fishing is a matter of skill and luck," she said placidly. "A smart fisherman learns not to become frustrated."

Jake looked at the little watch we'd brought along. "From what we know, the Yeerks will start arriving in an hour to clear the area."

Rachel nodded. "Even if we catch a fish now, we won't have time to test the morph."

<Maybe we should back off for today,> I suggested. <You really ought to test out the fish morph. You guys all know how much trouble a morph can be at first.>

Jake shook his head firmly. "I don't think so,

Tobias. We'd have to wait till we had another day off. Tomorrow's no good because I have stuff with my parents. So does Marco. Which means we'd have to wait a whole week."

<So we try again next weekend. What's the hurry?>

"The hurry is that the Yeerks can't keep coming to this same lake forever. Sooner or later the level of the water will start dropping, from them taking so much. They must use one lake for a while, then move on to another. It could take forever for us to find where they move to next."

It made sense. But that didn't make me feel any better about it.

<This is the first water animal any of us have morphed. You don't have any idea what it's going to be like.>

"I know," Jake snapped. "Look, Tobias, I know it's not exactly ideal."

"Hah!" Cassie yelped. She yanked at the line she was holding. "I believe we may have a fishy."

It took just a few seconds to haul in the fish.

"Trout," she said, looking it over as it flopped in the shallow water. The hook was poked through its lip. It was about ten inches long, not very big.

The four of them stared blankly at it.

"We have to become *that*?" Marco asked.

"It's a fish," Cassie said. "What did you expect?"

Marco shrugged. "I don't know. Something more like *Jaws.* This is just a fish. I mean, we could clean him and eat him with a little lemon juice. Maybe some fries on the side."

The others turned and gave him a dirty look.

Cassie reached down into the water and took hold of the squirmy gray thing. She concentrated. Her eyes closed halfway. She was acquiring it. The fish DNA was being absorbed into Cassie's body.

The gift of the Andalite. The curse of the Andalite — the power to morph.

CHAPTER 19

<I don't like this plan,> I blurted.

Jake looked up at me in surprise. "Tobias, you were in on the planning right from the start."

<Look, don't you guys realize how dangerous this could be?>

"I realize," Marco said. "I realize it plenty. But I thought you were the big, gung-ho Yeerk-killer. Suddenly now you're afraid?"

<I'm not afraid for me,> I said. <I'll be flying around safely while the four of you go up into that ship.>

Cassie nodded. "It's hard standing by while someone else is risking their life," she said. "I understand how you feel. But there have been times when *you* were the one taking the risks."

"Look, we don't have time to debate this," Jake said. "We have a plan we've all agreed to. Let's get on with it before the Yeerks show up." Jake gets peevish when someone questions things after everything has already been decided. Usually it's Marco getting on his nerves.

"We'll be okay," Rachel said confidently. Rachel took the fish in her hand. The fish went limp, as usual, while the acquiring was happening.

Suddenly I couldn't watch anymore. I'd just had a flash of memory, watching the four of them straining to get out of their wolf bodies. What if they were trapped in fish morph?

The idea of being trapped was still not something any of them really understood. I mean, they knew it had happened to me. But people are funny — they never think something bad will happen to *them.* I knew it could happen.

And to be trapped as a fish? It made me sick just thinking about it. The rest of your life in the body of a fish? Being trapped in a hawk's body seemed downright pleasant by comparison.

<I'm going to go upstairs and see if anyone's coming,> I said. I caught a small breeze and flapped hard to clear the treetops.

It was tough work gaining enough altitude to get a good view of the area. It was mostly dead air all around. But I was glad for the workout. It took my mind off imagining what life would be like if my only friends in the world were trapped as fish in a mountain lake.

I would have laughed if it weren't so serious. I mean, come on, how many kids have to worry about all their friends becoming fish? Life had definitely gotten strange since that night when we saw the Andalite landing in the construction site.

I circled higher and higher till I could see the entire lake and most of the surrounding area. No Park Rangers. Yet. I wondered if Jake was right and maybe the Yeerks would move on to another lake. Maybe they already had.

Then, there, way down below, on a branch . . . the hawk. The female I had freed from captivity.

She was watching me. I could see her eyes follow me across the sky. In part, I knew, she was merely watching me for the simple reason that I was in her territory. Hawks are defensive about their territory. They don't want strangers coming and grabbing all the best prey.

But I had the feeling that there was something more going on. She wanted me to join her. I don't know how I knew that, but I did. She wanted me to fly down to her.

Some people think hawks mate for just a season. Some people think they mate for life, and I don't really know which is true.

One thing I knew for sure: I wasn't ready to settle down with anyone. Especially not a hawk.

And yet there was this feeling in me. Like . . . like I *belonged* with her.

I looked away. I would be glad when this mission was over and I no longer had to come here to her territory. She confused me.

Suddenly, movement!

I had let myself be distracted.

Trucks! Jeeps! They were rolling down the road. They were within a mile and moving fast.

I looked frantically for my friends. There they were! I shrugged off the wind beneath my wings and dropped toward them.

<Here they come!> I cried. <Get to the cave!>

They ran for the cave. But it was harder to crawl inside in their human bodies. The wolves' thick pelts had protected them against the scratches and tears of the bushes.

Thwak thwak thwak thwak thwak!

Helicopters skimming above the trees!

Too fast. My friends were still struggling to make it to the shelter of the cave. One of the helicopters was on a straight line to them.

<Oh, man,> I muttered. I still had a lot of my

speed from the dive. I flapped hard, powering up to maximum speed. Straight at the helicopter.

Straight at it.

I could see the pilot. A human-Controller. Beside him sat a Hork-Bajir.

Straight at them!

The chopper was doing ninety. I was doing a little less. The distance between me and the chopper's windshield shortened very fast.

They weren't going to pull up!

CHAPTER 20

Thwak thwak thwak thwak thwak!

The sound of the rotors was a roar.

They were not going to pull up! We were going to hit.

But then, a flicker of the pilot's eyes, a twitch of his hand on the control stick.

I cranked right.

The helicopter cranked left.

It blew past me like a tornado. The backwash of the rotors caught me and tumbled me through the air.

I fell, upside down. I folded my wings, flared my tail, and spun around. I opened my wings and swooped neatly between two trees.

I banked left and flew over the cave. Rachel was the last one in. She was still clearly visible. The helicopter would almost certainly have seen her.

I watched till she was safely inside.

<Okay, you guys, I don't think anyone saw you. Be cool till I tell you it's time.>

They couldn't answer, of course. They were still fully human, so they could hear my thought-speech, but could not respond in kind.

The Yeerks went through the familiar routine. The phony Park Rangers fanned out around the lake with automatic weapons ready. The helicopters buzzed around until they decided the area was free of witnesses.

The helicopters landed and the Hork-Bajir jumped out. They seemed extra careful. Probably Visser Three had given them all kinds of grief over the guy I had helped to escape the day before.

Visser Three was not a creature you wanted mad at you.

Then, I felt it. The emptiness in the sky. The sense of something monstrously huge moving slowly through the air.

It was above me.

Slowly it appeared, shimmering into reality like some kind of magic trick.

You could never get used to how big that thing was. It felt like someone was hanging a small moon over your head.

I flew out from under it, over closer to the cave. <It's here,> I announced.

From behind the truck ship came the usual guard of Bug fighters. Only instead of two Bug fighters, there were four. The Yeerks were definitely nervous this time. Two of the Bug fighters remained on patrol. The other two landed in the clearing beside the helicopters.

Why? Why the extra security? Was it just because of the guy I had helped to escape?

I felt something new in the air above the hovering truck ship. Another cloaked ship!

Not as large, but from that emptiness in the sky I felt a dread that I had felt before.

The cloak shimmered out and the ship appeared.

Black within black, an outthrust spear, razor-edged — I had seen this ship before. The Blade ship! I had seen it first at the construction site where the Andalite had been murdered while we cried helplessly.

No wonder the Yeerks were nervous.

The Blade ship lowered toward the landing area. The Hork-Bajir on the ground and the Park Rangers were in a frenzy now, searching the woods as if their lives depended on it.

Tssewww!

Someone had fired a Dracon beam. I looked and saw a deer in mid-leap sizzle and disappear. The Yeerks were shooting anything that moved.

The doors of the Blade ship opened. More Hork-Bajir poured out, Dracon beams leveled. Behind them came a pair of Taxxons, slithering and shimmying on their needle legs, undulating their gross caterpillar bodies.

And last, he stepped out: dainty Andalite hooves. Deadly Andalite tail, like a scorpion's. The mouthless Andalite face. The two small Andalite arms with too many fingers. The two mobile eyes mounted on antlerlike stalks that turned this way and that, always searching, so that the large main eyes could focus on one thing at a time.

An Andalite body.

But not an Andalite mind. For in that Andalite body lived a Yeerk. The only Andalite-Controller. The only Yeerk ever to enslave an Andalite. And thus, the only Yeerk to have the power to morph.

I dropped down into the trees. I waited till a patrolling Hork-Bajir had walked past the cave where my friends hid.

When I was sure no one would see, I fluttered down and into the cave, scraping the bushes on either side.

"Tobias? Is that you?" Jake whispered.

<Yes.>

"What are you doing here? That's not the plan."

<Forget the plan. *He's* here.>

No one asked who. They all knew from the way I had said it.

He was here.

Visser Three.

CHAPTER 21

"What is *he* doing here?" Cassie asked in a low, frightened whisper.

<I guess he just came to oversee this trip. Maybe it was because they let that guy get away.>

"He's here to kick butt on his boys," Marco said, trying to sound tough. "They screwed up and now he's here to make sure they don't do it again."

<It doesn't really matter *why* he's here,> I pointed out. <He's here. And there are extra Hork-Bajir and the whole crowd is way nervous. One of the Hork-Bajir Draconed a deer that just happened to be walking by.>

"A deer?" Cassie cried. "Those stupid jerks. Deer never hurt anyone."

<The plan was for you to sneak down to the water, morph as soon as you got there, and head out for the ship's water-intake pipe,> I reminded them. <It was always a dangerous plan, but now it's impossible. Four of you walking down to the water, then morphing? That's not going to happen. Not as alert as these guys are now.>

"Not with Visser Three hanging around," Marco agreed.

"I disagree." It was Rachel. "I think we should still try this. Look, if we pull this off, if we manage to get inside that ship and disable the cloaking device while they're over the city . . . this whole thing will be over."

Jake jumped in to support her. "We've always said, if there was just some way to show the world what was happening . . . well, this is the way. This would be way too big for the Controllers to cover up. I don't care *who* they are. Even if the mayor and the governor and the entire police force were Controllers, they couldn't cover up something like this."

<Jake, you're not listening. I'm telling you: There is no way you four can cruise down to the lake. You'll be dead before you take five steps!>

For a while no one spoke. It was Cassie who finally broke the silence. "There may be a way," she said. "See, a fish can survive out of water for a couple of minutes. And the fish we're morphing is small." She looked at me. "Small enough for a red-tailed hawk to carry."

Well. That idea got everyone's attention, I can tell you.

"Excuse me?" Marco shrilled. "Are you saying you want me to not just morph into a fish, but to morph into a fish *out of water* and then be carried through the air by a bird?"

Cassie bit her lip. "I'm just saying it could work."

"It would work," Jake said. He and Rachel exchanged a slightly insane look that said, "Okay, let's try it!"

<No way,> I said. <You guys are crazy. No offense, but this raises the danger level way beyond what it was to start with.>

"I know it's dangerous," Jake said. "But we may never get a chance this good."

Marco whined. I argued. But in the end it was three against two. Besides, Jake was right: We had a chance to seriously mess up the Yeerks.

I have watched Marco morph into a gorilla, Rachel become an elephant and a shrew and a cat, Cassie become a horse, and Jake become a tiger and a flea (man, was *that* weird!). But this was the first time anyone had tried morphing into an animal that lived in water.

Cassie insisted on going first. "It was my idea," she pointed out. She did not point out that she was also the best morpher.

"If you feel like you're suffocating, you have to back out of the morph," Jake told her. He took her hand. "Are you listening to me? You have to back out if it gets bad. You can't pass out halfway into a morph."

Cassie smiled. "I will. Don't worry about me."

She closed her eyes and began to concentrate.

I've told you that Cassie is always the best at controlling a morph. She has an almost artistic talent, where she can make it all look kind of cool and not so gross.

But not this time.

As I watched, her hair disappeared completely. Her skin began to harden, like it was coated with varnish or something. Like she had been dipped in clear plastic.

Her eyes swung around to the side of her head. Her face bulged out into a huge mouth that gaped and seemed to be blowing invisible bubbles.

As this happened, she was shrinking. But not fast enough. I could still see every nightmare change in her body. The way her legs shriveled up, smaller and smaller, till her legless body fell to the ground.

From her lower back her body stretched out, elongated.

"Ooohhh!" Rachel cried.

A tail had just suddenly spurted from Cassie's behind. A fish tail.

Now her varnished-looking skin cracked and split into a million scales.

Her ears were gone. Her arms were shriveling. She was no more than two feet long, lying helpless, a monster, on the floor of the cave.

<So far I'm fine,> she said, but her thought-speech was shaky. <Still . . . breathing . . . with my lungs.>

But at that moment, two slits appeared in her neck.

Gills.

<*Aaaah!*> she cried.

"Cassie, pull out of it!" Jake cried in an urgent whisper.

<No. No. Almost done. Tobias . . .>

<I'm ready,> I said grimly.

She was tiny now. Less than a foot long. All that was left of her human body were two very tiny doll hands. They made little fins.

Cassie flopped wildly. Her mouth gasped silently.

"Go!" Jake said.

I closed careful talons around Cassie's squirming fish body, aimed for the small sliver of sky that I could see through the cave's opening, and flapped my powerful wings.

I burst out of the cave into fresh air.

<Are you okay, Cassie?>

<Fish mind . . . panicky . . . water. Water now!>

<Hang in there. You've been through this before. You know how it is when you first go into a morph. You have to get control of the fish's instincts.>

<Water! Water! I can't breathe!>

I was about ten feet up, racing for the water's edge. Suddenly, below me, a Hork-Bajir.

He looked up and saw me. A bird with a fish in his talons.

I doubted the Hork-Bajir would realize that red-tails don't catch fish. At least I hoped he wouldn't.

I swooped down over the water. The huge Yeerk ship was just lowering its intake pipes into the water. I dropped behind a stand of trees that hugged the shoreline.

<Get ready!> I warned Cassie. I let her go like one of those old World War Two planes dropping its torpedo.

She hit the water with a small splash.

<Are you all right?>

No answer.

<Cassie! I said, are you all right?>

<Y-y-yeah,> she said at last. <I'm here.>

<Are you dealing with the fish okay?>

Again, no answer. Then, <Whoa. Cool! I'm underwater!>

I relaxed. <Yes, you sure are underwater,> I said with a laugh.

<I was scared,> she admitted. <I . . . I know this sounds crazy. But I just keep seeing myself. Fried. With a wedge of lemon and some tartar sauce.>

CHAPTER 22

Jake was next. He morphed and I flew him over the heads of two patrolling Park Rangers who did not even seem to notice me.

Then came Marco. When I exited the cave with him I practically ran into a big Hork-Bajir. He didn't take any notice of me, either.

Cassie's plan was working. Even with all the Controllers on maximum alert, it never occurred to them that their enemy might be a bird with a fish in its talons.

Back in the cave, it was just Rachel.

<So far so good,> I said.

"Yeah. I guess so."

<Are you nervous?>

"I'd have to be crazy not to be nervous. Oh well. Here goes."

She started to morph. I'd seen three others do it now, so it wasn't a surprise to me. But it was still horrifying to watch a friend, someone you cared about, twist and deform and mutate before your eyes.

I don't think any of us will ever get used to morphing. Maybe the Andalites are used to it. I don't know. But I'll bet it creeps them out, too, when they have to change.

I looked away as Rachel began to get strange and hideous.

She was almost completely a fish when it happened.

Crash! Crash! Someone was forcing their way through the bushes at the mouth of the cave.

"Heffrach neeth there." A Hork-Bajir!

"Yes, I see it," a human voice said grumpily. "You know, these human bodies aren't blind. Just because you're in a Hork-Bajir, don't get delusions. Use those blades of yours to hack some of these thorns out of the way."

I heard a sound like fast machetes, slicing away the vines and thorns.

"Better not find anything in here," the human-Controller said. "The Visser will do to you what was done to that poor fool yesterday who let the human escape."

411

I looked at Rachel. It was too late for her to morph back.

<What's going on?> she asked.

<Yeerks! A human-Controller and a Hork-Bajir-Controller, right outside the cave.>

"Go in fergutth vir puny body. Ha ha."

"This was *your* sector to check. You didn't even notice this cave. Keep getting on my nerves and I'll tell *him*!"

"He gulferch you and eat your lulcath. Ha ha."

Suddenly a human head appeared, followed by shoulders. He was wearing a Park Ranger's outfit.

<We have to make a break for it!> I told Rachel. <Here they come!>

"Yeah, there's a cave in here, all right. There's some kind of a bird — "

I grabbed Rachel, now fully in fish morph. But the human-Controller blocked the narrow entrance.

Well, I thought. It worked with a helicopter . . .

With a rush of wings I flew right at his face.

"What the — " He fell back, beating at the air. I scraped past him.

The Hork-Bajir slashed at the air with one of his wrist blades. He shaved an inch off my tail.

But I was in the air now, and moving faster. Only it was hard with Rachel. The weight of a fish is more than a red-tail can carry easily. And I had already carried three. I was tired.

Fortunately, I was also very scared. Fear can make you strong sometimes.

Ssseeeewww!

A Dracon beam sizzled the air above me!

Unfortunately for the Hork-Bajir who had fired, the Dracon beam did not stop when it buzzed by me. No, the Dracon beam hit the underside of the vast truck ship. A small, neat, round hole appeared in the bottom of the ship. It was too small to amount to anything.

But suddenly the Hork-Bajir lost his interest in me.

"Fool!" the human-Controller cried. "Visser Three will have your head for dinner!"

While they were busy panicking, I dropped Rachel into the water with the others.

<Good work, Tobias,> Jake said. <Be careful up there, my friend.>

<You, too,> I said. <Good luck, you guys.>

I could just barely see them, a small school of fish in the shallows. They swam off and disappeared into deeper water.

As I've told you, there are limits to how far thought-speech can reach. We don't really know what those limits are. But I wanted to stay as close to them as I dared, in case they needed me. Not that there was much that I could do to help someone underwater.

I didn't want to stay right over them. I figured that would look suspicious to anyone on shore. It was hard to figure out what to do. The monstrous bulk of the truck ship was overhead, leaving only a few feet open above the surface of the water.

I decided I had to chance it. I flew under the ship, skimming the dappled water below and practically scraping the metal belly of the ship above me.

It was a very difficult flight. I had to stay almost totally level. I couldn't rise or fall by more than a couple of feet.

<You guys still okay?>

<Tobias? I can't believe you can still thought-speak with that whole ship between us,> Rachel said.

I guess I could have told her the truth. That I was within a few feet of them. But then Jake would have just gotten all mad and told me not to take stupid risks.

I figured that between the time it had taken through the entire morphing process, and carrying them one at a time to the water, plus now the time spent swimming out to the big intake pipe, Cassie had been in morph for just over half an hour. Jake had ten minutes more, then Marco and Rachel.

<What are you guys doing now?> I asked.

<We're looking at the bottom of this intake pipe. There's tremendous suction,> Rachel reported.

<I'll go first and look around. See what's what,> Jake announced. <Here goes. Whoooaaaaa! Man! Whooooaaa! Yah!>

<Jake! Jake, are you okay?> Cassie cried.

<Oh, yeah! What a rush! They should have a waterslide like that at The Gardens. It's like being sucked up a straw by a giant.>

<Cool,> Rachel said. <I'm next.>

<No, let me look around first,> Jake said. <I seem to be in some kind of big tank. It's not very deep. At least not yet. It's filling up. With these lame fish eyes I can't see beyond the surface of the water very well. But I think up in the ceiling there's an opening. Like a grate or something.>

<Up on the ceiling? How are we going to get up there?> Marco asked.

<Well, I think if they fill this whole tank, we'll be near the top eventually. We should be able to morph to human, let ourselves out, then morph into something more dangerous than our human bodies.>

<Excuse me,> Marco said. <But does anyone else ever stop to realize that some of the things we talk about doing are totally INSANE?>

<What? Turning into fish, so we can be car-

415

ried by a hawk and let ourselves be sucked up the pipe of an alien spaceship, so that we can then turn into tigers and gorillas and whatever, and overpower the creepy aliens?> Rachel said. <Is that what you mean by insane?>

<That's it exactly.>

<Yep,> Rachel said. <It is insane.>

<Well, okay,> Marco said. <As long as we all know we're nuts. Let's do it!>

CHAPTER 23

There was nothing to do but wait. Wait while the water level inside the ship rose and carried my friends toward the top of the chamber. Up to where the grate was.

I could not maintain my level flight beneath the ship any longer. I said good-bye to my friends and zoomed out the far side. The open air was a blessing. I soared high on a nice thermal pattern created by the ship itself. I rose high up and over the top of the ship.

The Park Rangers were all around on the ground. The helicopters and two of the Bug fighters were still parked on the ground in the little clearing. The Blade ship was there, too.

Two other Bug fighters continued zipping around at treetop level.

While I watched, they brought the Hork-Bajir who had carelessly fired off the Dracon beam. They dragged him before Visser Three.

We'd gotten so we thought of Hork-Bajir as these totally fearless, deadly monsters. But this Hork-Bajir was not looking very brave. He collapsed on the ground before Visser Three. I almost felt sorry for him.

It was one of the terrible things about our battle against the Yeerks. See, our enemy was just the Yeerk slug that lived in the heads of Controllers. That Hork-Bajir may have been made a Controller totally against his will. He had lost his freedom to the Yeerk in his head. Now, he was about to lose his life, for something that he had no real control over.

I couldn't hear what was happening down on the ground. But I could see. My hawk's eyes could see far too well.

I turned away. I won't tell you what was happening to the Hork-Bajir. That memory will be my own private nightmare.

But when next I looked, the Hork-Bajir was gone. And in his place was a sudden rush of other Hork-Bajir and Taxxons and humans, all surrounding Visser Three. The Visser looked angry. He was pointing at the sky.

Within a few seconds, the helicopters were lifting off.

The two Bug fighters powered up and took off.

I had a very bad feeling that I knew what had happened. The doomed Hork-Bajir had told Visser Three about the bird he had fired at. And some other Controller had probably said, "Oh, yeah, I saw a bird acting suspiciously, too." And someone had no doubt said, "Hey, wasn't it a bird that distracted the Hork-Bajir yesterday and let that human get away?"

Visser Three had put two and two together. An animal acting unlike an animal meant just one thing to him: Andalites in a morph.

I guess I should have been flattered that Visser Three believed we Animorphs were true Andalite warriors. But it didn't make any difference whether he thought I was an Andalite or a human. He was sending his creatures into the sky. Looking for a bird that was no bird.

Me.

A Bug fighter skimmed over the trees. Its twin Dracon beams fired again and again in short, sharp spears of burning light.

My heart was in my throat. They were killing every bird they saw!

The hawk! This was her territory.

But then, behind me, a helicopter! *Thwak thwak thwak thwak! Ssshhhheewww!*

A Dracon beam. A near miss. I couldn't get away. Between the Bug fighters and the helicopters, they were too numerous, and too fast.

But there was one place no one was going to risk firing a Dracon beam. Not after what Visser Three had just done to the careless Hork-Bajir.

I let go of the air beneath my wings and dropped. Down, down, down. Toward the vast truck ship, spread below me like a steel meadow.

In an instant they were all on me. But the angles were wrong. I was too close to the ship. They couldn't fire!

I landed on top of the hovering ship. I planted my talons on the hard, cold metal surface. It stretched in every direction around me. The surface curved down and away from me so that I couldn't even see the edges. It was as if I were standing all alone on a metal moon. Over my head hovered helicopters and Bug fighters. I could see human and Hork-Bajir and Taxxon eyes all focused on me.

I knew the look in their eyes. The look of the predator.

And me, their prey.

CHAPTER 24

It was not looking good for me. If I tried to fly off that ship I would be Draconed ten different ways before I could get away.

It was an eerie scene. I stood on the vast metal plain while over my head they hovered, a swarm of deadly predators.

Then things got worse. A lot worse.

It floated up into my vision like a dark moon — the Blade ship of Visser Three.

It hovered just a few hundred feet up. I felt my last reserves of courage beginning to fail.

Tobias, old buddy, I said to myself, *you are not going to get out of this alive.*

But they just all hovered there. Slowly I began

to realize the truth — they didn't know *what* to do about me. They couldn't shoot me without hitting the ship.

<Andalite!>

The voice in my head made me reel. I almost took wing out of sheer fright.

He had never spoken directly to me before. It was a voice of such absolute power. Such utter confidence. The mere silent sound of it in your head makes you want to obey. Makes you quiver and fear. It is the voice of dread. The voice of destruction.

<Andalite. Fool. Do you think I don't know what you are? A true bird would fly away.>

Say nothing! I ordered myself. Nothing! If I tried to reply, he might know me for a human. I would not tell him that. I would not give him *anything.*

I closed my mind. But I could not shut out that dark voice.

<Give yourself up, Andalite. I will give you a quick and painless death. As soon as you tell me where the others are.>

I had seen what Visser Three did to the Hork-Bajir who displeased him. The memory was fresh in my mind.

<Have it your way, Andalite. I am patient. I can wait here for as long as it takes. And then you will die. Quickly by Dracon beam. Or, per-

haps, if we can snare you, more slowly here in my Blade ship. Much more slowly.>

Just then, I heard another voice in my head. A very different voice. It was faint. As if it were far away.

<Tobias? Tobias, can you hear me?>
Rachel!
<Yes, I can hear you!>

<Tobias! We're trapped! The tank is full, but the grate won't open. Cassie and Jake have already morphed back to human, but they can't get it open. We're trapped in here!>

<Rachel! I . . . What can I do?>

<We can't get out,> Rachel cried. <Listen to me, Tobias. We're trapped. There is no way out. This ship will take off soon. They'll find us when they get to the mother ship and unload the water. Tobias? We . . . we don't want to be taken alive.>

My blood ran cold. My head was whirling. <What are you talking about?>

<Listen, Tobias, we can't be taken alive! Do you understand? If there's anything you can do . . . anything!>

<Rachel! What can I do? I can't get you out of there!>

<I know,> Rachel said. <We *all* know. But if there's some way to . . . if the ship could be destroyed. We know it's probably not possible. I . . . just if there was some way — >

<No! No!>

<I have to morph to human. We'll tread water here. We have to be ready for when we get to the mother ship. Then we'll morph into other animals and go down fighting.>

<This can't be happening,> I cried. <This can't be happening!>

<I guess Marco was right all along,> Rachel said sadly. <I guess it always was insane to think we could fight the Yeerks.>

<Rachel . . . I never told you . . .>

<You didn't have to, Tobias,> she said. <I knew. Good-bye.>

She fell silent. In my mind I could picture her regaining her human shape. Treading water with the others, unable to escape. Expecting only the worst. Praying that I might find a way to make their end swift. As Visser Three had offered to make mine.

We had lost. The Yeerks had won, finally. And when we were gone, the last hope of the human race would die.

Above me the Blade ship waited like . . . like a hawk watching a rabbit. Ready to swoop down and finish me.

Only I wasn't a rabbit.

Visser Three was a predator? Well, so was I.

And I no longer had anything to be afraid of. If my friends were to die in the mother ship, I would be lost and alone in a world where I belonged nowhere.

I had nothing more to lose.

Just then I saw something that should have terrified me. Across the metal plain of the ship they crawled and slithered toward me. All around me. A dozen of them. Giant worms. Centipedes with a hunger for living flesh.

Taxxons.

They had come from the inside of the ship on Visser Three's orders.

If I stayed put, they would catch me. If I flew, the hovering Yeerk ships would fry me.

The Taxxons closed the circle around me.

<It looks as if you have run out of time,> Visser Three said in my head. He laughed. It was not a nice laugh.

Ah, Visser Three, you ruthless predator, I thought. *Very clever. You have me trapped. Trapped like a rabbit.*

But a trapped rabbit is one thing. And a trapped hawk, a hawk with the mind of a human being, is a whole different matter.

The nearest Taxxon leveled a hand-held Dracon beam at me. He watched me with two of the circle of red globs they have for eyes.

I pushed off with my feet. I beat the air with my wings.

I flew straight for those red Jell-O eyes.

He raised one of his feeble forearms to shield his eyes. The wrong move! I trimmed a shade right, raked my talons forward and struck like I was hitting a mouse in a field.

My talons closed around the Dracon beam. The Taxxon's weak grip was no match for my speed. The Dracon beam tore loose from his grip.

<Get him!> Visser Three cried. I could practically see the Blade ship rock from the force of his rage.

But I did not take to the air. I flew fast but hugged the surface of the ship's metal curve. They could not hit me without hitting their precious ship.

I knew just where I wanted to go. Wingtips actually hitting the ship on each downstroke, I raced toward the ship's bridge. Toward the tiny windows where I had seen the Taxxon crew.

I could not save my friends, perhaps. But I could try to grant Rachel's last wish. I could try to bring this ship down.

Even if it meant the end of my friends.

CHAPTER 25

<T ake off! Move!> Visser Three commanded the crew of the truck ship.

Almost immediately, the huge thing began to move forward. Very slowly at first. But as it moved, it created a headwind. The bridge was moving away from me. The ship was rising as it went. A hundred feet up now. Two hundred!

<Ha! Not so easy, Andalite!>

Right then I had a powerful urge to shock the evil monster and say, <Guess what, creep? Not an Andalite at all. The name is Tobias!>

But I wasn't ready to start bragging. The truth was, it was looking bad. The ship was slowly picking up speed.

I flapped harder, harder. I gained again. But it

427

was painfully slow. I was wearing out. The Dracon beam weighed me down. The headwind was building.

Ahead of me, just a few feet away, I saw the bulge of the bridge.

I gained a foot. Another. Another.

I landed and folded my wings. I couldn't fly any more. But I could still pull myself along with my talons, gripping the small edges and ridges that ran along the top of the ship's bridge.

I was there! Below me, transparent plastic. I could see the crew on the bridge. Taxxons stared wildly up at me.

With one desperate lunge I propelled myself into the air. I had to fly full force to stay ahead of the onrushing windows of the bridge.

Then, with one sharp talon, I pulled the trigger on the Dracon beam.

<Fry, you worms!>

There was no recoil. Not like a regular gun at all.

But a beam of intense red light lanced from me to the bridge. It burned a hole through the window, sliced through a fat Taxxon, and began slicing up control panels and instruments like a hot knife going through butter. I squeezed that trigger for as long as I could.

At last, exhausted, I could do no more.

The Dracon beam slipped from my talon and plunged toward the earth below.

But I had done it.

It was an incredible and terrible thing to see. The ship, big as a skyscraper, vast beyond belief, shuddered as though it had hit a speed bump.

Still it rose, sharply upward into the sky, as if it were a whale breaching. It aimed for space, its natural home. But it was clear that it was no longer under control. It rolled suddenly onto its side.

BOOM! A ball of orange flame!

The out-of-control ship had smashed recklessly into one of the helicopters. The chopper fell in ruins.

The Bug fighters and the Blade ship scurried quickly out of the way. But too late.

KA-RUNCH! BA-BOOM!

One of the Bug fighters had slammed into the side of the ship. The Bug fighter was finished. The Blade ship and the remaining Bug fighter withdrew quickly.

And then I saw the hole.

A tear a hundred feet long had been opened in the side of the truck ship. From the hole, the water of the lake gushed. It was a waterfall from the sky. Millions of gallons hemorrhaging out.

<Oh, boy,> I whispered.

We were maybe seven hundred feet up over the forest now, when I saw them.

Cassie first. Then Rachel and Marco together. And Jake. They fell, fully human, from the torn side of the ship.

They plummeted, helpless, doomed, to the uprushing ground!

<Noooo!>

I knew there was nothing I could do. I *knew* it. But still I hurtled after them. Hurtled with all my speed to them as they fell, arms flailing, mouths open in screams of terror.

CHAPTER 26

They fell.

But as they fell, they began to change.

Cassie and Marco were first. Feathers sprouted from their skin. Their morph was an osprey. A distant cousin of the red-tails.

They fell, and as they fell, they became less and less human.

Rachel had previously morphed a bald eagle. Bald eagles are huge birds, much bigger than red-tailed hawks.

As I watched, long wings replaced her flailing arms.

Jake had morphed a peregrine falcon. Peregrines are so fast they make red-tails look like they are standing still.

As I watched, a peregrine's beak grew from Jake's mouth.

Not enough time. Not enough time! They would hit the ground before —

Shwoooop!

Cassie opened her wings and skimmed above the treetops. Marco barely made it. He fell down into the forest, out of sight. I was sure he had been too late.

But then, up from the trees floated a bird with a six-foot wingspread and a proud white head.

<YES!> I cried.

In the sky overhead, the huge truck ship stopped climbing. It rolled again, onto its back this time, and plunged back to Earth.

<Man, that was WAY too close!> I heard Marco yell. <That does it. I have had it with this Animorphs stuff!>

<You're not safe yet!> I told him. <Look!>

With the truck ship out of the way and falling to Earth, the Blade ship and the Bug fighters came after us.

<Quick! Into the trees! Out of sight!> I yelled.

Like a well-trained fighter squadron, we swooped down into the forest. Down below the tops of the trees, where the Yeerks could no longer see us.

BOOOOOM!

An explosion like a bomb going off. The truck ship had hit the ground.

The concussion rolled us over like a tidal wave of air.

I rocketed into a tree, but was able to avoid being hurt. <Everyone okay?> I yelled.

One by one they said yes.

But the explosion had disturbed every animal in the forest. The birds had all either hidden or flown away during the earlier fighting. Those few birds still left now took wing, startled.

I saw her take off. The hawk. She was scared and wanted to run to the sky.

But the sky was not a sanctuary for her.

I don't know which ship fired the Dracon beam. Whether it was one of the Bug fighters, or the Blade ship.

You see, they'd had a good long look at me. And she looked just like me.

The Dracon beam sizzled. It burned off a wing.

And she fell to Earth, never to fly again.

CHAPTER 27

The Yeerk truck ship burned. What was left was eliminated by the Yeerks. No evidence was left behind. No proof that we could show to the world.

But we had destroyed it. And a Bug fighter as well. And we had gotten out alive.

Most of us.

It was a day later when I went to see Rachel again. It was like she was expecting me.

"Hi, Tobias," she said. "Come in. It's safe."

I hopped through the window and fluttered over to the dresser.

"How are you doing?" she asked.

<I'm okay,> I said.

She looked unsure of what to say next. "Look,

um, Tobias . . . maybe this seems crazy. But Cassie and I were thinking, you know, that maybe we'd go back up to the lake. Try and find . . . her body. The hawk. You know, and at least bury her."

<No, that doesn't sound crazy, Rachel,> I said softly. <Not crazy at all. Just human.>

She looked keenly at me. "Well, we are human. *All* of us."

<Yes. I knew I was human when I realized how . . . how sad I was that she was killed. See, a hawk wouldn't care. If she had been my mate, I would have missed her, been disturbed. But sadness? That's a human emotion. I know it seems strange, but I guess only a human would really care that a bird had died.>

"If you helped us look, maybe we could still find her body."

<No. Her body will be eaten. By a raccoon, or a wolf, or another bird. Maybe even another hawk. That's the way it is.>

"That's the way it is for wild animals, Tobias. Not humans."

<Yeah. I know. That's how I know that you are wrong, Rachel, at least partly. I *am* a human, yes. But I am also a hawk. I'm a predator who kills for food. And I'm also a human being who . . . who grieves, over death.>

She looked terribly sad. She's very human, my friend Rachel.

435

I went to the window. It was a beautiful day outside. The sun was bright. The cumulus clouds advertised the thermals that would carry me effortlessly to the sky.

I flew.

I am Tobias. A boy. A hawk. Some strange mix of the two.

You know now why I can't tell you my last name. Or where I live. But someday you may look up in the sky and see the silhouette of a large bird of prey. Some large bird with a rending beak and sharp, tearing talons. Some bird with vast wings outstretched to ride the thermals.

Be happy for me, and for all who fly free.

Follow the Path to More Adventures

GREGOR the OVERLANDER

BY SUZANNE COLLINS

When eleven-year-old Gregor descends into the Underland, he must face giant talking cockroaches, ridable bats, and an army of rats to save his family, himself—and maybe the entire subterranean world.

CHARLIE BONE

BY JENNY NIMMO

Enter Bloor's Academy, where young Charlie Bone is thrust into a crash course on magic and sorcery. As Charlie discovers powers of his own, as well as those of his fellow students, he encounters one bone-chilling adventure after another.

Available wherever you buy books.

SCHOLASTIC

www.scholastic.com

FILLFAN2